Bad Boy

Bad Boy

MAYA REYNOLDS

HEAT

HEAT

Published by New American Library, a division of
Penguin Group (USA) Inc., 375 Hudson Street,
New York, New York 10014, USA
Penguin Group (Canada), 90 Eglinton Avenue East, Suite 700, Toronto,
Ontario M4P 2Y3, Canada (a division of Pearson Penguin Canada Inc.)
Penguin Books Ltd., 80 Strand, London WC2R 0RL, England
Penguin Ireland, 25 St. Stephen's Green, Dublin 2,
Ireland (a division of Penguin Books Ltd.)
Penguin Group (Australia), 250 Camberwell Road, Camberwell, Victoria 3124,
Australia (a division of Pearson Australia Group Pty. Ltd.)
Penguin Books India Pvt. Ltd., 11 Community Centre, Panchsheel Park,
New Delhi - 110 017, India
Penguin Group (NZ), 67 Apollo Drive, Rosedale, North Shore 0632,
New Zealand (a division of Pearson New Zealand Ltd.)
Penguin Books (South Africa) (Pty.) Ltd., 24 Sturdee Avenue,
Rosebank, Johannesburg 2196, South Africa

Penguin Books Ltd., Registered Offices:
80 Strand, London WC2R 0RL, England

First published by Heat, an imprint of New American Library,
a division of Penguin Group (USA) Inc.

First Printing, April 2009
10 9 8 7 6 5 4 3 2 1

HEAT is a trademark of Penguin Group (USA) Inc.

LIBRARY OF CONGRESS CATALOGING-IN-PUBLICATION DATA:

Reynolds, Maya.
Bad boy/Maya Reynolds.
p. cm.
ISBN 978-0-451-22601-3
I. Title.
PS3618.E976B32 2009
813'.6—dc22   2008047095

Set in Centaur MT • Designed by Alissa Amell

Printed in the United States of America

As always, it takes a village to produce a book. I owe special thanks to my marvelous editor, Tracy Bernstein, who stuck with me through this project—even when I was making life tough for her. Thanks, too, to Jacky Sach, my ever-patient agent.

Thanks to everyone who critiqued this book for me. Huge baskets of flowers to Linda Lovely, who did yeoman's labor when I was in a time crunch. And to Red Garnier for being a great cheerleader when I needed one.

And, finally, thanks to my mother. She is slipping away from us now and will never get to read this book, which is probably a very good thing <G>.

Mom did not drive when I was a child, but I can remember her putting my brother and me into a red wagon and heading down the hills of Atlantic Highlands, NJ, to the local library, piling that wagon full of children's books and lugging it back up the hills. She read to us every day, communicating her love of books and reading. I love you, Mom.

Chapter One

The naked girl danced on the twelve-foot-square stage, her only accessory a length of red satin. She twisted it around her twirling body, teasing the audience with momentary glimpses of her gleaming skin. A single breast, her flat stomach, a lightly muscled leg—all appeared and then vanished behind the flashing strip of red.

Klieg lights surrounded the stage, creating the illusion of a bright island floating on a sea of shifting shadows. Beneath the lights' glare, the dancer's body glowed.

Word had spread among the regulars that Katya would be performing this Wednesday night, and the 69 Club was packed. Patrons sat at small tables or in easy chairs scattered around the large room and watched her with hot, predatory eyes.

The well-dressed crowd included a few couples but was primarily composed of single men, nursing their drinks and their fantasies. They paid little attention to the scantily costumed waitresses who moved among the tables. Katya's spell was too strong; no other woman stood a chance while she was onstage.

In a private box against the rear wall, fifteen feet above the floor, Leah Reece looked down at the crowded room and shivered. *How can she bear to have all those men ogling her—naked and alone?*

At the same time, she coveted the caress of that flashing red satin. *I wonder how it feels to be the focus of so much desire?*

Her nipples tightened, rubbing against her green silk blouse. *She's like a slave girl dancing for a sultan's court. But does she feel powerful or powerless?*

Leah pressed her thighs together and tilted her upper body a few inches forward. The tiny movement shifted her center of gravity so that her pussy pressed against the seat's cushion and the cloth of her panties rubbed against her labia. The light friction sent shards of pleasure through her. She bit down on her lower lip. *It's been too long.*

Ten months, to be exact. Over three hundred days since she'd had sex with anything but her vibrator. *I need a nice no-strings-attached hookup. And I don't need to be watching the floor show in a sex club.*

She'd rented a six-seat box at the 69 Club for herself and her two guests. It had been worth the extra money to have the privacy in which to scribble notes. She doubted the club's management would welcome the news that their cabaret was soon to be featured in *Heat* magazine.

Leah glanced at her best friend. Sandy Prada's face was inches from the window that separated their box from the open club below. Sandy was clearly mesmerized by Katya's performance.

When Leah first announced her plan to write about the secretive Dallas sex club, Sandy tried to talk her out of doing the story. Sandy's husband, Zeke, a Dallas cop, agreed with his wife. Then when Craig, the reporter who was going to accompany Leah, backed out at the last minute because of a stomach bug, Sandy and Zeke nominated themselves as her escorts. Leah yielded, reasoning that a threesome would stick out less in a sex club than a single woman.

Sandy's profile, sweetly curved in the final month of pregnancy, made Leah smile. *She looks so happy.*

Leah noticed the vacant seat beside Sandy and blinked in surprise.

Zeke was gone. *He must be in the restroom. Damn, that man can move quietly. I didn't even notice him leave.*

She stole a surreptitious peek at her watch. Nine thirty. According to her informant, the real action started in another hour. And she needed to get Sandy and Zeke out of the club and on their way home before then.

Too restless to sit still, Leah slid her pad and pen into her bag, stood and moved toward the door. *Time to check in. Aggie Curtis should have arrived by now.* Leah was anxious to learn whether *Heat*'s guest art director for the next issue had made her flight in from Los Angeles.

Still absorbed in Katya's performance, Sandy didn't react to her friend leaving the box.

Outside in the hall, Leah fished her cell phone out of her jacket pocket and punched in the number for the front desk at *Heat*. Mike, one of the two security guards on duty, answered on the first ring. "*Heat.* May I help you?"

"Hi, Mike, it's Leah. Has Aggie—"

To her right, the door to the next box opened, and a middle-aged man scowled at her, clearly unhappy to have his enjoyment of Katya's performance interrupted by a telephone call.

"Hold on a second," she said to Mike while signaling an apology to the annoyed patron. She moved down the hall and entered the stairwell.

The 69 Club was located in a restored mansion located in Oak Cliff, a suburb to the south of Dallas. Built by an industrialist in the late nineteenth century, the palatial residence had fallen on hard times during the Depression. Too expensive to maintain as a single-family dwelling, the Mediterranean-style mansion had been subdivided into apartments. Years later, when the building could no longer pass inspection, the owner abandoned it.

Rumor had it that the club's owner had paid less than thirty thousand dollars for the property, and then spent more than a quarter of a million to renovate it for his special needs.

"Has Aggie Curtis checked in yet?" Leah stopped on the landing and rested her back against the stuccoed wall. She kept one arm outstretched on the fire door to prevent anyone from opening it and banging into her.

"Yes, ma'am. Felix carried her stuff up to her room and he's helping her settle in."

A murmur of voices below suggested she wasn't alone in the stairwell. Leah dropped her voice. "Great. Anything I need to know?"

"Only that the lady had five big boxes she said were filled with sex toys. Felix took them to the studio."

Leah grinned. *Heat* held its spot as the number-one e-zine—electronic magazine—by staying on top of the latest trends. Aggie Curtis had contracted to do a spread on "How to Spice Up Your Sex Life."

"Make sure Felix locks the studio. We don't want the staff walking off with the merchandise before the story's finished."

"Yes, ma'am, I surely will." She could hear the smile in Mike's voice.

Leah snapped her cell shut and was about to return to the hallway when she heard a familiar voice. *Zeke.* He was below, talking with another man.

Although she couldn't make out the words, the hushed conversation aroused her journalistic instincts. She moved quietly down the stairs. When she was ten steps above the two men, she cleared her throat.

"Hey, Zeke, I'm not interrupting anything, am I?"

The two men had been so intent on their conversation they hadn't heard her approach, and they looked up, startled.

As her gaze rested on Zeke's companion, Leah's breath caught in her throat. *Damn, he's hot.*

The stranger looked Latino; he had a dusky complexion and high, sharp cheekbones. A thin scar ran down his left cheek from temple to jaw. *That's a knife scar,* a tiny voice inside her brain whispered.

His black hair was combed straight back from his forehead, and he had a five o'clock shadow that made him look disreputable and a little dangerous.

Great! A bad boy. Just my type. While Leah's brain screamed warnings, her pussy twitched with approval. After all, it had been over three hundred days. And he looked so damn sexy.

Although she had difficulty judging his height from her position, he appeared to be as tall as Zeke, which would make him at least six feet two.

A black T-shirt and dark jeans emphasized his broad pecs, tight stomach and narrow hips. Tattoos decorated the muscles on both arms.

Mr. Sex-on-a-Stick stared at her, his gaze intense, penetrating and . . . hungry.

The breath she had been holding since first seeing him whooshed out in a soft exhalation. *Hold it together, girl. Don't drool right in front of him.* Embarrassed by her thoughts, she glanced at Sandy's husband.

Zeke frowned, not pleased by her sudden appearance. "Leah, this is Quin," he offered in a grudging tone, giving the name a Hispanic pronunciation so that it sounded more like "Queen" than the English Quinn.

Leah moved closer. "Hi. I'm Le—"

The stranger interrupted. "Leah Reece. I know. I read your

column in *Heat*. Your picture runs above it." His voice was dark and husky. But he didn't seem to be trying to match her face with the head shot from her e-zine. His gaze roamed up and down her body, and he didn't appear to care that she knew it.

Leah felt warmth flood her cheeks, but she refused to look away. Instead, she challenged him, staring boldly at the bulge at the juncture between his legs. "I'm so glad to hear you read *Heat*," she said. "I hope you enjoy it."

She raised her gaze to his face, and his smile turned her legs to rubber. Gleaming white teeth raised his sexiness quotient from a ten to a fifteen . . . minimum. She grabbed the banister with one hand to steady herself.

Quin smirked as if he understood his impact on her. "I enjoy *Heat*, all right. You've got a great imagination."

She swallowed to clear the lump clogging her throat. When she was certain her voice was under control, she said, "Oh, all that imagination isn't mine. The credit goes to the writers and editors."

He quirked one eyebrow. "I said I read your column, not your whole magazine. After I finish with you, I'm not interested in anyone else."

The innuendo rocked her. She moistened her suddenly dry lips with the tip of her tongue. Realizing the gesture might signal nerves—something she'd be damned if she'd show him—Leah transformed the act into a come-on. Slowly and deliberately, she licked her lips like a cat tasting cream.

His eyes darkened and his torso stiffened, making him stand a tad straighter.

Her turn to smile. *A direct hit.*

He shifted his feet, spreading his legs a bit farther apart, as though his jeans were suddenly too tight.

She flicked another glance at the juncture between his legs. *Let's see how Mr. Macho likes being treated like a sex object.*

Now that she'd made her point, she looked at the man beside him. "Where do you know Quin from, Zeke?"

Zeke opened his mouth, then hesitated. "I . . . he . . . ah . . ." His voice trailed off.

Surprised, Leah narrowed her eyes. Zeke Prada was one of the most self-assured men she knew. She'd never seen him at a loss for words before.

Quin broke the silence. "He's trying to tell you that he's the cop who arrested me." His voice was neutral, carrying no anger.

"Arrested you! For what?"

Quin's lips twitched with amusement. "Ask him. He'll tell you all about it." He nodded toward Zeke. "Catch you later, man." Looking back at Leah, he smiled again, a lazy, sensual smile that made her stomach leap.

"I'm sure we'll see each other again, Princess. I'll look forward to it." Touching his right hand to his forehead, he offered her a small salute before he opened the door and stepped out of the stairwell.

Cocky bastard. Leah grinned at her unintended pun, but watched him leave with regret.

Chapter Two

Leah turned her attention to Zeke. "*Who* was that?"

"No one you need worry about." He came up the steps, seized her elbow and directed her toward the second-floor landing.

"Why did you arrest him?" She stopped moving and pulled her arm free.

He shrugged. "For assault."

"Assault? On whom?"

"A scumbag who had it coming. Come on." He grabbed her elbow again and propelled her up the stairs.

"If the scumbag had it coming, why did you arrest him?"

"Because citizens can't go around beating up people and putting them in hospitals."

They'd reached the landing.

"Why were you talking to him just now?" she pressed.

Zeke didn't answer. He put his hand on the door's crossbar to open it.

She stopped him by touching his wrist. "I'm not going to quit asking, so you might as well tell me."

He sighed. "Fine. Quin and I have known each other a long time. We grew up together."

"Here in Oak Cliff?"

He nodded. "The other side of the tracks from you." He peered into her face. "Satisfied?"

"For now," she said. "And let me remind you, I may not have grown up in Oak Cliff, but I live here now."

He grinned, and they returned to the box in a companionable silence.

Sandy greeted them with a smile. "I thought the two of you had eloped. One minute you're both here, and the next I'm all by myself."

Zeke grinned. "I went to take a leak, and your girlfriend here was nosing around the joint."

"You're missing the best parts," his wife complained.

"You're the voyeur in the family, baby, not me." He rested his hands on her shoulders as he sat down behind his wife and stretched his neck to look out the box's window. "What's going on? . . . Hello!"

His tone prompted Leah to move closer to the glass partition. "Whoa!" she said, plopping into a chair.

In their absence, two nude men—one black, one white—had joined Katya on the stage. Their bodies were heavily muscled and gleaming with body oil.

The trio had positioned themselves to form a rough letter *N* using their bodies. The two men faced each other, and Katya formed the crosspiece connecting them.

Katya's legs were draped over the Anglo guy's shoulders, while the African-American hunk gripped her waist to provide support. With her outstretched arms snaked through the black man's spread legs, she cupped his taut cheeks while she licked his testicles. Meanwhile the white guy's face was buried in her pussy.

Leah was so taken aback that it took a moment before she recognized the music playing overhead was "In the Drink" by the Barenaked Ladies. *Someone has a funky sense of humor.*

She stared at the stage, imagining her legs draped over Quin's shoulders and his tongue teasing her clitoris. Her eyelids drifted closed as she gave into the fantasy.

"Oh, baby, as soon as the Frogman is born, I want to try that," Zeke said, interrupting her daydream.

"Are you crazy?" Sandy asked. "I'm not Elastic Girl, and who are we gonna get to play catcher?"

Leah started to giggle, but Zeke leaned forward to carefully study the trio. "We don't need a catcher, baby. You could rest your shoulders on the couch and put your legs over my shoulders."

"Zeke, honey, I wasn't that limber before Froggie." Sandy laughed. "We'd have to put a chiropractor on retainer."

Since they'd viewed his first sonogram, "Froggie" and "Frogman" had become the couple's affectionate terms for the soon-to-be-born Zeke, Jr.

"Okay, okay, guys. Too much information," Leah protested. "Let's leave me with some illusions."

Zeke snorted. "Yeah, right. This from the Queen of the Sleazy Tabloid."

"Zeke!" Sandy snapped. "You take that back."

"It's okay, Sandy. He's not saying anything I haven't heard before."

Zeke wore a stricken expression. "Leah, I didn't mean—"

She waved his apology away. "Believe me, my dad has said a whole lot worse. And that's when he was being nice." She glanced at her watch. "It's nine fifty. The show ends in ten minutes."

Sandy sighed. "Froggie and I are ready for bed."

Zeke stood. "Then let's leave."

"Did you get what you needed for your story, Leah?" Sandy asked.

"Absolutely," Leah said, relieved she wouldn't have to persuade them to leave. "Come on. If we go now, we'll avoid the traffic jam out front."

The trio gathered their things, left the box and clambered down the stairs, with Zeke in front to break Sandy's fall if she slipped.

Heavy black draperies covered the windows on the first floor, preventing any free peeps from outside.

The 69 Club was a private operation, open only to members and their guests. Leah had heard rumors about its existence for years but couldn't verify them. After cell phone photos surfaced on the Internet, one of her researchers finally got confirmation that the club was real. It still took months to discover its location and to find someone willing to wangle an invitation for Leah—for a price. Her research staff eventually located a kitchen worker willing to show Leah around the club. That informant, Consuelo, was the reason Leah planned to remain behind after Sandy and Zeke left.

With Katya's show in the middle of its grand finale, the front hallway was deserted except for club personnel. After Leah handed the key to her box to a hostess, the security guard opened the front door to let them exit.

The mansion sat on two acres of land separated from its neighbors and the street by a black wrought-iron fence. A long, wide circular drive led up to the house. Club patrons parallel-parked in single file along the curve of the drive, leaving an open lane. The small group walked to Leah's Honda Accord.

"Thanks for coming with me, guys." Leah hugged Sandy and Zeke each in turn. "I really appreciated it."

"Will you be okay?" Sandy asked.

"Sure. *Heat* is less than ten minutes away." Leah patted Sandy's forearm. "Take Froggie home and put him to bed."

Leah climbed into her car and pulled out, turning right and circling the block. She parked on a side street with a clear line of sight to the boulevard. In less than a minute she saw Sandy's Explorer go by, heading west.

Once the Pradas were gone, Leah returned to the mansion and parked again. After taking three hundred dollars out of her wallet and retrieving her invitation, she tucked her purse under the front seat. She got out and approached the entrance again.

She hated deceiving her friends, but she knew they'd never have driven away if they knew her plans.

The same guard was on duty. He looked about twenty-five and had the build of a heavyweight boxer. She smiled and gave him the invitation she'd paid five hundred dollars to obtain. "Hello again."

He glanced at the engraved pasteboard before handing it back. "I'm sorry, ma'am. This is for one night only."

"Yes, tonight. I was going to leave with my friends, but I changed my mind. You remember me."

He nodded. "Yes, ma'am, I remember you. But it says on the back of the invitations that they don't include in-and-out privileges. I'm sorry." He lifted his arm to block the entrance, as though he expected her to try to run past him.

Leah stared with frustration at his adamant expression. *The policy is probably meant to prevent a cop like Zeke from going in, witnessing the floor show and then coming back with reinforcements.* She glanced at the doorman's name tag and reached into her pocket to pull a fifty-dollar bill from the stack she'd brought. "Are you certain, Martin?" she asked, waving the bill in front of him.

He stared at the money with real regret. "Yes, ma'am, I'm afraid I am. I could lose my job."

"I was gone for less than five minutes. Can't you stretch the rules this one time?" she pleaded.

"No, ma'am, I can't."

"Something wrong?" a familiar voice asked.

Quin appeared in the doorway behind Martin. "What's going on here?"

Chapter Three

"Just a guest looking for a readmit, Quin." Martin obviously wanted to be seen as in control of the situation. "I was explaining the rules."

Quin works here? Why didn't he kick me out before? He knows who I am. Before the guard could put his own spin on her story, Leah spoke up. "My friends had to leave, and I decided to stay a bit longer. I didn't realize I couldn't come back in once I'd stepped out." She flashed Quin a pleading smile. "Can't you make an exception this one time?"

He shook his head, his expression impassive. "Sorry, Princess. This isn't your kind of joint anyway. Run along and find some other playpen to roll around in."

His words made her spine stiffen. She hated condescending men—even sexy ones.

Before she could find her tongue, a new voice, one with a heavy Hispanic accent, interrupted. "Let her in."

The trio at the door turned to stare at the man behind them in the entry hall.

"Yes, sir, Mr. Gutierrez." Martin, the doorman, practically saluted. He lowered the arm blocking Leah's path into the mansion.

Carlos Gutierrez, manager of the 69 Club. In her mind's eye, Leah saw the words on the report her research staff had prepared. Before Quin could change Gutierrez's mind, she moved forward, past him and Martin.

Gutierrez was about three inches taller than she was, making him five feet eight. He wore a gray-green Pachuco suit—a style that had originated in El Paso and later migrated to Harlem, where it was called a zoot suit. The high-waisted, wide-legged *tramas* and long *carlango* coat with its broad lapels looked custom-made.

Leah smiled at him. "Thank you for your help, Mr. . . . Gutierrez?" She looked back and forth from the doorman to him, as though seeking confirmation of the name.

The man extended a hand. "Carlos Gutierrez at your service, beautiful lady." When she took his hand, he bowed, allowing her a top view of his slicked-back dark hair.

"Thank you. My name is . . . Lee." She paused, waiting to see if Quin would correct her, but he remained silent. *He's not going to out me. Why?*

"I need to get back to the ballroom." Gutierrez released her hand. "I am the emcee this evening. Perhaps after the show, we could have a drink together?"

Leah smiled and nodded. "I'd like that," she lied.

"Quin, please take care of Lee for me." The manager didn't look at his employee; he was too busy leering at Leah. "I'll come find you afterward," he said to her.

Without waiting for her to respond, Gutierrez walked toward a group of men on the other side of the marble floor.

The entry hall was filling with patrons pouring out of the ballroom.

Katya's performance must have ended. Leah moved away from the entrance. "You don't need to babysit me," she said to Quin. "I'll just go back up to my box."

He shook his head. "Sorry, Princess. That box is long gone. They go like hotcakes during second shift."

"But I just turned the key in." She intercepted the nearby hostess. "Is box two still available?"

The young woman shook her head. "No, we had a waiting list tonight. Sorry."

Leah glanced at her watch. Five after ten. She was supposed to meet Consuelo in the kitchen at eleven. *Where do I go for the next hour?*

"Where do I go?" she repeated the question out loud to Quin.

He shrugged. "Depends on whether you plan on watching or participating. If you just want to watch, you can come up to my office. It's got a view of the floor."

He knows I'm a journalist. Why is he offering to help me? She stared up into his handsome face. *Zeke said he went to jail for assault. Should I risk being alone with him?*

Quin grinned. "Scared, Princess? You can leave. I'll tell Carlos it was past your bedtime." His eyes held challenge and the flash of something else. Was it regret?

Leah had never turned down a dare in her life. Not even to jump off a tall bluff into a lake when she was nine.

"Make up your mind, Princess. Otherwise, you may find yourself part of the show."

That did it. "Thank you. I'd like to watch from your office."

"Come on." He directed her up a different stairwell to the second floor. She was very conscious of him behind her on the stairs and deliberately put an extra wiggle into her walk.

Once they were upstairs, he escorted her toward a door marked PRIVATE.

While his office was twice the size of her private box, a similar plate-glass window overlooked the ballroom and stage. The wall to her left held a bank of television screens monitoring what appeared to be empty rooms. The opposite wall held a desk, chair and file cabinet. A large mirror on the wall permitted the desk's occupant to check the TV screens without turning around.

In front of the window, a love seat and two chairs were positioned to provide comfortable seating for viewing the club floor below.

As with the boxes, low-intensity filtered lights and one-way glass prevented anyone downstairs from seeing inside the office.

"Have a seat." Quin waved toward the love seat.

Leah hesitated, still a bit uneasy at being alone with him while watching the 69 Club's second course. She moved toward the window, but did not sit.

Downstairs, only about two dozen men milled about. Perhaps not every club patron knew about the "second shift."

Leah had wondered whether the spectators for the next show would be different from the earlier crowd, and they appeared to be a significantly smaller group and all male. So why did Gutierrez admit *her*? And why hadn't Quin reported her?

She glanced over her shoulder at him. "What's your role here?"

"I work for the owner." He perched on the edge of the desk and stretched his long legs in front of him, clearly at ease.

Damn, he's fine-looking. Desire licked at her nerve endings, reminding her how long it had been since she'd had sex with a live man. Even though she'd stayed busy with *Heat*, she'd been aware of her growing physical tension. "Gutierrez is the owner?"

"No." He didn't elaborate.

"County records show this property is owned by the Sixty-nine Real Estate Trust, but I couldn't find the trust listed anywhere else. Care to give me the principals' names?"

"Nope."

She took a step toward him. "Why didn't you tell Gutierrez who I really was?"

"Because you're flirting with trouble, *chiquita*, and I'm trying to save you from a world of hurt." He wasn't smiling now.

Leah felt a shard of ice slither down her spine. "Are you saying the owners would harm me if they found out I was writing a story on this club?"

"I'm saying you ought to go home and forget about this place. You're in over your head."

She shook her head. "If these guys are so bad, what are you doing here?"

He shrugged. "Not many businesses are willing to hire a guy who just finished serving ninety days in lockup for assault."

"What do you do here?"

Quin shrugged a second time. "Driver, bodyguard, whatever's needed." He grinned—that same devastating grin she'd seen earlier. "Do you have any needs I can fill, Princess?"

Her mouth went dry, but she tossed her head, making her shoulder-length hair swirl like a blond cloud—a gesture she'd mastered at sixteen. "You wish. Did you bring me up here to threaten me, or to put the make on me?"

"A bit of both." He waved toward the window. "Maybe I just wanted a partner for the show."

Leah's heart contracted hard, sending blood rushing through her body. She could hear the reverberation of her heartbeat in her ears, and the pulse in her neck began to pound. Quin could probably see it throbbing. *A partner. He wants a partner.*

Her mind filled with images of Katya and *her* partners; for a moment, she felt light-headed. *Maybe he's right. I'm headed for trouble.*

Her mental film reel shifted. Now she was seeing a naked Quin. Imagining him touching her, stroking her. . . .

She shook her head, trying to dislodge the dangerous image.

He watched her, a knowing expression on his face.

"Want to change your mind, Princess, and get out before things get . . . exciting?"

He's trying to scare me. That thought added steel to her spine. She lifted her chin.

"If you're trying to run me off, it won't work."

"I just want to be sure you know what you're getting into."

His warm fingers wrapped around her wrist like a handcuff, but then he paused, as though waiting for her to protest or try and snatch her hand back. "*Do* you know what you're getting into, Princess?"

She was saved from having to answer by blinking lights and Gutierrez's voice on a speaker. "All right, everyone. We're ready to start. Take a seat, please."

Leah tilted her head. "The show's about to begin. Shall we watch?"

Quin leaned forward and whispered in her ear. "I want to do a lot more than watch. How about you?"

His breath was hot on her skin, and his scent enveloped her. She recognized the fragrance of sandalwood. But Quin's scent was spicier than the typical men's aftershave; she detected a hint of cloves.

Almost without realizing it, she swayed toward him, trying to absorb his scent into her pores. She inhaled, drawing that delicious smell into her . . . inside her body, where she wanted him to be.

Much closer now, he blew lightly in her ear.

She couldn't help it; she shivered. Not because she was afraid. No. Leah shivered because she wanted what he offered. She wanted his mouth on her lips, his hands on her breasts, and his cock buried deep inside her body. She trembled for want of him.

His tongue grazed the lower part of her ear and then traced a path slowly around the entire lobe.

"Mmmmm," she sighed.

The voice on the speaker intruded. "Please, take your seats. The auction is about to begin."

Quin's lips abandoned her ear to follow her jawline to her mouth. He tilted his face toward hers and kissed her, so lightly she barely felt his lips.

"Ready, Princess?" he asked.

"Yes," she murmured, not caring what he was asking her to commit to.

Without warning, Quin stepped back and away, freeing both her mouth and her wrist. He put his hands on her shoulders and turned her body around so she was facing the window. "This is what you wanted to see."

It took several seconds for Leah's brain to make the switch. She blinked rapidly, trying to erase the haze of heat that enfolded her and to focus on the strange scene below.

The white guy who had earlier performed with Katya stood on the stage beside Gutierrez. Still naked, his enormous erection jutted proudly in front of him.

This time he had accessories. His right hand was raised above his head, where he held a silver tray with two glasses and a squat bottle of what looked like brandy.

Around his neck was a thick band of black leather. As Leah

narrowed her eyes to focus, she realized it was a studded dog collar. "What . . ."

Gutierrez interrupted, speaking into a microphone. "Tonight we have only a dozen lots. I'm proud to present lot number one. A delicate yet delicious calvados brandy. An earthy taste, this lot is medium-bodied with a spicy flavor. What am I offered?"

Chapter Four

Gutierrez's words snapped Leah back to reality. "What is this?" she asked, not bothering to conceal her distaste.

"Exactly what it looks like."

"It looks like he's about to sell that man." She leaned forward to get a better view of the ballroom. Men were waving their auction paddles, shouting out bids.

"Who said anything about selling the man?" Quin moved to her side at the window. "The club owner has a promotional permit from the TABC—the Alcoholic Beverage Commission—and he's promoting Texas wines and beverages among his friends."

"Promoting Texas wines, my eye!" Leah snapped. "The only thing he's promoting is sex."

"And you have a problem with that because . . . ?" Quin looked amused. "It's just a bunch of wealthy guys having fun together. It's a game to them."

"Selling people isn't a game!"

"Well, the merchandise doesn't seem to mind." He nodded toward the stage.

He was right. The naked guy, lot number one, had swiveled his body so that his firm buttocks now faced the audience, while he looked backward over his shoulder with a sultry smile.

"Sold! For thirteen hundred dollars. Congratulations to our high bidder, number seventeen," Gutierrez announced. "Enjoy your prize."

As he stepped off the stage, lot number one offered a thumbs-up to the winning bidder, a lanky cowboy type in a flannel shirt and jeans. The winner brandished his auction paddle in a victory gesture. The two men walked together toward the entrance of the ballroom.

"Now for lot number two," Gutierrez said.

An African-American woman in her mid-twenties wearing nothing but four-inch black heels sauntered into view. Her dark hair had been plaited into braids with colorful beads at the end of each strand. She was solidly built—not fat, but not convention-ally thin either. The tray she held above her head included a bottle of red wine and two glasses.

The woman stepped onto the stage and grinned at the audi-ence, which clapped and cheered its approval.

"All right, gentlemen," Gutierrez said into his mike. "Lot num-ber two is a luscious full-bodied Cabernet Sauvignon with great color and a lot of appeal. Who wants to start the bidding?"

The audience erupted with shouts and waving paddles. Guti-errez kept the bidding brisk, pointing first to one man and then another.

Leah noticed for the first time that another man, wearing a headset, sat at a table beside the stage and took bids from the private boxes. He was shouting out the bids to Gutierrez.

Lot number two made the most of her time onstage, encour-aging the bidders with come-hither gestures and swiveling her hips from side to side.

Leah watched, completely fascinated by both the woman and the crowd's response. Like lot number one, this "merchandise" obviously didn't have a problem with the auction.

The problem was Leah's.

Although it was irrational, in a crazy kind of way she envied lot number two. The woman was at ease both in her body and in her sexuality. *Too bad I'm not as comfortable.*

Leah had a checkered history of relationships with men. She was drawn to those guys any other woman could tell with a glance should be avoided: guys with an edge, guys who skirted the law, guys who liked to take chances.

Trying to keep from hooking up with the wrong man, she had a habit of white-knuckling her way along before falling off the wagon with a completely inappropriate guy. Then, when the relationship went south, as they all inevitably did, she'd swear off men until the next time. Her last breakup had been the worst yet.

Quin has Bad Boy written all over him, so, of course, I find him attractive. What else is new?

Gutierrez announced the "Cabernet" had sold for twenty-eight hundred dollars. Lot number two stepped off the stage, laughing and waving to the crowd.

Leah stole a peek at Quin and realized his attention was on her instead of on the action below. "What?"

"You were surprised by the auction. Didn't you know what to expect?"

She blushed, more because of her thoughts about him than because of the show.

"I'd speculated, but it's still a little . . . outrageous."

He shrugged. "No more than a porn film. And about as interesting."

Leah frowned. "I thought all men were turned on by porn films."

He grinned. "I'm more turned on by opportunities closer to home. For instance, I like the way your nipples press against that silk blouse."

Before she could stop herself, Leah turned to look in the mirror over the desk.

Quin was right. She wasn't wearing a bra, and her tits were outlined against the fabric of the green silk. Her face was flushed, and he could probably see the hunger in her eyes. Her longing for him.

I should turn around and walk out right now.

But knowing what she should do and actually doing it were two very different things.

The sight of her own desire, and Quin's obvious admiration, made the heat pool in Leah's belly.

He stood behind her, and her gaze met his in the mirror.

"Look," he whispered, nodding at the reflection.

She looked in the direction he was gesturing. And froze.

In the mirror, she could see the television screens on the opposite wall.

On the first screen, lot number one and his now-naked cowboy looked like they were wrestling on a king-size bed.

On the adjacent screen, lot number two was kneeling in front of a tall thirtyish man in a business suit. She was going down on him.

Leah automatically moved to turn away from the intimate moment, but Quin put his hands on her shoulders and gently turned her toward the mirror.

"Go ahead. Look," he said. "I want to watch you watching them."

Hypnotized by the low, urgent growl of his voice, she looked at the reflection. The man's head was thrown back in ecstasy as the woman continued to suck on his cock.

The sight was unbelievably erotic. Leah's fingers twitched toward her breast before she could stop herself. She made a fist and forced her hand down to her side.

Quin bent forward, and his lips nuzzled her cheek from behind. "Go ahead. Touch yourself. I want to watch you doing it."

Needing only that small encouragement, she leaned into him. His hard erection pressed against the small of her back. *He's as aroused as I am. Sweet Lord.*

She shivered, her body's response to the idea of fucking him . . . and of being fucked by him.

His lips traced the long column of her neck. She moaned, wishing it were Quin and her in that bedroom, wishing it was her mouth holding his cock prisoner.

His right hand rested momentarily on her hip before sliding upward along her waist. *Yes, yes, touch my breast. Please.*

Leah almost cried when, instead of moving toward her breast, Quin's hand slid along her forearm to her closed right fist.

He pried her fingers apart and then pulled her hand toward her torso. Spreading his hand over hers, he moved her palm to her right breast.

Leah's heart began to beat a rapid tattoo. It was her hand actually touching her nipple, but it was his hand manipulating her fingers.

She raised her left hand, intending to grab his arm and pull it away from her body. But the second she wrapped her fingers around his muscled forearm, she forgot all about her plan. She could feel his coiled strength, and her primitive brain voiced its approval. A rush of moisture dampened her panties.

Lost in sensation, she barely registered the fact that the man on the screen had climaxed and lot number two greedily swallowed his cum.

Quin licked her neck and ear, all the while murmuring disjointed phrases in Spanish: "I want to fuck you." "Fuck you until you scream." His breath came in short, harsh pants, and he ground his cock into her back.

He grabbed at her skirt and began to drag folds of the material toward her waist, exposing her thighs. His hand burrowed under to find the bottom edge of her panties. He slipped his fingers between the silk and her skin to find her clitoris. Using his index finger, he drew tight circles around the tiny organ.

"Ohhhh," Leah moaned. She arched her back and threw her hands over her head.

With his left hand, Quin finally touched her breast, plucking at her left nipple while his other hand moved her closer to orgasm.

A rhythmic noise intruded. Leah heard it but was too wrapped up in feeling to recognize it. The sound grew louder. Then she realized: Someone was knocking on the door.

Chapter Five

"Quin, *el jefe te busca.*" The boss wants to see you.

With a snarled curse, Quin released her. *"Dame un minuto."* Give me a minute.

Dizzy with desire, Leah turned to face him.

Quin ran a hand over his head, brushing his hair back from his forehead. "Princess, I have to go. Stay right here. I'll be back as soon as I can." He leaned over and gave her a quick kiss before he left the office, closing the door behind him.

Whew! Another couple of minutes and I would have been ripping his clothes off. Trying not to obsess over the memory of his kiss, she checked her reflection in the mirror. *I look like a teenager who's been necking in the backseat of the family car.* She straightened her rumpled blouse and smoothed her skirt back down over her hips.

Her lower belly ached, a souvenir of all that unresolved lust. *The female equivalent of blue balls.*

Trying not to think of Quin, she checked her watch. *Another fifteen minutes before I meet Consuelo.* She looked out at the ballroom floor, where the auction continued in full swing.

This might be a good time to head downstairs.

Consuelo had faxed a hand-drawn map of the house with directions to the kitchen.

Leah hesitated before opening the door to the hall. *Okay, if I'm stopped, my story is that I'm looking for a drink of water or something to eat.* She popped the button lock in the doorknob so she could get back into the room if she needed to return.

After checking the hallway, she slipped out of the office. *If I'm lucky, maybe Quin will think I got tired of waiting and went home. I need to start focusing on my job and not on his oh-so-very-hot body.*

Consuelo had said the kitchen staff left at ten p.m. Since she did not have a key to the building, the only time she could show Leah around was when she was working. She'd suggested they meet in the kitchen while the rest of the place's attention would still be directed toward the stage.

At the end of the hall opposite the public staircase, Leah scurried down the servants' stairs, emerging in a narrow hallway with several doors.

After tucking the map in her pocket, she moved toward a swinging door. She peeked through a round porthole window but saw nothing in the darkened kitchen. She entered.

The only illumination came from a nearby streetlamp shining through a window over the sink. Leah could make out the light's reflected gleam on the stainless steel appliances. She bumped into a large island in the center of the room.

"Consuelo?" she whispered.

"*Aqui,*" a low voice responded. A woman stepped out of the shadows beside the refrigerator into the pool of light.

Consuelo was short, about five feet tall, and wore kitchen whites with an apron. Her gaze kept darting around, as though she were afraid someone would jump out at them from a darkened corner.

"I'm Leah Reece. Thank you for agreeing to speak to me." Leah took two steps forward and froze when an expression of horror crossed Consuelo's face. The little woman jumped backward.

Leah swiveled to look behind her just as the swinging door opened. A harsh voice asked, "What are you doing in here?" His arm snaked out to turn on the overhead light.

She blinked as bright light flooded the room, momentarily blinding her. When her eyes adjusted, she found a man standing uncomfortably close and glaring at her.

The newcomer was a very thin Hispanic dressed in a black long-sleeved silk shirt and beige pants. His face bore numerous old acne scars, and his eye sockets were sunk deep in his skull. The dark eyes studying her were as flat and unexpressive as those of a coyote. Leah felt a sudden chill.

"Who are you?" he asked.

"Uh . . . my name is Lee." She stumbled over the words.

"What are you doing in my kitchen in the dark, Lee?" He moved even closer, and she took an involuntary step backward.

He didn't see Consuelo. I need to keep him from finding her. "I was upstairs, watching the auction. I got hungry and came down here to see if there was anyone willing to fix me a snack."

"In a darkened kitchen?" he asked. Although his tone remained courteous, he made no effort to hide his disbelief.

She smiled to buy time. *Should I mention Quin or Gutierrez?* "To tell you the truth, I planned to sneak a peek in the refrigerator to see if there was something I could steal."

This man was not Gutierrez; a smile and flirtatious manner didn't impress him at all. "Who are you here with?" A note of menace crept into his voice, and his gaze raked her body from head to toe.

Her legs were trembling, and Leah had to struggle to keep her smile from faltering. She hesitated, afraid her voice would betray how deeply he scared her.

Before she could gather her wits to speak, a familiar face appeared in the porthole of the swinging door. Her limbs went liquid with relief.

The door opened, and her questioner swung with the swift-
ness of a rattlesnake, his hand going to his pocket.

"There you are, Lee," Quin said, glancing from her to the man
beside her. She could see him quickly sizing up the situation. Two
other men followed him into the kitchen.

"Quin! I thought you'd abandoned me," she cried.

"You know this woman?" her interrogator asked Quin, his
eyes narrowing.

"I met her tonight," Quin answered. He took three steps forward and grabbed Leah's wrist. "What are you doing down here?"
he asked her.

"I got tired of waiting for you," she said, putting a world of
feminine reproach into the sentence. "I was hungry." She turned
to stare at the first man. "Who is this guy anyway? He scared me
half to death."

"Miguel Lucero, owner of the 69 Club," Quin said.

"What are you doing, bringing *sus mujeres* into my club while
you're working?" Lucero asked Quin in a cold voice.

"She's not my woman," Quin replied. *"Pero me la quiero cojer."*
Although I want to screw her.

Leah had spent much of her childhood on her father's ranch
in west Texas, surrounded by Mexican cowboys. Her Spanish was
excellent, including the slang. She bit down on the inside of her
mouth to keep her face from registering distaste at Quin's vulgar
comment. *Don't let them know you understand what they're saying.*

"If she's not your woman, how did she get in?" Lucero
demanded.

"Gutierrez admitted her a second time on an invitation."

Lucero's lips tightened. "I see I'm going to have to have another chat with Carlos."

Leah's stomach turned over. *I'm glad I won't be here to see that little discussion.* While Quin looked dangerous, Lucero dripped menace.

"It's probably time for me to leave," she said aloud.

Lucero's attention returned to her. "I thought you were hungry." He waved toward the refrigerator.

No! I need to keep him from finding Consuelo. She pouted, shaking her head. "That was before you scared me, sneaking up behind me like that. You spooked the hunger right out of me." She made a show of looking at her watch. "It's late. I'll just head on home. I can eat there."

Lucero's gaze remained fixed on her face. "Quin, take Miss . . . what is your last name, Lee?"

"Reed," she said, anxiety rising.

"Take Miss Reed home."

"That's okay. I have my car here," she said.

Lucero continued as though she hadn't spoken. "Quin, you ride with Miss Reed. Ruben will follow in a car to bring you back here. We'll talk more in the morning." He turned away, but not before she noticed his large belt buckle. *That's real gold!* There was something engraved on the buckle, but she didn't get a good look at it.

Leah started to protest, but Quin's hand tightened on her wrist, and she remained quiet.

Lucero paused with one hand on the door to smile at Leah; it wasn't a nice smile. "I'll look forward to seeing you again, Lee."

Not wanting to risk saying the wrong thing, Leah just nodded.

Lucero snapped his fingers at one of the two underlings standing behind Quin. That man followed the owner out into the hall, leaving Leah, Quin and presumably Ruben behind—with Consuelo still in hiding.

I need to get these guys out of the kitchen. But Lucero had scared her so badly, she couldn't think.

Quin reached into his pocket and pulled out a set of keys. He tossed them to the other man. "Ruben, go get my Jeep. We'll meet you out front in five minutes."

"Wait!" Leah said. "You don't need to take me home. I'll be fine. If you'll just walk me to my car—"

Quin interrupted. "Boss's orders, Princess." He wrapped an arm around her waist. "What are you waiting for, Ruben? An engraved invite?"

The man scrambled to obey, leaving the kitchen.

"You want to tell me what's really going on here, Princess?" Quin asked in a low voice, freezing her with a penetrating look.

"What is it with you people? There's nothing going on." She pushed his arm away from her waist. "You left me high and dry, and I got hungry." She stomped toward the swinging door. "And stop calling me Princess. It makes me sound like a French poodle."

Chapter Six

Neither Leah nor Quin spoke again until they reached the entrance hall and one of the hostesses called out to them.

"Hey, Quin, where you going? I thought we were gonna go out when I get off?" Like all the women at the club, the girl wore a skimpy dress, heavy makeup and a sensual smile.

"Sorry, Dara. I'll have to take a rain check. I've got an errand to run."

The girl pouted while sizing Leah up with an unfriendly gaze. "Well, if you finish with your *errand* before two, I'll still be here." She fixed him with a sultry look. "I promise I can do more for you than she can."

Leah gritted her teeth to keep the rash words that sprang to her lips from escaping.

Quin grinned at Dara. "I'll see you tomorrow." He put his hand in the small of Leah's back as he directed her toward the entrance.

Leah waited until the door was closed behind them before slowly exhaling the breath she'd been holding. "One of your job perks?" she asked sweetly.

He shook his head. "She's a nice kid."

She started to reply sarcastically, then shut her mouth. *Men! Pollyanna was a nice kid. Dara was a conniving witch.*

But the encounter had planted a seed of doubt in her mind. *Does he sleep with all the staff?*

A small voice in her head responded, *What do you care? You're the one who wanted a no-strings-attached hookup. Let him count you as another scalp. You'll be gone, and it won't matter.*

They walked in silence to her Accord. Quin held his hand out for her keys.

Leah stared up at him. His dark eyes revealed nothing. She wanted to know what he was thinking. Repressing a sigh, she slapped the keys into his hand.

He didn't say anything, just opened the door for her and then walked around to the driver's side of the car. He got in, adjusted the seat for his taller frame and started the car.

When they pulled out onto the street, a Jeep Wrangler fell in behind them. Leah looked into the side-view mirror. She could see Ruben driving the SUV.

"We'll need to go south—" she started to say.

"I know where we're going," he said. "Are there any signs outside on your building announcing *Heat*?"

"No. We didn't want to advertise all our video and audio equipment to the local thieves."

"Good." He nodded and then lapsed into silence again.

Although the Accord usually felt roomy to Leah, Quin seemed to fill her car. She was very conscious of his muscled right arm inches from her. The scent of his cologne made her pussy twitch. *Quit feeling and start thinking,* she told herself.

"You covered for me again," she said. "Thanks."

"Lucero's a dangerous man, Leah. You need to keep your distance."

Always the journalist, Leah leaned toward him. "Why? What will he do if I don't?"

Quin took his eyes off the road to glance at her. "This isn't a game. Stop acting as if it were. You don't want to cross Miguel."

"Why? Tell me. I won't quote you."

He snorted and looked back toward the road. "Leah, if you keep digging around, people could get hurt. I helped you tonight. I won't do it again. You need to drop this."

She sat back in her seat. "I've got a story to do."

"*¡Chingado!*" he swore.

Although she knew it was childish, a small part of her was pleased to have ruffled his composure.

They completed the rest of the journey in silence.

When they reached the *Heat* building, she directed him to the adjacent parking garage. Quin rolled down his window and motioned for Ruben to wait on the street for him.

Quin pulled into the garage, and Leah pointed the way to her reserved space on the second level. After he'd parked the Accord, she jumped out without waiting for him.

He shut the ignition off, got out and came around to her side of the vehicle.

She watched him approach; he sauntered toward her with a predatory, sexy stride that reminded her of a cat on the prowl.

"What were you doing in that kitchen tonight, Leah? And don't give me that crap about being hungry."

For the last two hours she'd been torn between her desire and her fear of getting involved with this man. And now he was asking questions she couldn't answer. *I'm just trying to avoid his questions,* she told herself right before throwing her arms around his neck and kissing him.

He froze, but only for a second. She knew the exact moment when he surrendered to the kiss she'd initiated. He yanked her into a crushing embrace and thrust his tongue into her mouth. Their tongues twined together in a frantic, erotic tango.

He broke for air and whispered against her mouth, "What were you doing in the kitchen, Leah?"

"Looking for you," she gasped, covering his lips with hers a second time and bumping her hips against his.

His cock leaped to attention and pressed into her belly.

His hardness felt so good against her softness. She ached to wrap her fist around his penis and make him as crazy with wanting her as she was with wanting him.

He pulled free of her mouth and nibbled on her lips. "Who were you meeting?"

Leah felt a surge of anger. Here she was on fire with need, and he was conducting an interrogation. She tried to pull him closer by hooking her right ankle around his legs. But the moment she stood on just one leg, Quin slid his hands under her ass and lifted her off the ground. He pulled her closer to him.

She went eagerly, raising her legs to wrap around his torso, struggling to seat herself so that she could rub against his cock through their garments.

He groped for a second and finally positioned her where he could grind his erection against the juncture between her legs. His hands burrowed under her short skirt to cup her ass.

The feel of his large hands touching her skin so intimately made her pussy weep. She had never been interested in rough sex, but suddenly Leah wanted him to mount her right there and pound into her body.

"Take me," she begged.

He growled and swiveled so that he could balance her weight on the hood of her car. His fingers moved upward to find the lace trim that edged the top of her panties. He ripped the scrap of cloth in half and then shoved his hands under her ass to drag the two torn pieces down to her knees.

She shifted her hips to help him peel the panties off.

He dropped the scraps of cloth on the ground and immediately slid the fingers of his right hand into her pussy.

"God," he muttered. "You're so wet."

"Wet for you," she whispered. As he moved his hand in and out of her vaginal channel, she arched her back and rocked her hips. *So good. It feels so good.*

She leaned back, propping her elbows on the hood of the Accord. "Fuck me, Quin. Fuck me, please."

Quin stepped into the vee between her legs, fumbling with the front of his jeans.

A horn blared on the street below. Quin's head snapped backward, and his hands stopped moving. His passion-glazed eyes regained focus.

"What are you doing?" she gasped.

He shook his head. "No, Leah. Ruben is waiting. I don't want to fuck and run."

"I don't care," she moaned in frustration.

He removed his hand from her sex. "In another two minutes, Ruben will be walking up that ramp to see you lying on the hood of your car." He pulled her skirt down to cover her sex and bent over to retrieve her torn panties from the ground. "If we ever do this, I won't leave you feeling like a ten-dollar *puta*."

She slid off the Accord to the cement floor, smoothing her skirt. *He'd said "if we ever do this." Maybe he doesn't want me. Maybe all he wanted was to know what I was doing at the club.* No man had ever turned down a chance to have sex with her before. She didn't like it, not one bit. *Maybe he's saving himself for Dara.*

He held her panties out to her. She snatched the pieces and threw them down on the cement. Not meeting his eyes, she turned to walk toward the elevators. "Good night, then," she called over her shoulder.

"I'll walk you to your door," he said.

"This *is* my door." The horn sounded from below again, and she stabbed the elevator button. "Just follow the ramp back to the street." She pointed in the direction they'd come.

The elevator pinged its arrival, and she stepped on board. She didn't turn around to look at him.

Quin Perez watched Leah walk away. She didn't look back. He started to follow, but a long, impatient blast of the horn reminded him that Ruben was still waiting on the street.

His balls ached, and he felt like seven kinds of a fool. She was begging him for it, and he'd sent her away. What the hell was wrong with him? He shook his head in disgust.

No, I did the right thing. Ruben would've come looking for us. He'd have found me with my dick hanging out of my pants and Leah with her legs draped over my shoulders. I couldn't do that to her.

Dios, Perez. Could you possibly screw this up any more than you already have? Lucero's pissed, Leah's angry, and you have blue balls. Great work, man.

He'd only been with Lucero for three months; he couldn't afford to get fired right now.

But, damn, that girl was hot. He'd always been a sucker for *las rubias*, the blondes. As early as junior high, whenever there were girls available to be checked out, he'd always headed straight for the cool blondes.

And, Leah, *Dios mio*, she was a blonde and a half. She had a sexy body, a beautiful face and a quick tongue. And she wanted to be fucked and didn't care who knew it. What more could a man ask for in a woman? He'd been an idiot to walk away. He bent down to scoop up the tattered remnants of her silk panties.

Okay, so there were a few problems. She wanted to write about the club. Zeke had claimed Leah only wanted a light, sexy story, which was bad enough. But now Quin was less certain. He couldn't figure out what she'd been doing in the kitchen earlier. Only two things made any sense and both suggested plans for a longer, more detailed story, maybe even an exposé. Either she was snooping around on her own and ran into the kitchen to hide, or she was planning to meet someone, an informant.

No matter. If Lucero got wind of either possibility, she'd disappear, and no one would ever hear from her again.

Ruben pressed the horn again. *If he does that one more time, I'm going to wipe the sidewalk up with him.* But the noise got Quin moving down the ramp toward the street level.

Leah. He raised her torn panties to his face and held them in front of his nose. Her perfume—a light, flowery fragrance—filled his nostrils, but he could smell something else, too. A secret scent, beneath the other, almost overwhelmed by the perfume. A musky, feminine odor. Leah's essence.

He pressed the cloth to his face, trying to trap her fragrance, to breathe in her sum and substance.

Before she'd interrupted them in the stairwell, Zeke had alerted him to Leah's presence and asked Quin to keep an eye out for her.

Then Leah herself appeared on the stairs, and the woman who confronted them was nothing like Quin had expected. He'd known about the drop-dead-gorgeous part from her photo, and Zeke had told him about the tough magazine owner part. But nothing had prepared him for the fragile part. *That look on her face when she turned toward the elevator a minute ago. I hurt her feelings.*

"Fuck!" he muttered. "What the hell am I going to do now?" He stuffed the panties into his pocket and headed toward his Jeep.

Chapter Seven

On Thursday morning, Leah woke with a headache and the sense of having just averted disaster.

Damn, girl, you almost did it again. What's wrong with you?

She sat up and swung her legs over the side of the bed. *Who are you kidding? You haven't gotten laid in almost a year, and along comes Mr. Tall-Dark-and-Sexy. Of course you begged him for sex.*

The memory of her pleading with him made her wince. She stood and walked across to her bathroom, forcing the events of the night before out of her mind. *I've got a lot to do today.* She pulled a bottle of aspirin from the medicine cabinet and dry-swallowed two tablets.

In the shower, she thought about Consuelo. *I need to call and make sure she's okay. I hope she'll talk to me.*

After dressing and eating a cup of yogurt and blueberries, she threw herself into the day's activities. Her apartment on the fourth floor of the *Heat* building, just two flights above her office, made commuting easy.

Thursday's meetings did nothing to alleviate her headache. The graphics staff was feuding with the editorial staff, and nobody—reporters or columnists—seemed to be happy. The appearance of this month's guest, Aggie Curtis, and her too-large-for-her-face grin was a welcome sight late in the morning.

Aggie was a rail-thin thirty-year-old with frizzy orange hair, huge rimless glasses and a raunchy sense of humor. She walked into the conference room and dropped half a dozen items on the mahogany table in front of Leah.

"What are these?" Leah asked.

"Some of the sex toys we'll be profiling in the new spread. Thought you might like to test-drive a couple of them." An overbite dominated Aggie's broad smile.

Leah picked up two items. "Okay, I know these are nipple clamps"—she held up two alligator clips connected by a silver chain—"but what the heck is this thing?" She waved a peach-colored item made of silicone gel. "It looks like a mood ring on steroids."

Aggie laughed. "That's an expandable cock ring with a vibrating capacity. The ring part goes over the penis and the ribbed part on top rubs against the clitoris."

"Sweet mercy." Leah shook her head and dropped both items on the table. "I'm guessing I can figure out what this is." She picked up a long silicone tube studded inside and out with plastic nodes.

Aggie nodded. "Yeah, that's a penis sleeve. Helps a gal when her partner's equipment comes up"—she spread her thumb and forefinger three inches apart—"short. The sleeves are sometimes called 'extenders,' but they come with vibrators so the woman can say she's looking for the pulsing sensation instead of telling the guy he just isn't big enough to get the job done."

All this talk about sex reminded Leah of Quin. She dropped the penis extender on the table and got back to business. "Kevin tells me you want to do the spread like a schoolroom show-and-tell."

Aggie nodded again. "Yeah. Your photographer and I have been talking about the best way to display the items. We're thinking he'll shoot my hands against a black cloth background. That way, the readers will get a sense of the size of the items and also be able to concentrate on the toys themselves."

"Great," Leah agreed. "Let me know if you need any help."

Leah ate a late lunch at her desk while she checked her e-mail and returned phone calls. She telephoned Consuelo around two p.m. and left a message, giving her cell phone number.

Leah had grown up with publishing in her genes and in her blood. She'd had a front-row seat for her father's assault on publishing and his creation of a media empire.

As the legendary Tex Reece's only child, everyone—including Tex—assumed she would one day run the Reece Media Group. But a father-daughter spat led Leah to start *Heat*.

It had taken nearly a year and most of the inheritance from her mother to put together the first edition of the e-zine. She'd recruited young people like herself, interested in working on the cutting edge of the industry. Initially, the team members remained in their home cities and worked via e-mails and phone calls.

But recognizing the synergy produced when creative types are housed together, Leah bought a four-story brick building with an attached three-story garage in Oak Cliff, a depressed area rapidly undergoing gentrification.

The move had generated lots of free publicity for the new venture. While the bottom two floors housed *Heat*'s offices, the third floor offered a variety of employee perks, including a fully equipped kitchen, gym, hot tub, sauna and a dozen bedrooms where staff could spend the night when working against deadlines. Leah reserved the fourth floor for her own penthouse apartment.

By the time the first issue was ready for release, the entire team had transferred to Dallas. They quickly bonded, spending as much time together after work as they did during the day. Stories about Tex Reece's "maverick daughter" and her young staffers quickly spread. Leah was inundated with requests for interviews about the new enterprise. The *Dallas Morning News* ran a cover article on *Heat* and the "Workplace Playspace," implying that the staff used the third floor to hook up.

Anxious to keep *Heat* in the public eye, Leah responded to a reporter's question about the bedrooms by saying, "As long as *Heat* is produced, I'm not going to worry about brushfires along the way."

By six p.m., anyone going home had already departed the building. Those remaining had decided to hold a barbeque in Aggie's honor on the roof of the garage, where a dozen chaise lounges and five or six kids' wading pools flanked two large gas grills.

Leah retreated to her apartment to shower and change. Because the early May weather was mild, she decided to wear a turquoise sundress with white piping and matching sandals. Since she had not yet heard from Consuelo, she tucked her cell phone into the pocket of the dress.

She stepped out onto her wraparound balcony—the architects called it a terrace—and glanced over the side to see how the barbeque was progressing on the roof below her floor.

From the looks of things, it would be at least another hour before dinner became a possibility. Half the crew members were in cutoffs and bathing suits, sitting with their rumps in the wading pools and their limbs hanging over the sides. The remaining staffers were draped over the chaise lounges. All held glasses or beer bottles.

"At least they're not out driving drunk," she murmured.

Throughout the day, whenever her mind had drifted toward Quin and the night before, she'd ruthlessly concentrated on something else. Now, alone with her thoughts, she felt the burn of embarrassment return. *I offered myself like a cheap whore, and he turned me down flat. What's wrong with him? What's wrong with me?*

Restless and not in the mood to be subjected to her staff's

exuberance, she decided to take a quick walk around the block. It was still daylight. *The fresh air will clear my head.*

Fifteen minutes later, while she was crossing a street, her cell phone rang.

As she suspected, the previous evening had spooked Consuelo, who was having second thoughts about helping her.

Leah knew better than to push an informant. She suggested they wait and talk again the next day. Once some time passed, she hoped Consuelo would give more weight to the money she could earn than to the risk that went with it.

Just after seven p.m., Quin drove his Harley down the street toward the *Heat* building. The evening was warm and the wind against his face a pleasant relief.

This must be what schizophrenia feels like. He hadn't been able to get Leah out of his head. One minute he pictured her on the hood of the Accord and felt his cock harden; the next he reminded himself how catastrophic it would be to get involved with her while still working for Lucero.

With the evening off, he'd been enjoying a ride on the Harley when he found himself heading toward Leah's building. *Okay, I'm here. Now what?*

Quin braked diagonally across the street from *Heat* and parked in a spot that gave him a view of the entrance. He propped his elbows on the handlebars, folded his right hand over his left and rested his chin on his entwined thumbs.

This is a huge mistake.

He was still debating whether to present himself at the *Heat* desk and ask for Leah when he heard her voice.

"Quin?"

Chapter Eight

*L*eah approached the motorcycle from behind to stand beside him on the sidewalk. In her sundress, she looked as cool and delectable as a parfait.

All his good intentions flew out the window. "What are you doing out here?" he asked and immediately thought, *What kind of a stupid question is that, nimrod?*

"Taking a walk. What are you doing here?"

"I . . . uh . . . was wondering if you had plans for dinner."

He could see indecision dance across her face. She wanted to go with him, but her desire conflicted with her fear. *Damn, I saved her ass twice—first with Gutierrez and then Lucero—but she's still suspicious of me. Let her stew. We'll both be better off if she turns me down.* He refused to try to persuade her, sitting still, waiting for her to make up her mind.

"We're having a barbeque upstairs." She waved toward the garage. "Why don't you join us?"

She doesn't want to go off alone with you. Let it go, Perez. Ride away. He shook his head. "I spend every night surrounded by crowds of people. I'd like to go to a quiet place where we could eat and talk—just you and me."

If the sight of Quin sitting on a motorcycle down the street from her building surprised Leah, the invitation to dinner completely disarmed her. *What kind of guy shows up unannounced on a motorcycle to take you to dinner?*

She answered her own question. *A guy who doesn't care about the rules. My kind of guy.*

Leah made a sudden decision. "I need to run inside and put on some jeans. Give me five minutes."

His expression didn't change, but she caught the flash of surprise that glittered in his eyes before he nodded.

He didn't expect me to go. Good. My turn to catch him off guard.

Without pausing to think about what she'd done, Leah ran across the street. She waved at the guards and took the elevator to the fourth floor.

In minutes, she changed into jeans, a rust-colored T-shirt with an aquamarine scarf tied around her neck, tennis shoes and a soft leather jacket. *The aquamarine makes my eyes look more blue.* She swept her hair back into a clip. After transferring her wallet, brush and lipstick to a shoulder bag and her phone to her pocket, she started toward the door, then hesitated.

Retracing her steps, she went to the top drawer of her nightstand. She checked the expiration date on the box of condoms stored there and then tucked three foil packets into her purse. *I can't believe I'm doing this.*

Leah had already locked her apartment door and pushed the button to summon the elevator before the serious doubt set in. *How do I know where he's taking me, or what he has planned? The little I do know about the man doesn't qualify him as Citizen of the Year. What am I doing?*

Instead of waiting for the elevator, she retrieved her cell phone and speed-dialed the Prada residence.

Sandy answered on the first ring. She told Leah she was waiting for Zeke to call on his way home from work. When he'd learned he was to be a father, Zeke had obtained reassignment to the day shift.

Leah asked how Sandy and Froggie were feeling and then switched subjects. "Listen, honey, I need some help. Last night at the club, I met a guy Zeke knows. His name is Quin. . . ." She hesitated, realizing for the first time that she didn't know his surname. "He's waiting downstairs, saying he wants to take me out to dinner . . . on a motorcycle." She paused, trying to decide what to say next. "What I'm hoping you'll tell me is whether or not I can trust this guy."

There was a moment of silence. When Sandy spoke, her voice was cautious. "I've heard Zeke talk about Quin. They grew up together—"

"I know," Leah interrupted. "Zeke told me that. He also told me he'd arrested the guy. For assault. So should I get on a Harley with him or not?"

"Leah, you've always trusted your instincts with guys. Why are you calling me?"

An excellent question. "First, because he's downstairs right now. Second, because the guy's been to jail at least once, and he looks kind of dangerous." *But neither of these is the real reason.* "And, third, because last year proved my instincts are lousy."

"So this is really about Dale and not Quin?" Sandy asked.

"Probably. I don't want to get involved with another psycho. If he had killed Tex, it would have been my fault."

"No, it wouldn't. Dale was responsible for his own actions. And he didn't kill your father, thank God." Sandy used the soothing tone she probably employed when counseling clients. "But I'm wondering. What happened to your plan to only date safe business types? Why now, and why this guy?"

"I don't know." Leah glanced at her watch. Her five minutes

were up. "All I know is that I want to go with him so I called my best friend for help. What should I do?"

Sandy was quiet for a long moment. Leah waited, chewing her lower lip in an agony of indecision.

"Leah, this reminds me of the night I went to meet Zeke for the first time." Sandy ignored Leah's sharp intake of breath. "I wanted to go to him so badly, but my brain said I was crazy to trust a blackmailer." She chuckled. "I knew you were out on a date so I called your answering machine and talked to it instead. Do you remember?"

"Of course," Leah whispered.

"I can't tell you what to do, but . . . I can tell you Zeke once said that, when they were kids, there was no one he trusted more to watch his back than Quin."

Leah let out a long sigh. "Thank you, Sandy."

"You're welcome. Now, listen, this isn't free rein to be stupid. He works for some seriously scary people, and you need to be careful."

After the two women exchanged good-byes, Leah snapped her cell shut and stabbed the elevator call button again.

She reached the lobby with Sandy's advice repeating in her brain. *"He works for some seriously scary people, and you need to be careful."*

I need to be smart and careful. Quin has already admitted his boss is dangerous.

She strode to the security desk and asked Felix, one of the guards, to follow her outside and write down the license plate on Quin's motorcycle.

Alarmed, Felix said, "Is there a problem? Do you not want to go?"

She smiled. "Oh, I want to go with him, Felix. I really want to go. I just need you to get a look at the driver and record the number of his Harley."

Felix exchanged a look with his partner before picking up a pad and pen. "Lead the way."

Quin sat sideways on his motorcycle, the calf of one leg resting on the thigh of the other. Once again, he was dressed all in black: T-shirt, jeans and biker boots. The garments clung to his lean frame. *God, he looks hot.* Her skin began to tingle, imagining him touching her body.

When he saw her approach with Felix, Quin lowered his right leg to the ground. "Bringing a chaperone?" he asked, his tone wry. "I'm not sure this bike has enough room for three."

"Think of it as my insurance," she retorted. "Felix Warner, please meet Quin . . . you never did tell me your last name."

"Medina," he answered. "Quin Medina." He extended a hand toward Felix, who ignored it. The security guard was busy taking notes.

Quin turned toward Leah. "So how does this work? If I don't bring you home by midnight, does Felix send out a search party?"

"When I lived in my father's house, my curfew was two a.m." She smiled at Felix. "If I haven't called you by two, call the police and give them our description."

"Yes, ma'am." The dark-skinned guard, who was at least eight inches shorter and twenty years older than Quin, gave the other man a hard stare. "You take good care of her, hear?"

Quin nodded, with no hint of mockery on his face. "I assure you, Mr. Warner, I will protect her with my life."

Felix frowned, but obviously couldn't find anything objectionable in Quin's response.

Leah walked to the Harley. Quin swung his long leg over the

saddle and then leaned forward to make it easier for her to climb aboard. She spent a few seconds scooting around to get comfortable on the seat and then put her hands on his waist.

Quin gunned the motor and took off.

Felix stood in the street watching as they rode away.

Chapter Nine

When the motorcycle accelerated, the momentum pushed Leah backward. She instinctively tightened her grip on Quin's waist.

He guided the bike around a corner. As her body started to tilt to the right, Leah wrapped her arms around him. The more intimate position pressed her torso into his body and flattened her breasts against his back.

"Where are we going?" she shouted.

"Not far," he answered. "Do you like Mexican seafood?"

"Yes. Are you thinking of El Camarón?"

"Yeah."

"I love it."

Mention of the well-known local eatery eased some of Leah's tension and allowed her to enjoy the ride. It had been years since she'd been on a motorcycle, but Quin handled the Harley with the confidence of a seasoned biker.

Riding on a motorcycle was a much more immediate experience than riding in a car. Her leather seat was higher than Quin's, allowing her to look over his shoulder. If she wanted to do so, she could lean forward and lick his earlobe. *Of course, he'd probably go right off the road if I did.*

The roar of the engine blocked out other sounds. A brisk wind dried her lips and assaulted her hair. Strands kept escaping the clip at the nape of her neck and whipping across her face.

The wind also brought Quin's now familiar scent to her nostrils. She took a breath, drawing it in. Her nipples tightened. *I'm turning into Pavlov's dog. One whiff of Quin and I begin salivating. I wonder if he can feel my tits against his back?* She had an insane urge to rub her face against his T-shirt, like a cat scent-marking its territory.

They arrived on Jefferson Boulevard in minutes. Quin parked in a lot behind a block of buildings that included the restaurant, and the couple dismounted.

Leah wanted to make casual conversation as they walked toward the entrance, but she couldn't think of anything to say. She still hadn't quite absorbed the fact that she was with Quin. Her pussy was busy celebrating, while her brain was having trouble organizing thoughts.

El Camarón—the Shrimp—occupied a building that had once housed a factory. The cavernous first floor featured a bar in its center that was popular with the after-five crowd. A raised platform ran around the perimeter of the room and held tall saltwater aquariums. Restaurant patrons sitting at tables in the dining area enjoyed spectacular views of fish normally seen only in the ocean.

The maître d' escorted the couple to a table and made a production of helping Leah remove and drape her jacket over the back of her chair.

An awkward silence followed the host's departure. Suddenly self-conscious, Leah ran her fingers along her hairline, checking to make sure the wind-whipped strands weren't sticking out in all directions. She tried to think of something to say, but discarded every possibility as inane. Looking down, she pretended to be studying her menu.

Quin spoke first. "What are you thinking?"

"I was surprised to see you." At his quizzical expression,

she faltered. "I mean, after last night . . . when you told me to leave . . ." Her voice trailed off uncertainly.

Quin frowned, tiny creases appearing on his forehead. "Never think that I didn't want you, Princess. Letting you go last night was one of the hardest things I've ever done."

"It was?" she whispered.

"Oh, yeah." His voice dropped several octaves. "I wanted to fuck you more than I wanted to breathe."

She sighed, but before she could say anything, the waiter arrived with a tray bearing water.

Since both of them were already familiar with the menu, they ordered their food along with drinks. Quin chose shrimp tacos, and Leah ordered the calamari.

When they were once again alone, Quin shook his head. "Leah, how could you believe I didn't want you? I'm risking a lot to even be here."

"What do you mean?"

He hesitated. "I'm putting my job on the line by getting involved with you." He realigned the knife and fork in front of him, putting them exactly parallel to each other. "And I'm worried that I could put you in danger. Or"—he looked directly into her eyes—"*you* could put us both in danger."

Taken aback, Leah looked down, not wanting to meet his gaze. "I don't know what you're talking about."

"Come on," he rasped, and she looked up. "Let's not game each other, Leah. You're planning a story about the club for *Heat.* We both know that. Don't pretend."

"I'm not pretending. I *am* doing a story, but I don't see how that should make a difference. I'm not asking you for anything." She jutted her chin forward defiantly. "And you're not the only one taking a chance here. I'm the one who went off alone with a man who admits to spending time in jail for assault."

The second she said the words, Leah wished she could call them back.

Quin's hands tightened into fists, but he didn't say anything. She watched as he worked to get control of his temper.

After several seconds of silence, he exhaled a deep breath and unclenched his fingers.

"You're right. I did go to jail, but not for hurting a woman. I beat the shit out of a pimp who was trying to recruit a sixteen-year-old boy." His right hand jerked as he started to reach across the table toward her, but then he pulled back. "I'd never hurt a woman, Leah. Especially not you."

"Why not me, especially?" she asked, conscious of how whiny and insecure the question made her sound.

For the first time since they'd arrived, Quin smiled, a very rueful smile. "I can't believe you're even asking. In the twenty-four hours since we met, I've lied to my bosses, put my job in jeopardy, almost fucked you on the hood of a car and then sat mooning like a lovesick teenager in front of your building." He shook his head. "I've never done any one of those things before, and you have me doing all of them at once." His smile faded. "Why don't you believe me?"

"I don't know." It was Leah's turn to confess. "I guess it's because I'm always attracted to the wrong guys for all the wrong reasons."

His grin was lopsided. *"Muchas gracias."*

She winced. "I didn't mean it that way. It's just that I don't trust myself with men. Believe me, I have good reason."

He leaned forward and placed his hand over hers on the white tablecloth. "Your past is just that, Princess. Your past. When my cock is buried deep inside your pussy, you won't be thinking about any man but me."

Oh. My. God. A flood of heat rushed over her, and her stomach tumbled off a cliff. She felt it drop.

Not willing to let him simply assume the upper hand, she locked gazes with Quin. "Big talk, mister. Are you sure you can deliver?"

Perhaps recognizing the challenge in her voice, he smirked. "No question, Princess. Satisfaction guaranteed."

Leah pulled her hand from his. She raised her arms, bent them at the elbows and laced her fingers together behind her head. The movement lifted her breasts, which pressed against the thin T-shirt. "What exactly do you plan to do with me?"

His grin turned wolfish. "I'll start by peeling that shirt off you and licking your nipples."

"Just licking?"

"At first. I'll lick your nipples and then the rest of your breasts and maybe suck on them, too. After that, I'll nibble on your tits."

The tits in question tightened, and Quin leaned forward. "Do you want me to nibble on your nipples, Leah?"

Not trusting her voice, she simply nodded.

She could read the smug satisfaction on his face, and it awakened a little devil inside her. Remembering his previous reaction to seeing her tongue, she deliberately slid the tip of it out to moisten her upper lip.

She was rewarded by his sharp intake of breath. "What about you, Quin?" she asked. "How would you like to have me suck on your cock?"

He swallowed convulsively, and she saw his Adam's apple bob.

"Oh, yeah. I'd like that a lot." His gaze was on her mouth; his grin was gone. "Please."

Before she could speak—or leap across the table toward him—the waiter appeared from nowhere with their drinks. The man seemed to realize he'd interrupted something. He put the two glasses on the table and quickly left without speaking.

Leah stood. "I need to visit the ladies' room. Why don't you wait a minute or two and then join me there?"

His exhalation of breath was an audible hiss.

She turned and walked toward the back of the restaurant, her heart pounding with excitement. *What's gotten into me? I've never done anything like this before.*

She looked over her shoulder toward the table to see if Quin was watching her. He was, with a look of stunned disbelief on his face.

With her gaze still fixed on him as she entered the alcove leading to the restrooms, she bumped into a large blue-collar type who was hanging up the pay phone.

"Excuse me," she murmured, trying to maneuver her way around his bulk.

"Hey, hold on, pretty lady. Let me buy you a drink." He grinned at her.

"No, thank you. I have someone waiting." She could smell liquor on him, but he didn't look dangerous. Just lonely. And probably hungry for a woman. While the bar at El Camarón really got hopping on a Friday or Saturday night, this was Thursday. Not a good night for pickups.

The burly blond held her forearm, not tightly, just firmly. Before she could employ the twist she'd learned in her self-defense class, a large hand clamped itself over her new suitor's wrist.

"I believe the lady said no," Quin growled.

Leah stared at him. His eyes were blazing and his jaw looked granite-tough. He must have been squeezing the other guy's wrist hard enough to hurt because a wince rippled across the blue-collar worker's face.

"Quin, we're fine here. Let him go," she said. *Don't ruin everything with another assault charge.*

He looked her over, obviously checking to make sure she was okay before releasing the other man and slowly backing out of his way.

The blond moved past without another word to either of them.

"What did you think you were—" She didn't get the rest of the sentence out. One second she was standing in the alcove; the next, he'd swept her into the ladies' room and shut the door behind them.

The two-stall restroom was empty. Quin eyed the entrance doorknob.

"No lock," he muttered. "We'll just have to make do." With his hands on her shoulders, he angled their bodies so that he stood with his back to the door and she was standing in front of him, with her back to the sink.

"Now, where were we?" he asked.

In spite of the situation, Leah started to giggle. "You're insane."

"Are you trying to tell me you're a tease?" he asked. "Did you or did you not suggest I meet you right here, where you would suck my cock?"

"Okay, okay." She waved her hand in surrender. "But if I kneel on these hard mosaic tiles, you're gonna really owe me."

Without hesitation, he yanked his T-shirt free of his pants, pulled it off and dropped it on the floor. "Use this."

She froze, staring openmouthed at his torso.

His shoulders were broad, his chest sculpted. And he had stylized tattoos in black ink along his biceps and across his pecs. With his caramel-colored skin, the tattoos looked spectacularly sexy.

Unable to help herself, she reached out to trace one of the designs with her fingers.

"*Chiquita,*" he growled. "We don't have time for sightseeing. Any minute now, someone's gonna try this door."

Without a word, Leah dropped to her knees in front of him and looked up.

His wide shoulders narrowed to a slim waist. But the bulge between his legs wasn't slim at all.

She unbuckled his belt and then unsnapped his jeans. Slowly, with her head tilted back so she could watch his face, she opened the jeans zipper. She could feel the coiled tension of his body.

When she had the zipper undone, she reached in, burrowing past the opening of his briefs to wrap her fingers around his already stiff penis . . . and froze as someone pushed on the door that led to the bathroom.

Chapter Ten

The restroom door banged closed, unable to move more than an inch because of Quin's body blocking the way.

"What the—?" The surprised voice was a middle-aged woman's.

"Sorry," Quin said in a matter-of-fact tone. "We've got a bit of a flood here. Please use the men's room."

"Oh, for God's sake," the matron snapped. But she went away.

"We'd better hurry," he said, his voice still calm.

Leah pulled his cock free. It sprang out like a jack-in-the-box, ready for action, and bobbed past her cheek to poke at her left ear.

She turned her head to the left and ran her tongue along the hard length.

Quin sighed. The sound was so heartfelt it struck an answering chord in Leah's own chest.

When she reached the juncture where the smooth shaft met the bulbous tip, she began to lap at the corona—the flared ridge that divided the shaft from the mushroom-shaped head.

"Oh, sweetheart," he breathed.

"Spread your legs a bit," she told him. He immediately obeyed.

She scooted backward to get in front of his jutting cock. Holding it with her left hand, she swirled her tongue over the tip of his shaft, capturing the first drops of pre-cum.

A shudder shook his entire frame . . . and someone tried to open the bathroom door again.

Quin's voice was not as steady as it had been before. "Sorry . . .

this restroom is . . . out of service. Please use the men's room," he said in a strangled growl.

"What? What's going on in there?" This time, the woman's voice contained suspicion as well as irritation.

We don't have much longer, Leah thought.

Quin apparently agreed because he put his hands on either side of her head and began plunging in and out of her mouth.

To control how deeply he could thrust, Leah tightened her grip on the base of his cock. She could hear him panting above her, his breath a harsh rasp.

"I'm coming," he groaned. "I'm coming."

I hope so because someone is going to be pounding on that door in about sixty seconds. Her stomach was leaping up and down with trepidation, practically climbing into her throat.

His thrusts became shorter and more rapid. He was grunting now, his vocabulary reduced to "Oh" and "Yes."

Leah heard several voices gather outside the restroom. But excitement now trumped anxiety; the electric current buzzing along her nerve endings took precedence over the acid dancing around in her stomach.

Someone pushed on the door. Hard. A male voice intruded. "Who's in there? What's going on?"

Quin and Leah were too busy to respond. Quin's orgasm shook his frame, and he cried out as his seed spurted.

No question what we're doing in here, Leah thought. She concentrated on swallowing every precious drop. *Breathe through your nose.* She pulled back slightly to create more space and keep the semen from spilling out of her crowded mouth.

"This is the manager. Open this door right now!" Despite his outraged tone, the man wasn't shouting.

He doesn't want to draw attention to what's going on in here, Leah thought. *Not good for business.* But the manager continued to shove on the door.

After one particularly vicious thrust against his back, Quin staggered forward a few inches. He bent from the waist and dropped his hands to Leah's shoulders to brace himself and push back with his hips. His breath sounded as though he'd just run a long-distance race.

His now-shriveled cock slipped from Leah's mouth. She reached up to tuck it back into his pants and zip him up.

Quin straightened and offered a hand to help her stand. He gestured toward his T-shirt with his other hand.

"Don't make me call the police," the manager hissed through the door.

"We'll be right out," Quin responded. He spread his legs to help anchor his body against the door, pulled Leah to her feet and grabbed his shirt from her. Keeping his hips against the door, he bent forward to yank the tee over his head.

Leah checked her reflection in the mirror and ran one hand over her hair, smoothing down the strands Quin had ruffled. In the mirror, her face appeared flushed and her eyes wide with passion.

"Ready?" he asked.

Thinking of what waited outside the door for them, she found her mouth too dry to speak. She nodded instead.

Quin wrapped his right arm around her waist, gave her a reassuring squeeze and pulled on the door handle with his left hand.

The motion of the door swinging open knocked the manager off balance. He fell backward into the two waiters behind him. One of the waiters was theirs.

Oh, good. No cops. Even though her brain had told her the manager wanted to keep things quiet, her stomach needed confirmation that she wouldn't be splashed all over the ten o'clock news.

"Excuse me," Quin said. He escorted her past the three men. His polite nonchalance made Leah want to laugh. The tension drained from her shoulders, and she began to relax.

A middle-aged couple stood in the alcove entrance. The husband stepped aside to make room for them to pass.

"Well, I never . . . ," the woman started.

"Yes, I'm sure you haven't," Leah said in a sunny voice, and then winked at the man beside her.

The stranger raised his hand to cover his smile and, when his wife turned to glare at him, began to cough.

"That's my girl," Quin whispered as he guided her back to their table.

"We need to leave before the manager decides to get nasty," she responded.

"Probably a good idea," he agreed.

When they reached their table, their food was waiting.

Leah picked up her jacket and handed it to Quin to assist her with it.

While he was angling the jacket to capture her right hand, their waiter reappeared. Quin finished helping Leah and then reached for his wallet. "Do you suppose you could wrap these meals up to go? We've changed our minds."

"How are we going to carry the food on your bike?" Leah asked.

Quin removed a hundred-dollar bill from his wallet and held it in front of the waiter.

With his gaze fixed on the money, the server answered, "We have bags with handles."

Quin nodded. "That's what we want."

"I'll have this boxed up in two minutes," the waiter promised, picking up the platters as he spoke.

By unspoken agreement, neither Quin nor Leah sat at the table while they waited. She stole a glance around the room.

The only people watching them were the couple she'd spoken to and the manager, who now stood at the back of the dining room glaring at them.

"*Chiquita*, that was the best blow job I've had in my life," Quin said in a low voice, drawing her attention back to him.

"Tell that to your little friend Dara," she said before she could stop the words from tumbling out. She winced. *Take a great moment and ruin it by sounding like a jealous bitch.*

He grinned. "I thought your eyes were blue, not green, Princess."

"Do me a favor. Just forget I said that, would you?" She looked down at the table.

Leaning forward, he whispered, "At this moment, I would do anything you asked." He put two fingers under her chin and lifted her face toward him. "Thank you, Leah. That was one of the nicest things anyone has ever done for me."

She smiled at him. "You're welcome. Just remember, you owe me."

"I always pay my debts."

In less than five minutes, the couple headed out of the restaurant, leaving the waiter smiling at the hundred-dollar bill in his hand.

Where their trip into the building had been awkward and silent, the walk back to the Harley was full of laughter. As soon as they got outside, Leah gave in to the bout of giggles she'd been fighting, and Quin quickly joined her in laughing. They walked around the building, reminding each other of the outraged expressions on the faces of the manager and the matron . . . and the wistful look on the husband's face.

As they turned the corner to the parking lot, three shadows separated themselves from the darkness crouched at the foot of the building.

"Hey, wetback, I got some business with you."

Quin pushed Leah behind him while she was still gaping at the figure in the middle. It was the blond guy from the pay phone inside. Flanking him were two other men. Both of the newcomers were opening and closing their fists.

"Go inside, Leah," Quin said, his voice even.

"No," she responded. *Maybe if there's a witness, things won't get crazy.*

"Tha's right, honey. You stay right there." The blond slurred his words more than he had earlier. "When I get finished with Chico here, you and I kin go get tha' drink."

"Please, Leah," Quin said without turning around to look at her.

"No," she said for a second time.

The drunk's henchmen spread out on either side of Quin, making it difficult to keep track of all three at once.

One of the other men urged the blond forward. "Go ahead, Jake. Barney and I, we've got your back."

The third man said, "Yeah, Jake. Frank and I have you covered. Get the Mex."

"Leah, if you won't leave, give me some room," Quin growled.

Fear bubbled up Leah's throat, flooding her mouth with acid. Obeying him, she stepped to the left away from Quin and let her shoulder bag slide down her arm so she was holding it by the strap.

Lots of things happened at once. Jake, the blond from the restaurant, surged toward Quin. At the same moment, Frank made a feint forward. Quin threw the bag of food at Frank, spun out of Jake's path and grabbed his arm, pushing him past.

Jake stumbled and—too drunk to recover—fell, hitting the pavement hard. He fumbled around, trying to get up again.

Quin leaped forward toward the third guy, Barney. He grabbed him by the shoulders and pushed his head down at the same time, raising his knee to smash the man's face. Leah heard the sickening crunch of bone.

Seeing Frank move to jump Quin from behind, she ran at him, swinging her shoulder bag as hard as she could at his head. "No!"

"Bitch!" he yelled, fending off the bag.

She opened her mouth to scream for help from inside the restaurant, but he backhanded her, striking her chest hard and knocking the breath out of her.

The scream came out as a strangled croak as she went reeling. Quin twisted to catch and steady her.

"Don't call for help," he said as his gaze went beyond her to Frank, who was fumbling in his pocket.

"What?" she asked, disbelieving what she'd heard. She looked around at their attackers.

Barney was cradling his face and howling. "You broke my nose, you fucking wetback."

Jake had managed to get onto his hands and knees and to

crawl forward toward a nearby car. He was climbing to his feet with the help of its bumper.

Quin ignored the wounded men. "Don't call for help," he repeated. "I'll deal with this." His voice was hard, his eyes focused on the only man still looking for a fight.

Instead of taking advantage of Quin's distraction to escape, Frank had pulled a switchblade from his pocket. He stood his ground, holding the knife in his right hand. "Come on, Mex," he taunted. "Let me stick you."

Chapter Eleven

The blade gleamed evilly in the yellow light.

"Quin!" Leah cried. "He has a knife!"

"Shhhh. It will be all right," he soothed. "Give me two minutes, and I'll take you home." He pushed her toward the parking lot. Without taking his gaze off Frank, he leaned sideways to grab her shoulder bag off the ground.

"That's right, greaser," Frank sneered. "Snatch the lady's purse."

Quin didn't say anything. He just started circling to his left.

The guy with the broken nose, Barney, straightened and took a step forward.

Leah looked around for a weapon. She picked up a discarded beer bottle and then realized she didn't need it.

Barney, wearing a beard of blood, staggered a few feet to a Dumpster. He leaned one shoulder against the metal and then slowly slid down to sit in a heap on the ground, his legs splayed out in front of him. He was finished for the night.

She turned back toward the fight in time to see Frank lunge forward. Quin deflected the blade with her bag.

A few feet away, Jake had managed to get to his feet. "Wha's going on?" he muttered, shaking his head. His back was to the duel, his hands flat on the hood of the car he'd used to support himself.

Without hesitating, Leah ran at him with her arm raised. She brought the empty beer bottle down on the back of his head, and he fell face-forward again. He hit the car hood and slowly slid from it to the ground.

Leah stood over him, waiting, prepared to break the bottle over his head if necessary. But he didn't move any more.

She swung around to see how Quin was faring.

He was still circling Frank, holding her bag in one hand, but the halo of the streetlight revealed two long knife tears on the front of his T-shirt.

Her fingers went weak, and she dropped the bottle she'd been holding. *He could kill Quin right before my eyes. I need to run for help.*

Her desire to stay with Quin kept her frozen in place.

The silence of the two men was unnerving. She could hear the traffic on Jefferson Boulevard and music from a nearby club, but except for the scuffle of their boots on the pavement, Quin and Frank made no noise.

She'd watched for several moments before she noticed that Quin kept moving to the left, which forced Frank to do the same. Frank held the knife in his right hand. Since he was right-handed, the dance they were engaged in kept him slightly off balance. *Quin's been in a knife fight before.* She remembered the knife scar on his face. *Of course he has.*

Rather than alarming her, the realization calmed her. *If he knows what he's doing, maybe it will be all right.*

Frank leaped forward again, but Quin had somehow anticipated the move and was ready. He deflected the strike with Leah's shoulder bag, reaching for Frank with his left arm.

His opponent dodged and pulled back. Before he could stab again, a noise from the restaurant distracted both men.

The back door to the kitchen clanged open and a busboy came out, dragging two large plastic bags. He took one look at the two men and the knife, dropped the trash and ran back inside.

Quin grinned, but there was no humor in the expression. "You're running out of time, Frank. They're going to call the police. You're facing aggravated assault with a weapon. That's a felony."

Frank's face twisted into an angry grimace, and he charged at Quin, who was waiting for the move. He threw the handbag at the other man's legs.

The bag caught Frank in midstep; he tripped and then tumbled forward, his arms frantically windmilling.

Quin leaped on the man as he went down, yanking the knife arm back at an unnatural angle.

Frank screamed in pain and fury, but would not release the weapon. Quin moved to straddle the fallen man's body and continued to force the arm up and backward. Frank's shriek rose in pitch, but Leah could still hear the sharp crack of the break above his scream.

All the fight seemed to go out of him at once, like the air leaving a punctured balloon.

Quin dropped the arm he'd broken and pulled the knife from Frank's nerveless fingers. He snapped the blade closed before slipping the knife into his pocket. He leaned forward to talk to the sobbing man. "You won't ever use that arm to hit a woman again, will you?"

Frank didn't answer, and Quin placed his knee in the man's back.

"Quin, no!" Leah cried, not knowing what he planned, but guessing she wouldn't like it.

"You've still got one good arm," he told Frank. "Do you want to lose that one, too?"

Leah's anxiety, which had begun to drain away, returned, along with the sound of approaching sirens. "Quin, the police are on the way. Let him go."

Quin disregarded her, bending closer to Frank's ear. "You won't ever hit another woman again, will you, *amigo*?" He seized the assailant's left arm.

"No, no, I won't never," the broken man howled.

"Good." Quin released the guy, and Leah breathed a sigh of relief.

Quin straightened and glanced at the other thugs: Jake was still out cold on the ground, and Barney was holding his broken nose and whimpering.

"Okay, *chiquita*. Let's go." He scooped up her shoulder bag but ignored the restaurant bag, with its contents spilled all over the pavement.

They had just started toward the motorcycle when the squealing of brakes on the avenue warned of the arriving squad cars. Quin grabbed Leah's hand and pulled her back toward the buildings.

"Wait!" she said, tugging her arm from his. "Shouldn't we stay? We're the victims here."

"Princess, with my record, I'm guaranteed to spend the night in a cell while you tell your story over and over again until six a.m." He glanced in the direction of the crunching gravel. "Make up your mind fast. Is that the way you want our first date to end?"

Her teeth came down to chew her lip, but before she could make up her mind, he took the decision out of her hands. Grabbing her forearm, he hustled her into a narrow passageway between the restaurant and the club next door.

The alley was only about three feet wide, which meant they had to move through it in single file. The only illumination came from the glow of streetlights outside the openings at either end.

Quin pushed Leah in front of him so that his back was to the parking lot and the arriving cruisers.

About six feet into the passageway, he stopped and leaned forward to whisper into her ear.

"I'm not trying to force you, Leah. But those cops were about to take the decision away from you." He released her. "What do you want to do? We can go back out there, or head that way"—he indicated the mouth of the alley with his chin—"and catch a cab back to your place."

He may have just saved my life. And maybe kept me from getting raped. A night in a cell would be poor repayment. "Let's go," she whispered.

He nodded his approval, and they began to move quietly toward the mouth of the alley. Leah could see the traffic moving past the narrow sliver of space that opened onto Jefferson Boulevard ahead of her. She could also hear the officers' voices and the squawk of their radios coming from the direction they'd just left.

"What the hell happened here?"

"Looks like somebody jumped them when they came out of the restaurant. See the bag of food lying there."

"Well, they might have lost their wallets, but at least they're alive. Have you called a bus yet?"

"Yeah, it's on the way."

As if in response, Leah heard the wail of an approaching ambulance. The strident noise echoed off the tall brick walls, making the siren sound even louder.

They were about two-thirds through the passageway when Quin's hands on her shoulders tightened. She stopped and looked back at him. He nodded toward the mouth of the alley.

Leah had been so focused on moving quietly and listening to

the cops behind her that she hadn't even noticed a white car pulling up and parking on the street in front of them. The hood of the car was even with the passageway's opening.

She wrinkled her forehead. "So?" she whispered.

"It's another cruiser," he breathed into her ear. "It's standard practice to cover both entrances. We can't leave yet."

The ambulance siren abruptly cut off, and she heard vehicle doors banging open and more voices. The anxiety that had begun to settle down surged again. "But won't Frank tell them which way we went?"

His face was so close to hers, she felt the muscles of his face shift into a smile. "Not if he's smart, he won't. Right now the cops think he's a victim. If we're found, he becomes a perp." He chuckled into her ear. "Of course, if that busboy's powers of observation were as good as his reflexes, poor Frank may still earn a trip to Central Booking."

The adrenaline was wearing off. Despite the warm Texas night and her jacket, she began to feel chilled. She shivered.

He wrapped his arms around her. "Are you cold?"

"A bit," she answered.

He hugged her to his body, rubbing her torso with his large hands. "It won't be too much longer. We just need to stay quiet for another thirty minutes or so until they leave."

Leah allowed herself to relax against him. *Thirty more minutes. I can wait thirty more minutes.*

He nuzzled her ear. "You were quite the aggressor out there tonight," he whispered.

"*Me?* What are you talking about?" It took an effort to keep her outraged voice low.

"I saw you take out that guy with the bottle. Nice work."

She was glad it was dark so he couldn't see her blush. "I've never done anything like that before." Along with the fight, the memory of those minutes in the restaurant restroom came flooding back. "You've got me doing lots of things I've never done before."

He shifted his right hand inside her jacket opening to cover her left breast. "I like the sound of that. It makes us even." His thumb stroked her nipple. "Have you ever fucked standing up in an alley with cops all around?"

Leah gasped and tried to swallow the nervous giggle that threatened to escape. "Are you out of your mind?"

"Probably," he agreed. His breath warmed her ear as he whispered to her. "I need to know something."

"What?"

"Are you a screamer?"

"What?"

"Do you scream when you come? I need to know."

A thrill ran up her spine. She opened her mouth, but nothing came out.

A scream from the parking lot made her jump.

"Careful," an unseen male voice cautioned.

"The paramedics must have jarred Frank's arm," Quin said in a low voice.

"Ohhh," she sighed. She settled back against him.

He took her shoulder bag off her arm and, bending sideways, set it down on the ground beside them.

"What are you doing?" she whispered.

"It's payback time, Princess." He felt around her torso until he found the waistband of her jeans. Using that as a guide, he slid his hands to the front of her body, where he proceeded to unsnap her jeans.

"Not here!" she hissed.

"Why not? You have something better to do right now?" His voice held a hint of laughter as his fingers found her zipper.

The buzz the zipper made as he pulled it down seemed to resound in the confined space. Leah held her breath, but no one came running.

Quin slid his fingers into the opening of her jeans. "Damn," he groaned. "Another pair of panties. *Chiquita*, I'm going to have to take you shopping for new drawers."

"Don't you dare tear these panties," she warned.

"All right. If you say so." Bending over, he used both hands to pull her jeans and panties down together, letting them puddle below her knees.

She squeaked. There was no other word for it. She was standing bare-assed with her pants around her ankles in an alley surrounded by police.

Chapter Twelve

Still standing behind her, Quin stooped, burrowing under her jeans to find her right tennis shoe, which he untied. He lifted her foot and slipped the sneaker off. "Pick up your leg," he whispered.

Leah raised her right leg, and he helped untangle it from the pile of cloth.

"What are you doing?" she hissed.

"Helping you spread your legs," he responded. "Point your toes." When she complied, he put the tennis shoe back on her foot.

"That's good," he said with satisfaction. "Bend over a bit more."

She obeyed, and he helped her to shift her hips a little toward the right. The narrow alley made it difficult for him to stand behind her bowed form. She braced her left arm against the wall.

"Comfy?" he asked in a low voice.

"No," she snapped. "I can't believe I'm letting you do this."

He didn't answer. They both knew she was lying. Leah was more aroused than she had ever been in her life. Her pussy was thrumming; she could feel the moisture pooling between her legs. What with the sexual tension of just being around Quin and the prospect of discovery by the police, she was trembling with excitement.

Quin leaned over her, putting his lips to her right ear. "I'm going to touch you. Whatever you do, don't scream."

"I make no promises," she said.

"Think of seeing your photo like this in your father's newspapers," he threatened.

The mere mention of Tex was enough to make Leah click her jaws closed with an audible snap. She nodded.

He chuckled. The warm sound pulled at her insides and created a longing she didn't have sufficient words to describe.

Quin caressed her bare ass with one hand while parting her thighs with the other.

The juxtaposition of the public venue and the intimate touch made her a little dizzy. She was glad to have the support of the wall.

The fingers of his right hand skated down the cleft that separated her ass cheeks, circled the outside of her anus and moved on. He parted her labia and went straight for her clitoris.

Leah's knees almost buckled. She tipped forward and had to take a step to steady herself.

"That's my girl," he whispered. "Stay with me." His index finger found her pleasure button, and he began rubbing it. "You're already wet for me." His voice, though pitched low, was deep and rich.

Outside the alley, vehicle doors slammed, and an engine started. *Probably the ambulance,* she thought crazily.

Quin slid his left hand between her legs and inserted two fingers into her vaginal opening. He sawed them back and forth, in and out.

"Ohhhh," she groaned, unable to stop the noise from slipping out.

"Shhhh," he ordered.

"I can't help it," she whispered.

He pulled his hands from her pussy, and she moaned.

He bent over her. "Leah, you can't make a sound. They'll hear."

"Then stop touching me."

"Not gonna happen, Princess," he growled. He hesitated and then reached underneath the collar of her jacket. A second later, she felt the smooth slide of cloth as he pulled her aquamarine scarf free.

She sensed rather than heard his hands moving.

"Here," he said, thrusting a folded-up cushion of silk between her lips. "Bite down on this."

"My lipstick—" she started to complain, but it was too late. He'd already shoved the scarf into her mouth. *Maybe the cleaners will be able to get the stain off,* she comforted herself.

She could hear him fumbling behind her but couldn't tell what he was doing until she felt the warm press of his cock against her ass. He had opened his pants, but not lowered them. She heard a quick tearing sound and guessed he was putting a condom on.

"My jeans were getting uncomfortable," he said by way of explanation. He crouched behind her and slid his hands between her legs. "Now, where were we?"

Leah shivered as the fingers of his left hand returned to her vagina, while his other hand searched out her clit. He quickly found his rhythm: Alternating an in-and-out motion in her vaginal canal while circling her pleasure button.

Heat coiled in her stomach and spread out, down her legs and up her spine. Her hips started to rock back and forth in mankind's oldest dance. If she could have spoken, she would have begged him to slam his cock into her. Since she couldn't speak, she thrust down on his fingers, urging him to move faster. "Uhhhh," she whimpered around the cloth in her mouth.

He added a third finger to the two already in her vagina and increased the tempo of his in-and-out movement. Without warning, he leaned forward to run his tongue along the cleft of her ass.

The heat from his mouth in such an unexpected place pushed her over the edge. The orgasm came on so suddenly she wasn't prepared for it. She rocked forward, her legs gave way and she fell toward the wall.

Perhaps because she was standing—bending over was actually a better description—her world reeled, and she had the dizzying sensation of riding a roller coaster. A kaleidoscope of colors blurred her vision, and she felt strangely weightless. A series of spasms rippled from her core outward.

Quin's quick reflexes saved her. He must have felt her orgasm begin because he straightened and caught her before she crashed. Supporting her awkwardly with his left hand, he fumbled with the other hand as he tried to guide his cock into her.

The spasms had not yet subsided when he entered her from behind. Her warm wetness welcomed him, and he slid into her vagina as easily as a key into a lock.

Once he was firmly seated, he shifted position, fitting his groin against her ass like two pieces of a jigsaw puzzle. Holding her waist with both hands, he thrust his hips forward.

He filled her completely, and Leah almost swooned with pleasure. Seconds later, when he withdrew, she tried to scream "No!" but the scarf in her mouth allowed only a small squeak.

Quin chuckled and pistoned forward again.

The second orgasm came as suddenly as the first one had and was every bit as devastating. Waves of pleasure washed over Leah like breakers crashing on a beach. Her legs turned to rubber, and only Quin's hands at her waist kept her upright.

Maybe he was waiting for her second orgasm, or maybe the

after-tremors of her explosion were too much for him. Whatever it was, as she resurfaced, he began thrusting with greater urgency.

In and out, in and out, Quin pounded into her. He didn't speak, but she could hear his labored breath above her.

Her body teetered on the thin edge between pain and pleasure. Having him inside her and the continued friction on her already sensitized flesh was exquisite torture.

Leah felt her third orgasm approaching and tensed as the climax broke over her. Waves and waves of bliss cascaded through her body while colors danced in front of her eyes.

Her spasms must have triggered Quin's orgasm. He stiffened and slammed into her one last time. His hands shifted from her waist to her hips, and he emptied himself of his seed.

The weight of his upper body suddenly pressed onto her bent body, and Leah had difficulty remaining on her feet. In her crouched form, she couldn't lock her knees. She started to tip forward. "Uhnnnnnnn," she gasped through the silk of the scarf.

Either he heard her cry of distress or felt her slipping because he tried to brace himself. Unfortunately, he did so by tightening his grip on her and pressing down.

The added pressure made her knees give way, and Leah was in real danger of falling to her knees on the alley ground.

At the last moment Quin seemed to realize what was happening. He staggered backward, pulling Leah toward him.

The two fell back.

Because the alley was so narrow, Quin's shoulders made immediate contact with the brick wall behind them. The wall stopped their fall, anchored him and helped to stabilize them both.

Leah froze in terror, listening to see whether their mishap had been heard outside the alley. For ten tense seconds, they waited for the alarm to be raised. She could feel the sticky latex condom pressing against her ass.

Outside in the parking lot, the cops and paramedics milled around, talking and taking notes. She didn't hear an indication that anyone had noticed the unusual activity in the alley.

Very slowly, she pulled away from Quin and stood. She took the scarf out of her mouth and stuffed it into the pocket of her jacket.

Quin levered himself off the wall, bent and reached for the pants at her feet.

Her left leg was still encased in her jeans and panties. He reversed the process they had gone through earlier in order to help her pull her pants back up.

Once she was put to rights, he removed his condom and discarded it among the other detritus of the alley. She heard him pulling up his zipper.

At the mouth of the alley, an engine started. The police cruiser that had been parked on the street drove off.

"Come on," he whispered. "Let's get out of here." Taking her hand, he led her toward the lights of Jefferson Boulevard.

When they reached the street, he turned right toward the line waiting outside the club next door.

"Mingle with those people. You'll be safe there for a couple of minutes," he told her. "I'm going to get my bike."

"Why can't I go with you?" she asked.

"Because if that busboy noticed us in the restaurant or in the parking lot, he reported a couple. I'm counting on no one looking twice at a lone guy walking toward a motorcycle."

She pointed toward the knife slashes on the front of his T-shirt. "What about that?"

He frowned. "Fuck!"

Leah narrowed her eyes in thought for a second and then began to remove her leather jacket.

"That won't help, Princess," Quin said. "You're too small. I'll never get it over my shoulders."

"Go back to the alley, take off your shirt and reverse it so the cuts are on your back, and then sling the jacket over your shoulder until you get past the cops." She handed him the jacket with a smile. "I'll bet they won't look close enough to notice."

He leaned down to lightly brush her lips with his. "I knew there was a reason I keep you around."

She punched his shoulder, and he laughed.

"Besides the fabulous sex, I mean."

She watched him walk back toward the alley before she turned to join the crowd on the sidewalk waiting to get into the blues club.

"That your boyfriend, honey?" a thin black woman at the end of the line asked.

Leah didn't hesitate. "Yeah, he is."

"My friend and I were just saying that's one fine-looking man." The girl's voice was wistful.

"Thanks. I think so, too."

The woman's companion chimed in, "Girl, you'd better be watching your back because I know there are a lot of evil-minded females wanting to jump that man's bones."

"I know you're right," the first girl agreed.

Leah sighed. "Thanks for the tip." *As if I didn't already know.*

The second girl patted her arm. "You just keep giving him sugar, honey. He'll keep coming back for more."

Chapter Thirteen

When Quin returned on his bike to pick her up, he found Leah standing on the sidewalk talking with two African-American women. The three exchanged hugs before Leah joined him.

He draped her jacket around her shoulders, and she climbed aboard the bike behind him. Leah waved to her new friends as Quin gunned the engine.

The ride to her building was a lot more interesting than the ride to the restaurant had been. All Leah's tension appeared to have dissipated. She pressed her soft curves against his back and rested her chin on his shoulder. At one point, she leaned forward to lick the back of his ear, nearly sending him careening off the road.

When they stopped at a light, he looked over his shoulder. "Want to stop for something to eat?"

"No." She raised her voice above the engine's din. "I'm sure the barbeque is still going on at *Heat*. We can stop by and pick up some food to bring upstairs to my apartment."

No hesitation about having me in her place. We're making progress. A small flame ignited inside his chest, warming his heart.

Almost as though she'd heard his thoughts, Leah rubbed her cheek against his shoulder—like a cat expressing satisfaction with its owner.

The rooftop party was in full swing when they reached the *Heat* building. He could hear the laughter and music even over the roar of the motorcycle.

Quin drove his bike straight up the ramp into the garage and parked next to Leah's Accord.

She dismounted first, and he followed. Yielding to impulse, he pushed Leah against the wall, holding her prisoner with his body.

Surprised, she dropped her purse.

"Game over, Princess," he growled, placing his hands flat on the wall on either side of her head. "You nearly made me total my bike. You could have gotten us killed."

She giggled and then gasped when he slammed his mouth down on hers.

He thrust his tongue between her parted lips and, at the same time, pushed his hips against hers. Her body felt as if it had been fashioned to fit him.

Leah didn't hesitate. She wrapped her arms around his waist and pulled him even closer.

Their tongues and bodies twisted and teased, mimicking the sex act. His cock stirred to life.

He was first to break the kiss. "Stop!" he rasped. "You've already drained me dry. I need nourishment before I can perform again. I'm not eighteen anymore."

Leah laughed. "Let's go upstairs then. I'm hungry, too."

He released her, picked up her purse and handed it to her. They walked toward the elevator, holding hands.

While they waited, he pulled his arms out of the T-shirt and reversed it so he was once again wearing the front side forward.

Leah frowned at the sight of the slashes on the shirt. "I'm so glad you weren't hurt." She stood on tiptoe to kiss him. This time the kiss was sweeter, less frantic.

The elevator pinged its arrival. The door slid open to reveal a frizzy-haired redhead with glasses standing beside a geeky-looking guy holding a large cardboard box.

Leah frowned, although Quin was pretty sure she was only pretending to scowl. "What do you two have there?"

The geek looked abashed, but the redhead grinned, showing no signs of shame. "We've got a box of the sex toys I brought. I'm going to do a demonstration for your staff."

"Sort of like a Rubbermaid party—only with real rubbers," the guy chimed in helpfully.

Quin snorted, and Leah gave him a look intended to quell him. "Listen, we need those items for the photo shoot." She punched the CLOSE DOORS button. The elevator groaned into motion. "Don't lose or break anything."

"I know," the woman said. "We'll take good care of the merchandise."

The geek was eyeing Quin with a speculative gleam in his eye. "Hi, I'm Kevin Burke." He stuck his right hand out.

Quin shook hands with him. "Quin Medina."

"A friend?" Kevin asked Leah.

"No, a termite exterminator," she said. "He's making an emergency house call at"—she glanced at her watch—"just before ten p.m."

Kevin blushed. The elevator shuddered to a halt on the third floor, saving him further embarrassment.

The redhead smiled at Quin. "I'm Aggie Curtis. Are you coming to our party, handsome pest control guy?" She eyed the slashes in his dirty shirt with interest.

"Aggie, he's private stock. Hands off." Leah's warning held a peevish note. *She's jealous.* He was surprised at how much that pleased him.

The look of shock on Kevin's face reinforced Quin's suspicion that this wasn't a normal reaction from Leah. He felt a stir of male pride.

The elevator opened. Quin put a hand out to hold the door for Aggie and Leah.

The two women stepped off, and Kevin followed, still staring at Quin over his shoulder.

The three *Heat* staffers headed toward a door marked EXIT and up the stairs beyond. Quin followed.

Inside the stairwell, the noise from the roof was deafening; the enclosed space acted like a reverberation chamber in which the music and laughter echoed again and again. When they reached the landing above, Quin sighed with relief.

A brick propped the entrance to the rooftop open, leaving a gap of about three inches. Leah pushed on the door and stepped out to welcoming shouts from the partygoers. Quin heard affection in the voices of the *Heat* staff as they greeted Leah. It was obvious they liked and respected her. He followed Aggie and Kevin onto the roof.

Stepping out of the dim stairwell onto the rooftop was a disorienting experience.

A rectangle about half the size of the roof was enclosed by a three-foot-tall white picket fence. The two dozen or so attendees apparently honored the picket enclosure as the limits of their domain; no one was outside its perimeter. *Good idea. Keeps the drunks from falling off the top of the garage.*

Someone had strung multicolored Christmas lights along the top of the railing; the strands of color plus a mercury vapor light mounted on the *Heat* building provided light.

Two industrial-sized gas grills dominated one side of the

enclosure. Nearby, large plastic trash cans stood in puddles of melted ice. *Must be the drinks.*

The rooftop furniture consisted of kiddie wading pools, inflatable mattresses, cheap folding chairs and chaise lounges.

The partygoers wore everything from cutoffs and T-shirts to bikinis and Capri pants. No one looked over forty. The distinctive smell of marijuana came from somewhere to his left. Quin didn't turn to check on the tokers.

He was so preoccupied with the bizarre rooftop celebration that it was a few seconds before he noticed the silence that greeted his arrival. People stared at him, not bothering to hide their curiosity at his disreputable appearance.

Leah grabbed him by the forearm. "Everyone, this is Quin Medina. He's a friend of mine."

"And he's private stock. No poaching, I'm told," Aggie Curtis piped up as she accepted a bottle of beer from a guy who looked like he'd stepped off the set of a surfer movie.

"That's right." Leah nodded to emphasize the point.

A thin dark-skinned man approached Quin, grinning from ear to ear. "I want to shake your hand. I didn't think any man was ever going to get past my girl's defenses." He wrapped his left arm around Leah's shoulders to give her a hug.

"Hush, Roger," Leah said. "You'll have him thinking I'm some kind of freak. Quin, this is Roger Molson. He's one of our programmers."

"No freak, baby girl. Just discriminating." Roger fixed Quin with a penetrating look. "You take good care of our Leah, hear?"

"I will," Quin promised for the second time that night.

Leah addressed the sweating overweight guy manning the

nearest gas grill. "What do you have left for us to eat, Jeffy? We're famished."

"I got grilled chicken, some vegetable kebobs and those burgers." Jeffy waved a spatula at his various offerings.

"My hands are kind of dirty. Would you mind making a couple of plates for us?" She turned toward Roger. "Do me a favor and introduce Quin around while Jeffy helps me."

Roger nodded, and Leah smiled up at Quin. "You relax and mingle."

She's not embarrassed by the way I look. Good.

The staffers seemed friendly, and no one commented on the knife slashes on his now-grubby T-shirt. He made small talk with the half dozen people who drifted over for introductions.

Quin noticed one guy who bypassed him to make a beeline for Leah. The man differed from his neighbors in both costume and attitude. He wore preppie chino slacks and a dark blue Polo shirt. And when he leaned over to speak to Leah, he placed one hand below the small of her back—on the upper swell of her ass. Quin stiffened. *Who the hell does he think he is?*

Excusing himself, Quin walked away from his small group to rejoin Leah. He positioned himself on the opposite side of Leah and stared pointedly at the intruder. "Who's your friend with the wandering hand?" he asked, his voice flat.

Leah looked up, her eyes wide, and immediately stepped away from the Anglo.

The preppie met Quin's gaze with an unfriendly glare, but didn't speak.

"Quin Medina, meet Craig Carson, my CFO. Craig, this is my friend Quin."

"Medina," Carson said and nodded.

Quin didn't acknowledge the other man. He reached for the two plates Jeffy held out. "Ready to go, Princess?"

Leah looked from Carson to Quin, hesitated and then made up her mind. "Yes, let's go." She glanced sideways at Carson. "I'll see you in the morning, Craig."

"You don't have to leave," the preppie said with an annoyed tone.

"Yes, she does," Quin answered, stepping between Leah and Carson.

"Let it go, Craig," Leah said, her voice tight.

The couple was intercepted several times on their way to the exit. People expressed dismay that Leah was leaving so soon, and she responded in a light tone.

Kevin Burke held the door to the stairwell open for them. "Nice to meet you, Quin," he said.

"You, too, Kevin. See you around."

The pair didn't speak during the trip down the stairs. The music echoing in the stairwell would have made conversation difficult.

Leah didn't wait for Quin to hold the door on the third floor for her. She shoved it hard enough that it banged into the wall beyond; the clang reverberated through the garage. She stalked past the doorway toward the elevator with Quin on her heels.

"Exactly what did you think you were doing up there?" She swung around to face him as the stairwell door slammed shut behind them.

"I could ask you the same question," Quin responded.

"What?"

"Do you let all your employees put their hands on your ass?"

Her eyes narrowed. "First of all, his hand wasn't on my ass. And, second, even if it was, it's *my* ass." She stabbed the UP elevator button. "I've managed to get along for thirty-two years without having an overprotective, machismo-filled *man* in my life, and I don't want or need your jealousy. Is that clear?"

"Crystal." He continued in a conversational tone, "Let me be sure I have this straight. You're the only one who's allowed to be jealous, is that it?" Arguing while holding two plates filled with food wasn't easy, but he was too hungry to simply drop them.

"What?" She shook her head angrily.

"Did you hear me say a word when you twice identified me as 'private stock,' like I was a side of beef with your brand on it?" He watched with satisfaction as the barb struck home. *Bull's-eye.*

"That's . . . that's not the same thing," she said, but her voice wavered.

"It most certainly is the same thing," he answered, not hiding the smug note in his voice.

The elevator arrived while she was still searching for an answer. Quin straddled the doorway, holding the elevator open while he waited for her to respond.

"You're right," she said finally. "It *is* exactly the same thing. I *was* jealous, and I acted like a possessive witch. I have no right to criticize you for doing the same thing."

The clever cut he'd been about to utter died on his lips. Her acquiescence astounded him. He'd never known a woman who so readily acknowledged being wrong.

Her clear blue eyes met his. "Quin, I'm sorry."

"That . . . that's okay," he stuttered. In a burst of frankness, he continued, "This is all new to me, too. I've never played the possessive Latin before."

His remark stained her cheeks rose. "Do you still want to eat dinner with me?"

"Hurry up and push that damn elevator button while I try to remember how hungry we both are, because at this very moment, *chiquita*, the only thing I want to eat is you."

Chapter Fourteen

The abrupt end to their argument stunned Leah almost as much as Quin's generosity in not punishing her with anger. *He's right, of course. I was every bit as possessive as he was.*

When the elevator reached four, she guided him out and around the shaft to the fire door that led to the *Heat* building. She fished her card key out and swiped it across the reader mounted beside the door. When the indicator glowed green, she opened the door so he wouldn't have to rebalance the two heavily laden plates.

Leah was the fourth floor's only tenant. Quin trailed her to her apartment door and waited while she unlocked it.

Terra-cotta lamps on timers had switched on at dusk, and the room beyond was bathed in soft light. Leah looked around, wondering what Quin would think of her home.

The living room was one huge space that encompassed a formal sitting area, a dining area and a den.

During the building's renovation, Leah had asked the construction crew to remove the cheap interior drywall they'd found throughout the four-story structure. Underneath the drywall, they'd discovered the original red brick and wooden beams.

Although an interior designer had suggested replastering, Leah declined the recommendation. She liked the natural look the bricks and wood offered. Rather than cover the walls and hardwood floors, she ordered the construction crew to sandblast the brick clean and refinish the solid oak floors.

She loved the finished product. The aged bricks, exposed wooden beams and hardwood floors gave her a sense of stability as she started her very unstable business.

Her taste in furniture ran to overstuffed chairs and couches in warm earthy shades. The apartment seemed comfortable and appealing to her. *I hope he likes it.*

In that uncanny way he had of seeming to read her mind, Quin said, "Nice place. It looks comfortable."

"Thank you."

Instead of heading toward the formal eight-person dining table, she led him to the smaller, more intimate pedestal table already set with sea-grass place mats.

"What would you like to drink?" she asked as he put the plates down. "I have beer, wine, soft drinks and juice."

"What are you going to have?"

She smiled. "I drink a lot of Boston iced tea. It's a combination of iced tea and cranberry juice."

He grimaced. "I'll take the beer. Where's your bathroom? After tonight, I need to wash up."

She pointed toward the nearby hallway.

In the kitchen, she washed her hands, surprised at how grimy they were. *Well, you've been rolling around on the floor of a public restroom and in an alley. What did you expect?*

By the time Quin returned, she'd set the table, adding a bottle of beer, a pitcher of ruby-colored iced tea and a large bowl of fresh fruit.

"You've created a feast," he said, pulling her chair out for her.

"It was the least I could do after we lost that expensive dinner you paid for," she reminded him.

"*Chiquita*, I don't regret a penny of that meal. I'll remember it for a long time." His gaze met hers, and the warmth in his eyes made her want to sigh with happiness.

For a few minutes, they concentrated on eating. Leah was surprised by how hungry she was.

While she ate, she stole peeks at him.

His torn and smudged shirt only added to his dangerous, sexy mystique. The room's subtle lighting created shadows that made the white knife scar on his face more prominent.

"Did you get that scar in a fight?" she asked.

He wiped his lips with the napkin, taking his time before answering. "Yeah," he finally said.

"You're not going to tell me about it, are you?"

He pursed his lips, but then leaned forward to put his hand over hers. "Leah, I'm really curious as to why your staff was so surprised to see me." His grin was rueful. "I'll admit part of their surprise was probably because of the way I look." He glanced down and plucked at the front of his ruined shirt.

"Okay, you've made your point," she said. "You have your secrets, and I have mine."

He raised his gaze to hers and continued speaking as if she hadn't said anything. "But it was more than just my appearance, wasn't it? Your friends were shocked to see you with a man, any man." He paused meaningfully. "I'm going to wait until you're ready to tell me what that's about."

Leah pulled her hand free from his and lowered her gaze to the nearly empty plate. She focused on a small rip on the edge of the plate. *If I try to explain about Dale, he'll think I'm some kind of neurotic freak.* She began to tear at the rip, shredding the plate's colorful border.

The silence between them grew. Unable to bear it, Leah finally said, "It's because—"

He cut her off. "No, Princess. I don't want you to feel forced to tell me. I'll wait until you're ready."

Relieved, she raised her face to look at him again. "Thanks."

He smiled and stood. "Come on. Let's clear off the table, and then you can show me the rest of the apartment."

The paper plates made cleanup easy. Quin rinsed off their utensils and glasses while Leah put away the fruit and the pitcher of tea. When they were finished, she gave him the tour he'd requested.

Heat had been an enormous gamble for Leah. She had tried unsuccessfully to convince her father to invest in an e-zine, telling him electronic publishing would be the future of the empire he'd built.

Tex had not only refused, he'd mocked her proposed plan. His ridicule spurred her to prove that he was wrong and she was right.

Leah had sunk her entire net worth into the venture. For more than a year, she had pinched every penny and worked around the clock to make *Heat* a success. The only indulgence she'd permitted herself was in the design of her own apartment, her safe place.

Now, showing Quin around, she felt as though she were revealing important parts of herself to him.

She saved her bedroom for last.

Leah had furnished her personal space with the antique bedroom suite she'd inherited from her grandmother. The suite included an enormous mahogany four-poster bed, dressing table and chest of drawers. The massive furniture looked somehow natural against the brick walls and wood beams. She'd used a very feminine, lacy white bedspread and canopy to lighten the heavy effect of the bricks and dark wood.

Quin paused in the doorway. "Whoa. I know I've been calling you Princess, but I wasn't expecting this."

"What do you mean?"

"This looks like the bedroom of royalty. Expensive old furniture and lots of white lace. Is a peasant like me going to be struck dead if I enter?"

"Don't be silly. Come on." She tugged at his hand, trying to pull him across the threshold.

Without warning, he reached down, slid his arms under her knees and shoulders and scooped her up.

Leah shrieked in surprise. "What are you doing?"

"You look like a princess, and this room looks like a fairy tale, so I'm going to act like the handsome prince and carry you across the threshold." He grinned down at her startled face.

She put her hands on his chest and shoved. "You goofball. It's brides that get carried across the threshold, not princesses."

His smile turned wicked. "I never did identify with the handsome princes in those fairy tales anyway. They were always blond and blue-eyed—just like the princesses." He carried her into the room and toward the bed. "I identified more with the ogres. They were dark-skinned and dark-haired like me." He laid her on top of the bed and then reached over to switch on the bedside light. "And they said things like 'the better to eat you, my dear.'"

In one smooth movement, he jumped onto the tall bed, landing beside her on the mattress.

His face was inches from hers.

Leah chuckled. "Now you're confusing your stories. It was the wolf from 'Red Riding Hood' who said, 'the better to eat you, my dear,' not an ogre."

"My bad," he said and touched his lips lightly to hers. "I guess I'll have to play the wolf tonight, because I *am* going to eat you."

The wave of heat that washed over her body made her burn from her toes to her forehead. The idea of him licking and sucking her pussy . . . Oh!

She tried to push him off so she could sit up. "You can't. I have to take a shower. We had sex in that alley, and I need to clean up first."

Without much effort, he wrestled her back onto the mattress. "Relax, *chiquita*, we'll take a shower together later. For now, let me be your lady's maid. Lie still." He levered himself off the bed. "Do you have washcloths in your bathroom?"

Overwhelmed by the notion of someone else washing her private parts, Leah just nodded and then watched in silence as he disappeared into her bathroom. She saw the light come on and listened to the sounds of things being moved around, cupboards opening and closing, and water running. *He's serious. He's really going to wash me!*

She took refuge in practicalities. *We're going to ruin this bedspread.* She sat up, untied her tennis shoes and dropped them over the side of the bed. Next, she stood and yanked the lacy counterpane off the bed.

Quin returned as she was pulling down the top sheet on the bed. He was carrying her mirrored vanity tray with several rolled-up washcloths on it. "You couldn't relax for five minutes, could you?" he asked, shaking his head with a smile.

She blushed and stood there, suddenly awkward and tongue-tied.

He set the tray down on her nightstand. "Okay, Princess, since you're standing, let's get those jeans off you."

She instinctively backed up and bumped into the bed.

He didn't move, perhaps sensing her ambivalence. "Do you trust me, Leah?"

The fact that he wasn't rushing her helped to calm Leah. She reached for the snap at the top of her waistband.

The pleasure on his face at this signal of confidence reassured her. She unzipped the jeans and let them drop to her ankles.

"Let me. Please," he said.

She waited while he knelt in front of her.

Gently, and oh so slowly, he pulled her panties down and helped her step out of them.

Lifting the hem of her T-shirt, Quin pressed a kiss to her belly button. The warm touch of his lips made her shiver.

He rose and helped her pull the shirt over her head.

She stood before him naked while he remained completely dressed. Her mind flashed back to lot number two, the naked girl from the night before. *I envied how comfortable she was in her nakedness before those men. And here I am twenty-four hours later.*

"Are you okay, Princess?" he asked, as if realizing her thoughts had wandered from him for a moment.

"I'm fine," she answered, twining her bare arms around his neck and pressing her lips to his. With her kiss, she tried to say that she trusted him enough to follow wherever he wanted to go.

When she would have pulled back, he prolonged the kiss, turning it into a series of small pecks on her lips, her cheeks and her forehead. "Thank you," he murmured, acknowledging the gift she offered.

Without warning, he scooped her up and placed her on top of the mattress. "I don't want the warm washcloths to get too cold," he said. "It's time for your hand bath, Princess."

Chapter Fifteen

Quin watched as Leah settled onto the bed and spread her legs, making herself completely vulnerable to him.

He understood women and recognized that, for Leah, opening herself to him this way was a big step.

She fascinated him. She was an odd mixture of bravado and shyness, of confidence and uncertainty. He found it hard to believe that the woman who had offered him a blow job in a public restroom earlier that night was timid about allowing him to wash her pussy. But the evidence was in front of him, and he accepted it as real. *Go easy, Perez. Don't spook her.* She aroused a crazy kind of protective instinct in him. He wanted to make her happy.

Assuming a brisk, businesslike manner, he reached for one of the soapy wet cloths and brought it between her legs.

She flinched when he touched her for the first time, but remained still after that.

"You're a natural blonde," he teased, trying to get her to relax.

"Did you think maybe I wasn't?" she asked.

He grinned. "*Chiquita*, I've been surprised so many times, I no longer make assumptions." He leaned sideways for a better view of his work area. Her nether lips were still swollen from their earlier coupling . . . or perhaps her body was welcoming his ministrations. He gently parted the folds of her labia so he could reach the more intimate parts of her pussy.

"Mmmmmm," she purred.

He sat up and exchanged the soapy cloth for one he'd dampened in hot water.

This time, when he touched the cloth to her skin, she didn't recoil. Instead, she stretched her legs farther apart to allow him easier access.

He stole a peek at her face.

Her eyes were closed, and her expression was blissful.

Neither of them spoke while he continued the hand bath. He'd brought half a dozen hot cloths with him, and he took his time, using each of them in turn.

He knew exactly when the last bit of tension drained from her body; he felt the infinitesimal yielding of herself to the pleasure of the moment.

That was his cue to put the washcloths away. *Should I say something, or just touch her? She seems totally relaxed.*

He took a chance and started by touching his index finger to the pubic hair on her mons. Leah didn't move.

For some minutes he stroked the soft curls. When at last he slid his finger beneath the clitoral hood to touch her pleasure button, she rewarded him with a sigh.

Deciding that was a definite sign to continue, Quin withdrew his finger and shifted his body on the bed so his head was between her thighs. He lowered his face to her pussy, separated her swollen lips and ran his tongue from her vagina to her clit.

She shuddered, and he froze.

"Don't stop," she moaned.

Reassured that her trembling was a good thing, he returned to work. This time, he concentrated on her clitoris, running his tongue in circles around the tiny organ. He felt it harden and jut forward like a miniature penis. Pressing his mouth closer, he sucked on her pleasure button.

Leah's hips rose off the mattress and mashed against his face.

He raised his head to look up at her. "Like that, do you?" he asked.

She opened her eyes to stare directly at him.

He was startled by how brilliant the blue of her eyes was at that second.

"More," she whispered.

Smiling, he lowered his head again. Using his tongue instead of his fingers to probe her labial folds, he licked and sucked for several minutes before separating the lips and plunging his tongue into her vagina.

Her hips immediately began a rhythmic back-and-forth motion, replicating the sex act. He planted his hands on her two thighs to prevent her from moving too dramatically. *You'd have a hell of a time explaining how your nose got broken while you were making love.*

"Quin," she gasped.

He didn't respond, just continued his in-and-out assault on her vagina.

Her urgency grew. She rocked her hips so fast that his tongue couldn't stay in place.

Sensing she was close to orgasm, he used his teeth to nibble on the inner lips of her labia, hoping to send her over the edge.

She grabbed handfuls of the sheet, perhaps seeking to anchor herself in the world. Then she jerked, almost dislodging him from between her legs. "Quin," she gasped.

He tightened his grip on her thighs, holding her so he could continue his sweet torment.

She stiffened, digging her heels into the mattress and lifting her body six inches off the bed.

Quin pulled back in order to see her face as she came. He watched with delight as her normally porcelain skin flushed rosy red. She thrust her hips upward, pushing against his hands while an unseen cataclysm shook her slender frame.

When at last she collapsed on the mattress, he put a hand on her belly, where he could feel the tremors still rippling through her body.

Quin shifted position from the foot of the bed to sit beside Leah.

Her eyes were closed and tendrils of damp hair were stuck to her sweaty face. He brushed the strands off her forehead. Her overheated face in repose reminded him of watching his niece sleeping when she was a baby. He felt the same sense of tenderness he'd felt then.

He let his fingers trail down her cheek and neck. Leah's breasts were small and high—just the way he liked them.

There was an odd intimacy about watching her in such an unguarded moment. He liked that she trusted him enough to enjoy the moment and not immediately leap up from the bed.

When she opened her eyes, he smiled and asked, "Are you okay?"

She nodded and closed her eyes again.

He stretched out beside her, caressing the breast nearest him, squeezing and mapping her personal geography. "Do you know how beautiful you are right now, *chiquita?*" He lifted her hand and kissed her palm.

Leah's return to the real world came slowly and with great reluctance. She felt as though she'd been flying among the clouds and, once she opened her eyes, she'd be condemned to be earthbound again.

When Quin kissed the palm of her hand, she opened her eyes.

His expression was so tender, her heart stuttered.

She reached out and touched his cheek, the one without the scar. "Thank you, Quin. That was simply wonderful."

"I'm glad. I liked watching your orgasm. It was a beautiful thing to see."

"I've never had one that went on and on like that one did," she admitted.

His expression changed to one of pure male satisfaction. "I like hearing that."

Remembering their conversation from earlier, Leah decided to come clean. "I told you before that I haven't always made the best choices when it comes to men."

"You don't owe me an explanation, *chiquita*." The smug expression disappeared. "I'm happy just to know that I've given you pleasure."

"I want to tell you, Quin. It may help you understand me a bit better." She paused while gathering her thoughts. "About a year ago, I met a medical supply salesman named Dale Freeman." She pushed herself into a sitting position. *If I'm going to talk about it, at least I'll be comfortable.*

"At first, everything was great. He was attentive, and he cared about everything I did." She began twisting the moonstone ring on her right hand round and round.

"Looking back, there were signs that something was wrong. He hated for me to spend time alone with friends like Sandy, but when I tried to set up a double date with her and Zeke, Dale wasn't interested either."

"He was controlling?" Quin asked in a low voice.

"Yes." She nodded. "That's it exactly. He wanted everything to be his idea. The thing is, at first, I enjoyed his intensity." She smiled, but there was no humor in the expression. "There's something very seductive about being the focus of that much attention."

Quin stroked her bare thigh. There was nothing sexual about the gesture. He was soothing her, making it easier for her to tell him what came next.

"It took about a month, but I finally caught on. Even when he said it was all about me, the only thing that mattered was him. How he felt, what he wanted. . . ." Her voice trailed off.

"I imagine he wasn't happy to find out you were dumping him," Quin prompted.

"Not happy doesn't even come close. He went out of his mind." She shuddered at the memory. "I ended up taking out a restraining order to keep him from harassing me."

"But that wasn't the end of it, was it?" Quin's face was bleak, as though he knew what was coming.

"No," she whispered. "All the restraining order did was to send him underground. Instead of calling me sixty times a day, he followed me wherever I went . . . but he did it from a distance. I ignored him, hoping he'd get tired and go away."

"He didn't, did he?" Quin's voice sounded very sure. Very sure and something else besides. Leah glanced at him. The look in his eyes was somber, as though he'd heard her story before.

Wanting to get through the next part quickly, Leah spoke in a rush of words, "When my father is in Texas, we meet for lunch about once a month. During the period I dated Dale, Tex was spending a lot of time in Washington lobbying, so the two never met." She licked her suddenly dry lips. "Tex was in town, and he called me to suggest we meet for dinner instead of lunch. I agreed. We ate here in Oak Cliff. Afterward, he walked me to my car, and I kissed him good-bye." She paused, unable to go on.

"And Dale was watching?" Quin prodded.

She nodded. "He thought—and I don't understand why he would have entertained such a crazy idea—he thought that Tex was my new boyfriend. Dale . . . Dale followed him . . . to Love Field. Tex was supposed to fly back to Washington that night." She raised her gaze to meet Quin's. "Dale caught Tex by surprise when he was alone in an airport men's room. If someone hadn't walked in, he would have beaten my father to death." Her voice trembled for the first time since she'd begun the story.

Quin reached out to wrap her in his arms. Shivering, she went willingly.

"I remember hearing something about the story in the news," he said. "Your father insisted on testifying against Dale even though he was still in a wheelchair."

Leah nodded against his chest. "Yes. Dale was convicted and got twelve years."

"And your sentence?" he asked.

"What?" Confused, she lifted her head to look at him.

"I'm guessing you felt so guilty you haven't dated anyone since."

"That's not true. I have gone out on one or two dates." Her tone was defensive. She pressed her head into his chest again.

"But I'm betting never twice with the same guy, right?"

She didn't answer.

"Leah, am I the first guy you've slept with since the attack on Tex?"

"Yes." Her voice was small.

"Look at me, *cariña*." When she did't respond, he used two fingers to lift her chin. "Look at me."

Feeling exposed and raw, Leah met his gaze.

"Lots of women don't recognize psychopaths like Dale until too late. It could have been you he beat up and nearly killed." She felt the shudder that made his fingers tremble. "This was not your fault. You did what you had to. The rest was on Dale."

"That's what Sandy says."

"And she's right. This is no more your fault than a hurricane or an earthquake would be."

She managed a small, watery smile. "Thanks. And thanks for listening."

In the living room, the clock chimed twelve times for midnight.

"It's late," she said. "You probably have to be at work early tomorrow morning."

"Are you trying to get rid of me, *cariña*?" She could hear the smile in his voice.

"No, it's just that—" Before she could finish the sentence, he placed her hand on the crotch of his jeans.

An erection pressed against her hand.

"You're not thinking of sending me out in the cold with that, are you?"

Chapter Sixteen

"Do you know the Spanish word for 'penis'?" Quin asked.

Forgetting about her earlier decision not to let him know she spoke Spanish, Leah answered, *"Verga."*

Without warning, he released her, rolled off the bed and began stripping off his clothes.

Seeing his chest emerge from under the T-shirt, she decided she'd never get tired of seeing him undress.

When he was naked, he knelt beside her on the bed. "And what do you call these?" he asked, cupping his testicles.

She pushed his hand out of the way so she could hold them. "These are your *huevos*, your eggs," she answered. The short wiry hair that covered the sac containing his balls felt rough and very male.

"Careful, *chiquita*. I need those," he warned.

She smiled. "I'm not trying to steal them. Spread your legs for me."

He complied, and she released his balls. She scooted a few inches south on the bed. Then, using the tips of her nails, she lightly scraped the skin of his inner thigh just below the testicles.

Quin growled low in his throat.

"Like that, do you?" she repeated the phrase he'd used on her earlier. "Let's see what else you like." She grabbed his cock right below the engorged head. With her thumb, she rubbed the opening of his penis, milking him. A drop of pre-cum leaked out. She leaned over to lap it up.

Without warning, he surged up from the mattress and tipped her over onto her back. Before she knew what he was doing, he'd nudged her legs apart and positioned himself between her knees.

"What are you doing?" she gasped. "I was going to suck your cock."

"Sweetheart, the minute you take me in your mouth, I'll come. And I want to be in your *panocha* when I do that." His fingers circled her vaginal opening while he gauged her reaction, never taking his eyes from her face.

Lying there, with his probing gaze on her, Leah felt a sudden shyness. She looked away.

"Don't," he said, pulling his fingers from her sex.

She looked back to meet his eyes.

"Don't look away. I want to be sure that you know it's me who's here with you."

Something about his words hurt her heart. "Of course I know it's you, Quin," she replied.

"I don't want to be just another guy who satisfies your itch until the next time."

Her eyes widened with alarm. *How does he know that? How could he possibly know that?* "What are you talking about?"

His fingers played with the curls that protected her mons. "Ask me later. For now, trust me. Stay with me. Don't look away."

She nodded, biting her lower lip as she did so.

He smiled and maneuvered his fingers to find her clitoris.

An electrical shock ran through her body from her toes to the top of her head. Her spasmodic response almost dislodged his hand.

"Like that, do you?" He tossed their new catchphrase back at her. His thumb and index finger alternately rubbed and flicked the tiny organ.

"Stop. No, don't," she pleaded, not knowing what she was saying.

He didn't stop his torture of her clit, but he did insert two fingers from his other hand into her vagina.

"*Dios*, sweetheart. You're always wet. So wet for me. I'm going to give you three fingers." He held her gaze with his eyes while adding another digit.

Leah began shifting her hips back and forth.

Quin matched her motion, moving his fingers in and out of her channel.

Leah was having trouble keeping her eyes open and fixed on his face. Quin's two-pronged attack on her clit and vagina made it hard to breathe, much less to focus.

Her hips had taken on a life of their own. She thrust them forward again. "Please, Quin," she begged.

"That's it, sweetheart. Let yourself go. I'll catch you." He abandoned her clit to increase the speed of his hand movements in and out of her vagina.

One last quick thrust, and Leah went over the cliff and spinning off into space again. No longer tethered to the world, she fell into the cradling darkness that kept her safe.

Her return to awareness happened by inches. First, she recognized her bed. Then she smelled the musky scent of her own orgasm. Quin's voice murmuring endearments finally pierced the fog that surrounded her.

Leah opened her eyes to find him smiling down at her.

"How are you, *cariña?*"

"Mmmmm, just wonderful," she murmured.

"You just came apart. I love to watch you come."

"But I wanted to please you. I've come twice, and you still haven't had an orgasm."

"Sweetheart, as primed as I am right now, I was afraid I wouldn't last long enough to satisfy you. I needed to make sure you wouldn't be disappointed," he said.

She reached up and stroked his cheek. "I can't imagine you disappointing me, Quin."

"Don't say that, Leah." He shook his head. "I'm not perfect, and I will screw up."

"I'm not naïve. I know you will. I will, too. Everyone does. How about if we agree to try never to screw up at the same time?"

"Damn! I was hoping we might try a simultaneous screw right now." He took her hand and put it on his cock. "My friend here has been waiting ever so patiently." He flopped over onto his back.

Leah laughed. "Poor baby. I have neglected him. Let's remedy that." She inserted one finger in her mouth, wet it, then slowly drew the glistening digit out. She repeated the performance with a second finger.

"A warm-up exercise," she said as she reached down to rub the mushroom-shaped head of his penis.

"Oh, sweetheart," Quin groaned. "He really, really likes that."

"Is there something else he would like?" she asked in an arch tone.

Quin gripped his erect cock and waved it up and down at her. "He's really looking for a good home. Do you have room for him?"

Leah giggled. "Yes, I think I can accommodate him. Of course, he'll need his raincoat. If he doesn't have one, I've got extras in my purse."

"I was a Boy Scout. I'm always prepared." He rolled off the bed and retrieved his jeans. A few seconds of rummaging produced a small foil packet that he held up to show her.

She clapped her hands and watched as he opened the condom and stretched it over his penis. "You look like you've done that a time or two," she commented.

He waggled his eyebrows as he returned to her chair. "Stick with the experts. They get the job done."

Leah spread her legs apart in invitation. "Mr. Medina, I need your expert services."

He knelt between her thighs. "*Cariña*, I'm all yours."

She reached for his shoulders and pulled him toward her.

He placed his hands flat on either side of her and locked his elbows so that he was supporting his own weight above her.

She caught his face between her hands and kissed him. This time, she took the initiative, thrusting her tongue in and out of his mouth to simulate the sex act.

Quin broke the kiss and gasped into her mouth, "Leah, sweetheart, please tell me you're ready because I'm gonna explode."

"Whenever you are," she whispered.

He needed no more encouragement. Shifting his weight to balance on one arm, he gripped his cock with his right hand and entered her in one smooth movement. "Ahhh," he moaned.

Leah gulped and held her breath as her body accustomed itself to his invasion.

Quin held very still, although she could tell by his panting that the effort cost him. "Are you okay, *cariña?*" he gasped.

Rather than answering him with words, Leah rotated her hips.

"Oh, sweetheart, I can't hold back anymore."

"I don't want you to," she replied. "I'm ready."

The words were barely out of her mouth when he began pushing forward—pistoning into her body with urgency.

His initial lunges went deep, actually touching the entrance of her womb, but her body welcomed him.

They quickly found their rhythm. His thrusts became more rapid and shallow, and their dance grew more and more frenzied.

"Are you ready?" he asked.

"Yes, yes," she cried.

"I'm coming! Come with me!"

Once again, Leah tumbled into that dark abyss, momentarily losing her connection to the world. She floated in a sea of pleasurable sensations.

With the aftershocks of her orgasm still rippling through her body, she closed her eyes and immediately fell asleep.

A buzzing sound wakened her. She was disoriented and a little scared until she recognized Quin's head on her chest.

"Quin." She nudged him. "I think my cell phone is ringing. What time is it?"

"Too late for anyone to be calling," he snarled. "Can you see my watch?"

She seized his left wrist and turned it so she could get a look at his watch. "I think it's one thirty," she said.

"Who the hell would be calling you at . . ." His voice trailed off. "It's Felix."

"Oh, God!" she muttered. "I forgot all about calling him. He should have seen us entering the building from the garage on camera. Let me up."

"No," he said with a sigh. "You stay there and I'll bring you the cell."

Moving laboriously slowly, he rolled toward his right off the bed. He picked up her jeans and handed them to her.

Leah fished in the jeans pocket for her cell, but the phone had stopped ringing by the time she found it. She flipped it open and pushed the MISSED CALL button. "It's not Felix," she said, looking up at Quin in surprise. "It's Zeke."

"Sandy's having the baby," he said. "Call him back."

"I am. It's ringing now."

"Leah," Zeke's voice greeted her. "I'm sorry to be calling so late, but—"

She interrupted. "Is Sandy okay?"

"Yeah, she's fine. She woke me up about an hour ago and said it was time to go to the hospital. We made it to Baylor in twenty minutes."

"Is the baby born?"

"No, not yet. She's still not fully dilated. . . . Listen, Leah, I really could use your help."

"What do you need?"

"Turns out one of the Labor and Delivery nurses is in my mother-in-law's Sunday school class, so, of course, she called Victoria to let her know we were here at Baylor."

Leah winced.

"What's wrong?" Quin asked.

She shook her head.

"And you know what happened next," Zeke continued.

"Victoria is there, and she wants to be in the birthing room with the two of you," Leah said.

"Yeah." Only someone who knew Zeke well could hear the anger beneath his flat tone. "I'd be happy to tell her she needs to go home and let us handle the Frogman's birth, but Sandy's all emotional. She doesn't want bad vibes around when she pops the kid out."

"So you want me to come down there and keep Victoria company in the waiting room until Froggie makes his debut." Leah was resigned to her fate.

"Yeah. I'll owe you a big one, babe."

"And don't think I won't collect. Where do I find you?" She listened to his directions. "Okay, I'll be there as soon as I can. Tell Sandy to put a cork in it until I get there." Ignoring Zeke's profuse thanks, she hung up.

Quin held her jeans out for her to put her feet in. He helped pull them up her legs and over her hips. "We can be at Baylor in fifteen minutes."

"You don't have to go. I can drive myself."

"At one thirty in the morning? Forget it. I'm going. We'll take your car." He finished fastening her jeans and stood. "I take it our job is to keep Zeke's mother-in-law away from him and Sandy."

"Pretty much." She nodded. "And Victoria Davis is one formidable woman. When she sets her mind on something, she makes Patton look like a piker."

"Great." He retrieved his own jeans off the floor. "At least do me one favor and make sure Felix is cool before he rains death and fire on my head."

Leah reached for him, resting her hand on his naked hip. "I'm so sorry this had to happen tonight, but I really don't have a choice. Sandy's my best friend."

He captured her hand and brought it to his lips. "That's okay, *cariña*. We'll have other nights together. Now call Felix. I don't want him putting me in the hospital alongside Sandy."

Chapter Seventeen

*L*eah slept until eleven a.m. After Quin dropped her off at six thirty that morning, she left e-mails canceling all her meetings before noon, but she needed to keep the luncheon date with her father.

Fortunately, Hattie's, where the pair was scheduled to meet, was a short drive from the *Heat* building. By hurrying, she made it to the restaurant on time.

Hattie's, in the Bishop Street Arts District, specialized in Southern Lowcountry cuisine. The restaurant also represented neutral territory for Leah and her father. Because Hattie's was located in Oak Cliff, Leah had home-court advantage. But because many of the dishes reminded Tex of his childhood on Pawleys Island in South Carolina, he had the comfort edge.

Tex was already at a table when the maître d' led Leah into the dining room. With his customary Old World charm, her father stood and remained standing until the maître d' seated Leah.

Other diners kept looking toward their table and at her father. Leah was used to this. No matter where he went, Tex Reece always dominated a room.

Tall with rangy limbs and weather-beaten skin, Tex would have resembled a cowboy if it hadn't been for the four-thousand-dollar suit he wore. To help create the dramatic effect he loved, Tex had a shock of white hair, which he wore longer than fashion dictated.

But it wasn't just his appearance. Tex radiated confidence and power. Men envied him and, although he was over sixty, he still attracted plenty of attention from women.

Father and daughter exchanged pleasantries while examining the menu.

Their time together followed a predictable pattern. Tex always began by critiquing her appearance, then grilled her on *Heat*'s performance, and ended with an interrogation of her love life.

After the waiter left with their orders—pecan-crusted catfish for Tex and the Carolina crab cake salad for Leah—her father studied her over the rim of his iced tea. "You look tired. Too many late nights?"

She shook her head. "Sandy and Zeke's baby boy was born this morning at five fifty."

He pulled out his BlackBerry. "I'll send flowers," he said, tapping the keys. "I take it from the shadows under your eyes you spent the night at the hospital. Why?"

"I ran interference between Zeke and his mother-in-law." She broke a roll in two and buttered one of the halves.

"Ah, dear Victoria. How is she?"

Leah flashed back to the memory of introducing Sandy's mother to Quin. Victoria did not even pretend to be polite; she stared with distaste at his tattooed forearms and torn T-shirt.

For his part, Quin treated Victoria with quiet courtesy but with complete indifference to her opinion of him.

"Victoria hasn't changed," she replied.

The new baby and the financial status of *Heat* provided enough fodder to keep Leah and Tex occupied through the entrees. By the time their coffee arrived, her father was setting his sights on Leah's love life.

"Are you still dating Don Davis?" he asked.

"I told you the last time I saw you that we weren't dating anymore."

"And my recollection is that I urged you to reconsider." He waved to an acquaintance being seated at another table. "I've known three generations of the Davis family, and Don will be governor one day. Being First Lady of Texas is nothing to sneer at."

"Oh, I'm not sneering at being the First Lady," she assured him. "It's marrying Don I have a problem with."

A thinning of his lips was the only indication that he'd heard her. They sat in silence for several minutes.

When Leah was younger, silent disapproval had always been one of Tex's favorite weapons against her. The twelve-year-old Leah would have done anything to avoid sitting under his tight-lipped scrutiny.

Over the years, she'd learned to see his manipulations for what they were. She'd come to accept that the same negotiating skills that made her father successful in business were not particularly useful qualities in a parent.

She let her mind drift while she waited for Tex to weary of his power games.

A baby at a nearby table cried, reminding her of the trip to Baylor that morning. She remembered Quin's earnest recommendation during the drive home.

"Listen, sweetheart. You gotta quit calling that kid Froggie. He'll need a psychiatrist before he enters kindergarten."

She smiled at the memory.

Her father cleared his throat. "So are you seeing anyone now?" he asked.

During her adolescence, Leah had honed the skill of aggravating her father to a fine art. If she told him she was dating a Mexican named Quin Medina, he would be furious. But she didn't want to use her relationship with Quin that way.

"No one that I've had more than one date with," she answered with perfect honesty.

At about the same time Leah was lunching with her father, Quin walked into the 69 Club and waved at Terrance, a member of the cleaning crew. The old man looked quickly around, then gestured at Quin to join him.

"What's up, Terrance?"

"Keep your head down, man. Lucero is seriously torqued."

Uh-oh. "Thanks. Do you know what the problem is?"

"Something to do with a woman reporter."

Quin's pulse speeded up, but he kept his expression calm. *Fuck.* "Thanks, Terrance, I owe you one."

He checked his watch. Twelve fifty. *I've still got ten minutes.*

Instead of going directly upstairs, he took a detour through the ballroom to one of the first-floor bathrooms. Entering a stall, he reached under his jacket for the Glock tucked into the waistband at the small of his back.

He checked the load. The Glock 19 had a fifteen-round magazine. With the bullet in the chamber, he had sixteen rounds.

His primary problem was where to carry it. Fully loaded it was too heavy to put in his jacket pocket, and he didn't want to walk into Lucero's office with it tucked in the front of his waistband.

After a moment's consideration, he returned the gun to its hiding place at the small of his back. Then he bent over and pulled his throwaway piece out of its ankle holster.

His Taurus 605 was only a five-shot revolver, but much smaller and easier to hide than the Glock. After checking it, he dropped the little gun into the right pocket of his jacket. *That's the best I can do.*

He left the bathroom and took the grand staircase to Lucero's office, his mind still churning with questions. *What clued him in to Leah? Could Lucero have had us followed? No, I would have seen a tail. It's got to be something else.*

The door to Lucero's office stood open, and the club owner sat behind his desk. The surface of the desk was clean except for one piece of paper that was perfectly centered in front of him.

"Morning, boss," Quin said.

"Come in, and shut the door."

Quin forced himself to breathe evenly as he obeyed. "What's up?"

"Have a seat." The club owner gestured to the chair across from his desk.

Sitting would make it harder for him to access either gun. *But I don't have a choice.* He settled into the chair, making certain not to sit on the jacket so he'd be able to reach his right-side pocket easily.

Lucero was dressed in a white silk shirt and beige pants. Quin knew there would be a leather patch on the man's right rear pocket with the word "Culiacán" on it. Culiacán was the name of Lucero's hometown in Mexico.

The club owner stared at Quin, his face inscrutable. "When Ruben followed you and that girl Wednesday night, he took down her license plate number."

Fuck! "So?" He kept his tone casual.

"So I e-mailed the plate number to a friend at the DMV." Lucero picked up the piece of paper from his desk. "Got an answer back this morning."

"And?" *Don't overthink. Just see it through.*

The club owner held the paper toward him. Quin reached across to take it.

One glance told him everything: Leah's full name and address below the logo of the Department of Motor Vehicles. He looked up at Lucero. "She wouldn't be the first girl to give a phony name when she goes slumming."

"That what you think?" The club owner raised one eyebrow. "I looked her up on Google. Turns out she's a bit more than a pretty face. She's the publisher of *Heat* magazine."

Quin shrugged. "Don't know it. She did say something about owning a 'zine.' I didn't have any idea what she was talking about."

"She told you she was a journalist, and you still let her into my club?" Lucero's voice went from cold to ice.

Quin shook his head. "I've already told you. I didn't let her in. Gutierrez did. You can ask Martin. He was the one on the door at the time."

"I've already spoken to Martin. Still"—the club owner's eyes narrowed—"you and she seemed awfully cozy. And Ruben said you spent a lot of time with her in the car when you took her home."

"Come on, Miguel." Quin allowed a trace of scorn to color his voice. "You got a look at her. Tell me you wouldn't want a piece of that."

"Perhaps." His boss sounded unconvinced. "One thing I *am* certain of. We cannot have any publicity about this club. As long as we stay under the radar, we can continue operating. A magazine story . . ." He stood and started to pace while he talked.

"Some of our club members are important men. Protecting

their privacy, and ours, has to be our first priority." He turned his attention back to Quin. "Have you talked to her since Wednesday?"

Careful, Perez. He could be setting a trap for you. Quin tried to look embarrassed. "As a matter of fact, Miguel, I did make a date with her. That's what I was doing for so long in the car. We went out last night." He paused to see if Lucero was buying the story.

The club owner stared at him the way a mongoose might eye a snake. "What did you tell her about my club?"

"Nothing, Miguel. She didn't ask. We were too busy fucking."

Lucero leaned forward. "Are you telling me she didn't ask anything about this club?"

Quin met his gaze without flinching. "That's exactly what I'm saying." He shrugged. "Now, maybe she thinks she's softening me up, but you have nothing to worry about. I know how to keep my mouth shut."

Lucero continued to stare at him. "When are you going to see her again?"

"Tonight probably. Why?"

"Maybe you need to bring her here so I can have a talk with her."

¡Chinga tu madre! "Sure, Miguel. If you think that's the right thing to do."

"What do you mean?" Lucero's gaze sharpened.

"It's just that she seems really well connected. Her father . . . he's like famous or something."

For the first time, Lucero looked disconcerted. "Shit. Maybe I need to ask around about her first."

"Whatever you say, Miguel. You know I'm up for it, no matter what you decide." He leaned forward in his chair. "While you're deciding, I'll keep an eye on her. She's hot for my *verga*."

He wasn't sure what Lucero might have said or done next. A knock on the door interrupted them.

"Who is it?" Lucero snarled.

"Carlos."

Lucero gestured toward the door, and Quin got up to open it.

Gutierrez entered, looking from one man to the other.

"Get out," Lucero told Quin. "Come back at three, and we'll finish talking about the cameras." He tapped his index finger on the e-mail sitting atop his desk. "We'll decide later what to do about your girlfriend."

Quin walked to the door. *It's time Leah and I had a serious talk.*

Chapter Eighteen

After saying good-bye to Tex, Leah drove to Baylor Hospital to check on Sandy and the baby. She arrived at the Maternity wing shortly after two thirty.

The door to Sandy's private room was open. Leah peeked around the doorjamb. "Anyone home?"

"Leah, is that you? Come on in." Sandy sounded wide awake and cheerful.

She was propped up in the bed, surrounded by pillows, and cradling the baby in her arms. Zeke sat on the edge of the bed.

The new mother looked radiant. Her hair was neatly combed, and she wore lipstick and eyeliner.

By contrast, Zeke looked exhausted. He needed a shave, his hair stuck out in all directions and there were shadows under his eyes. But he, too, looked happy.

"The perfect family unit," Leah said. "May I see the new arrival?"

That morning, when the nurse practitioner came out to say the baby had been born, Victoria went into the room to meet her new grandson while Leah and Quin quietly left. Leah had not yet met her godson.

Sandy tilted the bundle in her arms so Leah could get a look at him.

Zeke, Jr., was sound asleep, a tiny pink-faced miracle.

"He's beautiful," Leah whispered. "You guys do nice work."

"Not me," Zeke protested. "It's all Wonder Woman here."

"Well, no matter who gets the credit, he's gorgeous." She reached out to touch the baby's cheek with one finger. He was sleeping so soundly, he didn't move.

She felt a strange tug at her heart. *I thought I'd be married with a baby before Sandy.* She rubbed her knuckle down Froggie's soft skin. *If I keep going the way I am, who knows if I'll ever marry or have children.* Instead of a tug, there was now a fist around her heart.

"Zeke tells me we owe you big-time for keeping my mother occupied last night," Sandy said. "I'll give you anything except my firstborn in gratitude."

Leah backed up to sit in the recliner next to the bed. "It wasn't bad at all," she lied. "I had Quin with me, and we took her downstairs to the cafeteria for a cup of coffee."

Husband and wife exchanged a quick look, and Leah's stomach turned over.

Zeke spoke first. "Uh, Leah, Sandy told me you were out with Quin last night. Um . . . getting involved with him is not a good idea." He cast a nervous glance in his wife's direction.

Before Sandy could speak, Leah jumped in. "Well, it's a little late for that advice, Zeke. I *am* involved with him."

Zeke ignored both Leah's tone and Sandy's glare. "Look, I went along with that scheme of yours to visit the club and sneak a look at the show because I thought it was going to be a onetime thing. If I'd known you were going to get involved with . . . one of the staff, I'd have put a stop to it."

Leah felt her temper rising. "And just how would you have put a stop to it?" she demanded. "Dallas isn't exactly a police state."

Zeke held his hands up in the classic "stop" gesture. "Whoa! All I meant was that Sandy and I"—he threw his wife a plea for assistance—"Sandy and I, we would have talked you out of it."

"Don't you dare drag me into this," Sandy warned him. Her gaze met Leah's. "I pointed out to my husband last night over dinner that your business is none of his business." Sandy's gaze slid to meet Zeke's, clearly daring him to say anything else.

The vice cop threw his hands up in the air. "Hell, I may be dumb, but I'm not stupid. I'll keep my trap shut." He paused, as though choosing his words carefully. "Just watch yourself, Leah. Quin works for some very bad men."

"So he keeps telling me," she said, relieved that Zeke hadn't pushed the subject. She stood. "I don't want to overstay my welcome. I just wanted to be sure everything was fine and to welcome Zeke, Jr., to the world."

"It's so odd to hear him called that." Sandy made a minute adjustment to the baby's blanket. "He's been Froggie for so long, it's going to be hard to call him anything else."

Remembering Quin's words, Leah smiled. "Well, I have it on good authority that if you don't start calling him something else, he's going to need a psychiatrist before he makes it out of preschool."

"But that's the problem," Sandy said. "They can't both be Zeke. If I call 'Zeke,' how will they know which one should respond?"

Leah moved closer for one last look at the baby. "What about calling him Zee? It's cute, and it won't embarrass him later in life."

"That's a great idea. I love it," Sandy said. She looked at Zeke, Sr., and asked, "What do you think?"

"Well, I'd rather call him the Frogman, but you're probably right. Kids can be pretty cruel." He bent over his son and kissed his forehead. "Zee it is."

*   *   *

Leah was still smiling when she left the hospital.

On her way back to *Heat,* she glanced at the clock. *Just after three. Should I call Consuelo again? She'll probably be leaving for work soon. Maybe I'll wait until tomorrow. Give her more time to settle down.*

Her thoughts returned to Quin. When he'd kissed her good-bye at six thirty that morning, he'd promised to call later in the day. *Maybe tonight I should cook something.*

Reality set in. *Do you really want him to learn this early what a lousy cook you are? I don't think so.*

Her cell phone rang. She fished it out of her pocket and flipped it open. "Hello."

"Did you get any sleep?" Quin asked.

"Quin!" Her heart did a little jig. "Yes, I got about four hours. How about you? Did you get any?"

"Yeah, about two hundred and ten minutes."

Leah grinned at his obvious attempt to make the three and a half hours seem longer than they were, but his next words spoiled the effect.

"I want to prop my eyeballs up with a toothpick."

She laughed. "Are you working tonight?"

"No. I'm going to stay until the first show starts and then head home."

"You probably want to go right home to bed, don't you?" she asked.

"Well"—his voice dropped—"I was actually hoping we could go to bed together."

She sighed happily. "Oh, I like that plan. What about dinner?"

"About that." He hesitated. "My family is celebrating my niece's birthday tonight. I was wondering if you'd be willing to go with me?"

What is it with this guy? On the first date, he picks me up on a motorcycle. On the second date, he takes me to meet his family. No one else does stuff like this.

"Leah?"

"I'm here. Is your family going to be okay with my crashing your niece's party?"

He laughed. "They'll be thrilled. I never bring girls home. They're beginning to think I'm gay."

She digested that news in silence. *Why me? Why now?*

"I'll pick you up at seven. And, afterward, we need to talk." He hung up.

She sighed and slowed down to make a right turn at the next corner. *Guess I'll be shopping for a birthday gift instead of taking a nap. I wonder what he wants to talk about.* She frowned. *It's got to be my story. That could get sticky.* She slowed down to allow a jaywalking pedestrian to cross the street. *I don't want to lie to him, but. . . .*

This time when Quin picked her up, he drove the Jeep. And he came into the building to tell the desk he was there for her.

Leah came downstairs to meet him. The approval in his eyes when he saw her wine-colored sundress warmed her heart. Although it left her shoulders bare, the dress had a square neckline and inch-wide shoulder straps.

Quin leaned down to kiss her cheek. "Your coach awaits, Princess." He turned and gave Felix a casual salute.

I love his confidence. He's not arrogant, just very, very confident.

He was wearing poplin slacks and a pale blue dress shirt made of Egyptian cotton with long sleeves that covered his tattoos. *It's too hot outside for long sleeves. I wonder if his family disapproves of his tattoos?*

Outside the building, he asked, "How are you feeling?"

She offered him her most brilliant smile. "Fabulous!"

The relief in his eyes was evident. He grabbed her hand and squeezed it.

Once they were in the Jeep and on their way, he asked, "Are you familiar with the term '*quinceañera*'?"

"It's the celebration for a Hispanic girl's fifteenth birthday, isn't it? Sort of the equivalent of the Anglo debut party."

"Close." He nodded. "For Mexicans, it's probably more like the Jewish bat mitzvah than a coming-out party." He slowed to make a right turn. They were headed in the direction of West Dallas, where much of the city's Hispanic population lived. "The *quinceañera* includes a religious ceremony, recognizing the girl's coming of age, followed by a reception."

"We're going to church?" she asked, a little alarmed.

"No, I told my family I couldn't make the Mass, but that I'd come to the reception. I take it you're not Catholic?"

"My dad claims to be Baptist, but the truth is his only religion is publishing. He left churchgoing to my mother. Her family was Episcopalian." Leah looked out the passenger window. The houses on this street were smaller than the ones in her neighborhood, and their exteriors were aluminum siding instead of brick. "After Mom died, religion didn't play much of a part in my life."

"How old were you when she died?"

"Eleven."

"That must have been hard." His voice was gentle.

She shrugged. "Tex handled it by giving me a job. He made me a runner between departments at one of his papers. Kept me so busy, I didn't have time to think, much less grieve."

"Did it work?"

"For a while." He didn't need to know what a wild child she'd become. In an attempt to change the subject, she asked, "Tell me about your family."

Quin put his right hand on her thigh.

She covered his hand with hers.

He took his eyes off the road long enough to smile at her. Her stomach leaped. *He ought to come with a warning label: "May cause spontaneous combustion."*

"My family," he said. "I have a mother and father, two brothers and two sisters, all living in Dallas." He moved his hand up and down along her thigh, ruffling the sundress's skirt. She could feel the warmth of him through the cotton fabric.

For such a dangerous-looking man, he had the hands of an artist—long, slender fingers with well-kept nails. She loved the color of his skin; it reminded her of caramel candy.

He pulled up to a stop sign. Instead of proceeding through the intersection, he looked at her. "Are you listening to me?"

"Mother, father, two brothers, two sisters." She gave in to the impulse and ran her fingers along the back of his hand from his nails to where his wrist disappeared under his shirt cuffs.

He shivered. She felt the ripple that moved through him. *Good. It's not just me. You feel it, too.* She raised her gaze to meet his, allowing him to see her lips curve upward.

Without taking his gaze off her, he slid his hand to the right, turning his palm over so it was facing up with the back of his hand resting on her skirt . . . between her legs.

Although he didn't speak the words, his message could not have been clearer: *The ball's back in your court, Princess.*

She placed the fingertips of her right hand on the fingertips of the hand in her lap. Using her nails, she lightly scraped along his hand, down the palm and to his wrist. When she reached the cuff of his shirt, she stroked the inside of his wrist with her nails. Back and forth, back and forth.

His intake of breath was audible. She leaned forward to look at his lap.

The hard ridge of his erection pressed against the cloth of his slacks.

Leah squeezed her thighs together, savoring her anticipation of having him between her legs again.

With a quick twist of his hand, he captured her right wrist. "Touch it." He nodded toward his erection.

Before she could respond, the blare of a horn made them both jump and turn to look behind.

Chapter Nineteen

A middle-aged man in a green Cadillac was glaring at them.

Quin waved an apologetic hand at the guy and hit the accelerator. "What is it about us and car horns? Every time I think I'm going to score, someone honks at us."

"Maybe it's your guardian angel," she teased.

He snorted. "My guardian angel bailed years ago." He gestured ahead. "We're coming up on my parents' street."

Leah looked around curiously as the Jeep cruised down a tree-lined boulevard. The oaks were forty feet high, forming a dense canopy overhead.

Most of the houses were ranch style and looked to have been built during the post–World War II period. There were no sidewalks, but every yard had flowering bushes. Yellow and red roses seemed to be the most popular choices.

Both sides of the broad avenue were lined with parked cars.

"This looks like a huge affair," she said.

Quin nodded. "Normally we would have held it on a weekend, but Carmen's older brother is home on leave, and we had to make do. He'll be shipping out tomorrow afternoon."

He parallel-parked between a low-rider Chevrolet and a black pickup. Leah could hear the sound of live music and laughter even before he came around to the passenger side to open her door.

He took her hand to help her step down. When she was standing beside him on the street, he dropped a light kiss on her lips.

Leah moved into the kiss but, after a moment, Quin broke it off.

"If we don't stop, I'm going to jump your bones right here in front of the neighbors' house." He reached around her to open the center console and pulled out a small, beautifully wrapped oblong box. "Let's go."

She brought her own small gift box, but left her sweater on the passenger seat with her purse hidden beneath it.

They walked down the street toward the corner lot. The closer they got, the louder the sound of the music and voices grew. Quin walked on the outside of the road with his right arm around Leah's waist. She was not a short woman, but she felt petite beside him. *I like that.*

The house was set back from the street and surrounded by a six-foot adobe brick wall. The house, also built of adobe, had a red barrel-tiled roof. Black wrought-iron gates stood open to welcome them into the compound.

"Did you grow up here?" she asked.

"On this property, but not in this house. When the last of us graduated from college, my parents razed the old house and built this one. My father worked as a construction site boss before he retired."

They walked through the gates into a courtyard filled with a profusion of flowers. Beneath a covered patio, the front door of the house stood open.

"Someone loves to garden," Leah said.

Quin nodded. "My father has a large vegetable garden, and my mother plants the flowers."

As they approached the doorway, a huge chestnut-colored dog

with wavy hair lumbered out to greet them. When it saw Quin, the dog bared its teeth and emitted a growling sound.

Leah froze in place.

"Don't worry. That's just his way of saying 'welcome,'" Quin said.

"That isn't what it sounded like," she replied.

Quin handed her his wrapped gift and dropped into a crouch.

"This is Turbo, and he's a good boy. Aren't you, *perro?*" He rubbed the monster behind its ears.

The dog whined happily, bumping Quin's knee with his enormous head.

"I was expecting a Chihuahua," she joked.

"That's a racist statement, Princess." Quin stood, put a hand under her elbow and guided her through the door. "Turbo is a Chesapeake Bay retriever, or, as my father calls him, his *perro cobrador*, his collector dog."

The inside of the house was cool and dimly lit. To the left and right of the entry hall Leah could see a spacious living room and a formal dining room.

Turbo remained behind at the entrance while Quin led Leah down the hallway toward a door. They passed what looked like a hundred framed family photos on the walls along the way.

She could hear the excited noise of many voices ahead. Her fingers tightened on the wrapped gifts. *There's nothing to be nervous about.*

He pushed the door open into a large, brightly lit kitchen filled with people.

"Quin!" a dozen voices screamed at once.

Leah was overwhelmed by the rush of bodies toward them. She took an involuntary step backward.

Quin caught a small girl—perhaps four years old—around the waist and swung her up into the air. She screamed with delight.

They were surrounded by women and children, all hugging and touching Quin. Leah moved to the right, trying to keep out of the way.

A dark-haired woman holding a baby boy smiled at her. "I'm Maria Elena, Quin's sister."

"It's so nice to meet you. I'm Leah Reece."

"Welcome to my father's house."

"Thank you." She glanced over at Quin. He looked relaxed and happy . . . and something else. It took a second for her to find the right word.

He looked open. The guarded expression she so often saw on his face was gone. Everyone was peppering him with questions or trying to tell him stories, and she could tell he loved every minute of it.

His gaze met hers over the head of a girl about twelve. "Everybody, hold up for a minute. I need for you to meet someone." He reached across the children for Leah.

Leah shifted both boxes to her left hand and offered him her right. He pulled her to his side. All the smiling faces looked to her with expectant expressions.

"This is Leah, a friend of mine. I invited her to come with me tonight." He squeezed her hand in a reassuring way. "Leah, I'd like you to meet my mother and sister. Mamá . . ."

Over the next few minutes, Leah was introduced to more than a dozen women and children. When the introductions were finished, Quin's mother, a small white-haired woman with her son's dark eyes, clapped her hands.

"Everyone, Quin and Leah need to go outside and say hello

to our *quinceañera.*" She smiled at Quin. "Carmen has been holding court in the backyard ever since we got home from the church. Go. The cake should arrive soon." She waved them toward a door.

Quin guided Leah past the smiling faces and out of the kitchen.

He leaned down and whispered in her ear, "See, dogs, women and children all love me. I'm harmless."

"Ha! But you do have quite a fan club, I'll give you that." She smiled up at him.

"I'm hoping to make one more fan tonight." He waggled his eyebrows and whisked her outside.

Thousands of small white lights twinkled in the trees and atop the adobe walls that enclosed the backyard, creating a fairy-tale look.

To one side of the yard, a live band played pop tunes in front of a portable dance floor. Four teenage couples were dancing. The girls swirled in flowing violet gowns while the boys moved awkwardly across the floor.

On the other side of the yard from the musicians, uniformed waiters swarmed around food-laden buffet tables. A lighted party fountain bubbled with punch.

Guests flitted everywhere. Leah estimated the crowd at more than sixty people, but it was difficult to tell. She quickly lost count of the number of round tables dressed in sparkling white cloths. Most of the scattered tables had at least two or three people sitting at them—eating, talking and laughing.

Once again, screams of recognition accompanied Quin's arrival. A beaming teenage girl in a mauve ball gown shouted "Quin!" as she threw herself into his arms.

He squeezed the teen in a bear hug, then held her at arm's length. "Happy birthday, Carmen. You look beautiful."

She took a step backward and twirled for him. "I do, don't I?"

He nodded in grave agreement. "I want you to meet Leah." He turned. "Leah, this is our *quinceañera*, Carmen."

The teenage girl held out her hand, and Leah took it. The hand was damp, the skin soft as butter. Leah couldn't remember ever feeling as young and fresh as Quin's niece looked. "Happy birthday, Carmen."

"Thank you. It's nice to meet you. Thank you for coming." The girl eyed the gifts in Leah's left hand and cut her gaze over to Quin. "Are those for me, *Tío?*" she asked.

"Carmen!" snapped a middle-aged woman who bustled to the teen's side.

Carmen looked down, embarrassed, and Quin leaped in. "It's all right, Rita," he said. "Leah, this is my older sister, Margarita."

The girl's mortified. Leah could remember dozens of such instances when she was young and her father had scolded her in public. She jumped in to bridge the awkward moment. "I'm so pleased to meet you," she said, extending her right hand to Margarita as she passed Carmen's gifts back to Quin.

A young man in a marine uniform threw his arm around Quin's shoulders. "About time you brought a girl home to meet the family, Uncle."

Without the slightest bit of self-consciousness, Quin grabbed the young marine and hugged him tightly. "Domingo, it's good to see you. How are you doing?"

"Good, good," his nephew said. "Who is this?"

"My friend Leah Reece." Quin emphasized the word "friend" as he turned toward Leah. "This is Rita's oldest, Domingo."

Although she continued to look at her feet, Carmen peeked sideways at her uncle. "Will you dance with me, *Tío*?"

Quin glanced at Leah, who nodded with a smile.

"I'll be back soon," he said. "Domingo, take care of Leah for me." He led the birthday girl toward the dance floor.

"May I get you a glass of punch?" Domingo asked Leah.

"Yes, thank you."

"Come sit down," Margarita offered, pointing to a nearby table while the handsome marine headed toward the punch fountain.

As the two women sat, Quin's mother and other sister seemed to materialize out of nowhere. Suddenly Leah found herself facing all three women across the table. A fearsome jury.

Chapter Twenty

"So, how did you meet my brother?" Margarita asked.

Leah smiled. "Through a mutual friend. Perhaps you know him? Zeke Prada? He's married to my best friend."

It was as though Leah had spoken a magic password. All three women visibly relaxed, and Maria Elena said, "Oh, yes, we know Zeke very well. He and Quin grew up together. They're very close."

Good. Maybe now I can get some of my questions answered. "So I hear," Leah said, "but I don't remember seeing him at Zeke and Sandy's wedding."

"He was still overseas," Domingo answered, coming up from behind to hand her a cup of punch. "I brought you some appetizers." He put a plate of food, a fork and a napkin on the table in front of her.

"Thanks." Leah frowned. "Overseas?"

"He was a marine, too; didn't he tell you?" Domingo answered.

"No, no, he didn't." Leah looked at the dance floor, where Quin and Carmen were dancing to a cover of Lionel Richie's "All Night Long."

"He got out a few months after Zeke and Sandy got married," Maria Elena added.

"Really? He didn't mention it." Leah smiled across the lawn at Quin.

✳   ✳   ✳

Quin's heart lurched when he saw Leah sit down with his mother and sisters. *¡Ah, chingado! I shouldn't have left her alone.*

He looked around, trying to find inspiration. A teenage boy in a suit and tie was standing on the edge of the dance floor, watching Carmen. "Who's that?" he asked his niece.

"Michael. He's my *chambelane*," she said proudly.

He glanced at Leah, who was smiling at him. "You should be dancing with your escort, not with me." He took Carmen's hand and led her to the boy. "Michael, I'm sorry I stole your date. Here she is."

Quin handed his niece the boxes he'd shoved into his pockets. "Here, sweetheart. Happy birthday."

Her face lit up. "Thank you, *Tío*." She looked around until she spotted her mother. "Come on, Michael, let's go over there." She pointed to a spot well away from Margarita's prying eyes.

Grinning, Quin headed toward Leah and the women of his family. "What lies have you been telling Leah?" He assumed a mock ferocious scowl.

"Only good things," his mother said, smiling up at him. "About your two Purple Hearts."

"You didn't tell me you'd been to Iraq," Leah said.

"We hadn't gotten around to my life story yet," he protested.

"What kind of a child was he, Mrs. Medina?" Leah asked.

Quin suppressed a wince. He'd forgotten that Leah only knew him by his mother's maiden name. Mamá's forehead creased in confusion. "Never mind, Mamá," he said quickly. "You can give the family history later. Leah and I are going to dance. Come on, Princess." He grabbed her hand and pulled her out of the chair.

As he led her to the dance floor, he called to the band leader, "How about a slow dance?"

The leader smiled, nodded and said something to the rest of his group. They swung into a cover of John Legend's "Slow Dance."

Leah started to laugh, and Quin grimaced. "Everyone's a wise guy." He put his hands on her waist and pulled her toward him. "But the song will work."

She came into his arms willingly. Her head came to just below his chin. Her scent filled his nostrils. He could identify lemon, jasmine and vanilla. It was a sensuous fragrance. His cock stirred to life.

She sighed and moved closer, laying her head on his chest. He tightened his hold, tilted his head and rested his cheek on her hair. Her curves fit perfectly against his hard body. His cock pressed against her belly. He wanted to pick her up, carry her off and fuck her until she begged for mercy.

What the hell is wrong with you, Perez? You've never mixed the job and your personal life before. You've never brought someone you just met home before. Is it this job? Is all that sex on display at the club finally getting to you? Or is it Leah?

She whispered something he couldn't quite catch.

"What, sweetheart?" he asked.

She pulled her head from his chest and looked up at him. "I can hear the wheels and gears turning in your brain. Can't you just relax? And maybe enjoy the dance?"

"I'm sorry, *cariña.*" He pulled her close again. "You're right. Only a fool would let his mind wander from you."

He felt her face muscles shift as she smiled with her head nestled against his shirt.

"Damn straight, Medina."

The "Medina" put his head in a spin again. He needed to get her away from this party before she again called his mother . . . or

God forbid, his father . . . by his mother's maiden name. And they still needed to talk about the club.

The song came to a close. He leaned down to gaze into her eyes. "I want to leave. I want to go someplace where we can be alone. Are you ready to go?"

In her blue eyes he saw a reflection of the same hunger that was eating him from the inside out. Without another word, she nodded.

He pressed his lips to hers in what he intended to be a light kiss. Somewhere along the way it changed. Her mouth against his stirred the passion he'd been tamping down since she came off the elevator to meet him earlier that night. She answered a need inside him that he hadn't even realized he had.

The sound of applause pierced the haze. Leah broke the kiss off, and he lifted his head. They were alone on the dance floor. His family and friends were all staring at the two of them, clapping and whistling.

He looked down at Leah. A faint blush stained her cheeks, but he didn't think it was from embarrassment.

"Ready to leave?" he asked.

Her gaze met his, and her eyes shone. "Yes. Let's go."

He took her hand and moved off the dance floor.

"Quin, where are you going?" Margarita called.

"I'm not one of your kids, Rita. You don't need to keep an eye on me." He smiled at her to take the sting out of the words.

"But Papá, Rod and Ric aren't back with the cake yet," she protested.

"I promise I'll bring Leah back another time to meet them."

Leah tugged on his hand. "I must say good-bye to your mother," she said.

Groaning, he let her lead him to where his mother was still sitting with his two sisters.

"Mrs. Medina, I want to thank you for allowing me to share this occasion with your family." Leah offered her hand to his mother. "You have a lovely home and a beautiful family."

"My mother's nam—" Margarita's automatic correction of the family surname stopped dead at an admonishing look from his mother.

Mamá gave Quin a meaningful glance. Her inherent hospitality would not permit correcting a guest in her house, but she was sending him a message that he needed to explain the Hispanic patronymic system to Leah.

Thank God. Mamá thinks Leah has just mistaken which is my last name.

In Mexico, children were named with their father's surname preceding their mother's, even though the father's surname prevailed as the legal last name. Therefore, Quin's name was Quin Perez Medina, but his legal last name was Perez.

Mamá disregarded Leah's outstretched hand to stand and hug her. "Thank you for coming to my home, Leah. I hope you will return again, with or without my son."

Relieved to have dodged a bullet, Quin waited impatiently for Leah to say good-bye to his sisters. *I just had to fall for a polite Southern girl.*

That thought stopped him. *I've fallen for her?*

Not prepared to address that possibility while still in his mother's presence, he squeezed Leah's hand as a signal to speed it up.

She took the hint and brought her farewells to an end.

He leaned over and kissed his mother on the top of her white hair. She smiled at him and shook her head indulgently. "You need to come visit your father. It's been too long."

"I will, Mamá, I promise. Next week."

Across the yard, Carmen blew him a kiss. She was wearing the pearl necklace he'd bought her, and he could tell she was pleased with it.

He sketched a quick wave to his sisters and then headed for the back door. Wanting to avoid the complication of his father's imminent arrival, he led Leah across the kitchen and down the entry hall, making only one stop. He paused to seize a fork and spear a meatball from the platter sitting on the kitchen counter. When they got to the front door, he whistled for Turbo, who came lumbering toward them.

"Here you go, buddy. Knock yourself out." Quin deposited the meatball on the front steps and the fork on a nearby windowsill.

Leah shook her head. "That probably isn't good for him."

"Most of the best things in life aren't good for you if you overdo them. But when is Turbo likely to see another *quinceañera*?"

"You're crazy, you know?"

He swung around to grab her. "Crazy with wanting you." This time, when he kissed her, his tongue coaxed her lips to part. Once he'd breeched the sweet opening, he invaded, his tongue stroking the roof of her mouth with growing urgency.

When they came up for air, he was panting like Turbo. "Come on. Let's go. I can't wait another minute to rip that dress off you."

Visiting Quin's family had been a bittersweet experience for Leah. On the one hand, she'd learned that he was a twice-wounded and decorated marine who'd served in Iraq. What's more, his family held him in high esteem.

At the same time, watching the family stirred up memories of being an only child with a domineering yet emotionally absent single parent.

Quin's interactions with his mother, sisters and niece had opened the door to that empty room inside her. The cold void that filled her heart the day her mother died.

One minute she was fantasizing about Quin's body, and the next she was yearning to have what he had. Lots of family, unconditional love and acceptance.

While he'd grabbed a snack for the dog, she'd scolded herself. *Get a grip, Reece. You have family. It's the family you chose for yourself. Sandy, Zeke and now Zee, Dora and all your other friends. Quit yer whining.*

Then Quin grabbed and kissed her. Really kissed her. She forgot all about that empty room. Her world narrowed to the place where their bodies met and merged. As her tongue twisted around his, her yearning morphed into a raging desire.

He was the first to break off the kiss. He rasped, "Come on. Let's go."

His erection pressed against her stomach. She glanced around to make sure no one was watching and then reached out to touch the bulge in his slacks.

"What are you waiting for, cowboy?" she purred. "Let's do it." She gently squeezed him.

His body convulsed, and he leaned forward as though to protect his cock. "Knock it off," he rasped. "I told you I wouldn't put you in an embarrassing situation."

"No, you told me you didn't want to 'fuck and run.'" She grinned. "That may be the most romantic thing any man has ever said to me."

"You're killing me, Princess."

"Poor baby. That's not what I want." What she wanted right

then was to touch him. She slid her hand between his legs and slowly, oh so slowly, dragged it down his thigh.

He started to moan, seemed to catch himself and grabbed her wrist. "Look, if we don't go now, my father and brothers are going to show up with that damn cake, and we won't be able to leave for another hour."

"Then let's get out of here." She withdrew her hand and stepped off the front stoop. He followed.

They walked briskly down the front walk and along the road toward his Jeep.

He opened the passenger door for her, then climbed into the driver's seat and started the engine. In seconds, they were a block from his parents' house.

Quin reached across the console separating their seats to take her hand. "Do you have any idea how badly I want to fuck you?"

She threaded her fingers through his. "I hope it's as much as I want to be fucked."

They exchanged grins.

He turned right. She looked through the windshield and realized they were traveling south instead of east. "Where are we going?"

"My place is closer than yours. We're only a couple of blocks away."

Chapter Twenty-one

Quin's place surprised Leah. Instead of the apartment she'd expected, he lived in a redbrick ranch house that had probably been built in the early sixties. The trim and shutters were painted black, while the front door and garage door were a creamy ivory.

As he approached the house, he reached under his seat and pulled out a garage door opener. When they pulled in, an overhead light came on automatically.

The interior of the two-car garage was tidy. Tools hung on Peg-Boards and neatly labeled boxes sat in rows on the shelves.

They entered the house through the laundry room, and he led her past the kitchen and breakfast room to the den.

"Do you want something to drink?" he asked. "I can open a bottle of wine or mix a drink for you."

"A white wine would be nice if you have it."

"Coming up. Feel free to look around."

The house reminded her of the display rooms in a model home. The furniture was comfortable, but there were very few indications that anyone actually lived there. No live plants anywhere. Leah walked through the rooms: dining room, study, guest room, master bedroom.

When Quin found her, she was standing at the French door in the master bedroom, looking out at the backyard. She'd flipped on a light, which illuminated the wooden deck and a pool surrounded by an eight-foot privacy fence.

"Can we sit outside?" she asked, taking her drink from him.

"Of course." He put the bottle of wine and a second glass on a nearby dresser, retrieved a key from above the door frame and unlocked the dead bolt.

The backyard was pleasantly warm, and Leah picked a redwood chaise lounge with cushions to sit on. Quin pulled a matching Adirondack chair alongside hers.

Tall euonymus bushes circled the yard. Planted against the fence, they increased the sense of privacy.

"This is lovely," Leah said. "Have you owned it long?"

"I bought it seven months ago when I returned to Dallas. I got a great deal on it because it only has one bathroom. Most families want a second or third bath." He hesitated. "I'm not here much. I keep an apartment near the club."

She took a sip of her wine and raised her eyebrows. "Riesling?"

He nodded. "You said white wine, not Chardonnay. I can get you another glass if you'd rather."

She shook her head. "No, I like this."

"I'm glad," he said. "I spent some time convalescing on a base in Germany. My first day trips were visits to the Rhine Valley. I learned to appreciate the Riesling wines there."

She took another sip. "You're full of surprises, Quin."

He frowned, and for a moment she thought he was going to say something.

Without warning, he put his glass down on the deck and stood. He began to unbuckle his belt.

"What are you doing!"

"Going skinny-dipping." He kicked his loafers off, let his trousers drop to the ground and began to unbutton his shirt.

She stared at him, a smile threatening her face. "You're crazy."

"Very likely," he agreed. He dropped his shirt on the chair.

Leah watched him undress, content to enjoy the view.

She had a brief moment of distress when he knelt and unbuckled a sheath from his right leg. *That's a gun holster!*

He placed the holster on the deck and stepped out of his slacks.

Standing there, dressed only in a pair of white briefs and his wristwatch, he was gorgeous. His torso was lean and sculpted, his abs tight and well defined. The tattoos made him look even sexier.

Quin smiled at her and bent down to peel off his briefs.

His cock leaped out and pointed straight at her.

The jutting shaft became the focal point of Leah's attention. She pushed up off the chaise, instinctively drawn toward that cock.

"If you want me, you're going to have to come get me," Quin growled.

Turning, he crouched and then dove into the pool, the motion clean and knifelike. Leah caught a glimpse of his grade-A ass before it disappeared into the water.

She had no memory of moving, but the next moment she stood at the edge of the pool, watching him swim.

He cut through the water like a seal, without a lot of splashing or unnecessary movements. He was the most beautiful thing she had ever seen.

When he reached the shallow end, Quin turned and rested his back against the gutter, stretching his long arms along the side of the pool. His body bobbed gently in the water as he watched her. "Here I am if you want me."

Conscious of his eyes on her, Leah bent over to unsnap her sandals. Moving deliberately, she slipped off first one shoe and then the other.

When she straightened, for his benefit, she stretched her arms far above her head, as though she were trying to put something away on a high shelf. Her breasts strained against the confining material, her already hard nipples pressing on the fabric. She peeked at him. *Yes, I've got his complete attention.*

Next, she unbuckled the belt of her sundress. She moved slowly, methodically, as though performing a ritual. When the belt was undone, she removed it, dragging it off inch by inch.

After laying the belt down on the chaise, she bent over to grab the hem of the dress. She maintained her leisurely pace, pulling the wine-colored skirt up a fraction at a time . . . revealing her thighs, her panties, her flat stomach and her breasts.

Leah yanked the dress over her head and tossed it on the chaise. Her gaze returned to Quin, but . . . he wasn't where he had been.

In those few seconds during which she'd been removing the dress, he'd crossed the pool. He was now only four feet from her, his forearms resting on the pool's edge, his face turned up toward hers.

The dark hunger in his eyes made her heart leap. He looked like a predator waiting to pounce.

She stood before him, almost naked. She paused a moment before sliding her panties down her legs.

"*Cariña,*" he said, his voice so low she had to strain to hear him, "you look delicious. I could eat you with a spoon."

"Then we're even." She grinned at him. "Because I'm dying to taste you again."

He jerked as if pulled by an invisible string. "*Chiquita,*" he growled, "you need to come here right now."

"Or else?" she teased.

He put his hands on the deck and vaulted out of the pool.

Leah jumped backward and let out a startled squeak.

He stood in front of her, dripping water everywhere, looking like a sea god come to land to claim his human sacrifice.

She froze in place. *Oh, god. He's magnificent.*

Quin took a step toward her. She stopped breathing.

He put his hands on her waist. She could almost see steam rising from his fully aroused body.

He lifted her, swiveled and . . . threw her into the deep end of the pool.

Leah screamed as she flew through the air; her mouth was open when she hit the pool. She swallowed water and sank. And then she splashed frantically for a moment or two until she recovered her wits enough to swim to the surface, spewing chlorine and water.

With murder in her heart, she turned in the direction where Quin had stood. He wasn't there.

She floated, moving her hands and feet in a gentle motion while she searched for him on the deck and in the pool.

Without warning, he came up beside her from below.

"You," she sputtered.

He put an arm around her waist and pulled her toward him, covering her mouth with his and ending anything she might have said to him.

He pressed himself against her. His chest flattened her breasts; his cock cradled between their bodies. She could feel his penis pulsing against her belly.

Still holding her close, he swam toward the shallow end of the pool. When the water was below his hips, he stood and put her down. He ran his hands up from her waist to cup her breasts. "God, Leah, you are so beautiful."

She snorted. "Not likely. You've ruined my hair." She ran her hands through the wet strands, trying to tame the wild mess.

He leaned forward and licked a drop of water from her neck, following the water trail all the way up the column of her throat. "You're always so cool and put together," he murmured with his mouth against her skin. "I want to be the only one to see the wild woman underneath."

Leah forgot all about her hair. She rested her forearms on his bare chest. His skin felt hot. Using a forefinger, she traced the outline of one of his tattoos. She couldn't decide if the black inked drawing was an elaborate knife with multiple blades or a demon with spiny scales. "What is this?" she asked.

"An ancient god called Quetzalcoatl." He pronounced it "ketsal-ko-a-tl."

"What is he?" Leah pressed. "He looks like a snake, but I don't understand these things hanging off him. Are they fins?"

Quin shook his head. "No, feathers. Quetzalcoatl was known as the Feathered Serpent."

"Where?"

"Quetzalcoatl is found in both the Aztec and Mayan cultures." He stroked her wrist in an absentminded fashion. "The Hopi tribe in Arizona worships a similar god."

Leah wanted to understand him. *Maybe his tattoos will tell me more.* "Why did you choose this design?"

"When I was overseas, my unit was sometimes called to do street patrols." His gaze became fixed over her shoulder, as though he were seeing something far away. "It was dangerous duty, and whenever we survived our turn without losing a man, we'd celebrate by getting a tattoo." He fell silent.

She repeated her earlier question. "Why this design?"

"The guys were getting all kinds of crazy-ass things. Names of women, places they'd been, things they'd done." He shook his head. "I picked the symbols of my heritage." His gaze met hers. "Perhaps I was drawing on the strength of my race."

"Well, it worked. You came home."

He nodded. "So I did. And I'm grateful to whatever god brought me home so I'd have this." He took her face in both his hands, lowered his head and kissed her.

His lips were soft, and the kiss gentle. His mouth already felt familiar. *I know him, and yet I don't.*

She pressed closer, craving the heat of his skin. *Until now, I hadn't realized how hungry I was to touch and to be touched. I've missed it so much.* His warmth brought her . . . solace. *I know when I'm hungry for food. I just never recognized my body's need for the comfort of another's skin.*

Without warning, he bent, put his right arm under her knees and picked her up. Not trusting him, she threw her arms around his neck to prevent another dunking, but he simply walked toward the steps that led out of the pool.

He carried her across the deck to another redwood chaise lounge and gently laid her down.

Chapter Twenty-two

"I'm dripping wet," she protested.

"Water dries," he answered, kneeling so that he straddled her legs. Sliding his hands up her thighs and across her hips to where her legs joined, he began to play with the curls that hid her mons.

Looking up at him, Leah realized she wanted to know everything about him. *Did he have a favorite toy as a child? How old was he when he first kissed a girl? Why did he join the marines?* He'd refused to tell her about the scar on his face before. Now she reached up to touch it again. "Did you get this overseas?"

He started to jerk away, but then went still and allowed her to trace the scar from his temple to his jaw. "Yeah, at a checkpoint outside Fallujah."

"Was anyone else hurt?"

"A kid named Mal Meyers. He pushed me out of the way of a bullet. Saved my life. Lost his." Quin shook his head. "I don't want to talk about it now."

He twisted his fingers in her pubic curls. "I've always loved blondes." The change of subject could not have been more abrupt.

Although she wanted to know more, Leah was beginning to understand he couldn't be pushed. He would share, but in his own time. And he'd offered the same gift to her; he'd waited until she was ready to tell him about Dale.

Okay. New topic.

"Do something for me," she said.

"What?" His expression was guarded.

"Tell me a sex act you've never done with another woman. I want to do something with you that no one else has ever done."

She watched the expressions flit across his face: surprise, relief and a sudden intensity.

"Princess, I hate to tell you, but there aren't many sex acts that I haven't tried at least once. With a woman, that is. And I've never lusted after barnyard animals."

"Oh. Then I guess I can't help you blaze any new territory." She felt a little foolish.

He chucked her under the chin. "When I'm with you, everything we do feels new. If it isn't the first time, it's the best time."

He's good. Even if it was a line, he'd helped her to feel better.

An odd expression flitted across his face, but was gone before she could identify it. "What? You've thought of something," she said.

He shook his head. "It's nothing."

"Yes, it is. I saw it on your face. Give." She tapped his chest with an imperious finger.

"When I got my discharge from the service, the guys in my unit gave me a going-away party." He hesitated.

"Don't stop now. What?" she pressed.

"A couple of them were always complaining that I never had any trouble getting a date. As a joke, they gave me a box of anal sex toys together with a card that said 'Go fuck yourself.' I still have that box in a closet. Never used the toys."

Although Quin was acting very casual, she could tell that the idea of sliding his cock—his very large cock—into her anus held enormous appeal to him. *Okay, girlfriend, you just had to ask. Now what do you say?* She couldn't think of anything to say for a few seconds.

He tapped her lightly on the nose with one finger. "Hey, it's okay. No need to try the back door when the front door is so sweet."

She shook her head. "No, I started this. It's just that . . . um . . . I've never had a backdoor guest before."

He shook his head. "Forget I said anything, Leah. I opened my mouth before I thought it through."

"Does the box include plenty of lubricant?" She pushed him away so she could sit up in the chair.

He stood to move out of her way. "*Cariña*, I love that you want to please me, but not tonight."

"Why not?" The more reluctant he seemed, the more determined she became. *People do it all the time. How bad can it be?* She swung her legs off the chaise to stand, too. "Do you have any K-Y Jelly?"

His strained expression wasn't what she expected. "What's the matter, Quin?"

He grimaced. "We need to talk, Leah, and I'd rather we did it before we took a step like . . . like . . ." His voice faltered.

"Like anal sex?" she asked. *Oh my god! He wants to break up.* Fear closed around her heart like a fist of steel. *Not so soon. I'm not ready.*

"Yeah." He looked away and grabbed a towel, which he held out to her. "I don't want you thinking that I tricked you or misled you."

She took the towel from him with nerveless fingers. *Tricked me? Oh, Lord. He's trying to say he thought I understood this was just a one-night stand. I've scared him, talking about doing something I've never done before. Like he was taking my virginity or something. How freaking stupid can you be, Reece?*

She swayed, and he grabbed her upper arms. "Are you okay, *cariña?*"

"I'm fine. Just stood up too fast." She shrugged him off and rubbed her upper body with the towel. "I need my clothes. Would you get them for me, please? I'm cold."

"Let me find you something warm," he said. He hustled over to a narrow outdoor closet set into the back wall of the house and pulled out a long white terry-cloth robe. Returning to her side, he draped it over her shoulders.

She was so desperate to cover her nakedness—her vulnerability—that she accepted both the garment and his help in sliding the sleeves over her bare arms. His scent was all over the robe. She wanted to bury her face in the collar, take one final bit of comfort from his now-familiar smell.

Quin wrapped the too-large robe around her body and cinched the belt tightly. "Let me make you a cup of coffee. I'm sorry. I don't have any tea."

"I'm fine." She looked around for her sandals. "You wanted to talk?" *The faster we get this over with, the sooner I can leave.* She bent to snag a shoe from under the chaise.

He didn't answer.

She looked up from where she crouched, reaching for her second sandal.

He was staring at her, and the look telegraphed despair.

"Quin?" Leah forgot about her shoes and her speedy exit. His expression told her she'd miscalculated. She didn't know how, but she was certain she had. "What's wrong?"

"You're leaving." His hopeless expression left no doubt as to how he felt about her departure.

"I thought you wanted me to go," she said.

"Why the devil would you think that?" His features clouded with confusion.

"Never mind." Leah felt giddy with relief. She dropped the sandal. Taking his arm, she guided him toward the steps leading into the pool. Hiking up the hem of her robe to keep it dry, she plopped down on the top step and patted the deck next to her. "Sit down, and talk to me."

"Leah, what the hell just happened?" Seeming completely oblivious to his nude state, he dropped down beside her. "One minute you're asking me to fuck you in the ass, and the next thing I know you're scrambling around, looking for your shoes so you can run out the door."

She hesitated, not wanting to admit how much she'd feared he might want to break up with her. "It was a misunderstanding. No harm done." Rather than meet his gaze, she stared at the glassy mirror of water.

He gripped her shoulders and turned her to face him. "I know I scared you. I saw it in your eyes. But how?" He put two fingers under her chin and tilted her head up. "Tell me what I said that spooked you."

His gentle voice said the question was sincere. *I need to tell him.* She met his gaze. "When you said we needed to talk, I thought you were going to tell me we were through."

A frown creased his face, but he didn't speak.

"You're angry with me," she said.

He sighed and removed his hand from her chin. "No, not angry. I'm floored. What have I done to make you think I was that big a prick?"

"I don't think you're a prick, Quin."

"No, you thought I'd fuck you, and then tell you to get lost."

She winced. *Put that way, it sounds awful.* "It's not you, Quin; it's me. I don't like being left alone."

His eyes narrowed. "That doesn't make sense. Since we met, everything I've seen indicates you're usually alone. You spend more time out of relationships than in one."

Leah squirmed under the laser probe of his gaze. "I'm used to *being* alone. I've been alone since I was eleven." She looked down at her hands. "I just hate the part when someone leaves."

"You mean it's the actual act of breaking up that bothers you? Bothers you more than being alone?"

She nodded without answering.

"You don't like breaking up because . . ." His voice trailed off while he thought about it. "You said you've been alone since you were eleven. That's when your mother died, isn't it? You had no say in that breakup." His voice grew more certain. "If you leave, it's a preemptive strike. You want to decide when and where the breakup happens."

"Maybe," she admitted reluctantly. *Damn! I sound like a controlling, whiny bitch.*

Quin wrapped her in his arms and pulled her face against his muscled chest. "Oh, *cariña.*" He sighed. "What am I going to do with you?"

"I don't know," she whispered. A wave of relief flowed through her limbs. *It's all right. He called me* cariña. She snuggled closer, luxuriating in both his warmth and his spicy sandalwood-and-cloves fragrance.

He rubbed his cheek against her wet hair. "We still need to talk."

"About what?" She didn't care. *We can talk about anything as long as we're still together.*

"About Miguel Lucero. He knows who you are, Leah."

Her head snapped back. Alarmed, she studied his face. "How? You didn't tell him." It was a statement, not a question. She knew Quin hadn't betrayed her.

"No," he agreed with a small smile. "I didn't tell him. Ruben copied down your license plate Wednesday night. By this morning, Lucero knew your real name and that you were a reporter."

"A columnist," she corrected absentmindedly while trying to process the news. *Did Lucero find out about Consuelo?* "How much does he know?"

"About as much as I know." He tapped her nose, forcing her attention back to him. "He knows you're planning to write a story about his club, and he's thinking about how to stop you."

"Realistically, what can he do?" she asked. "Bribe me, or threaten to hurt me in some way?"

"Don't underestimate him, Leah. Lucero's ruthless. He suggested I bring you to him tonight."

Quin's face was hard as granite, and a shiver of anxiety ran through her body. "Bring me to him for what?"

"Probably just to scare you. For starters anyway." He shook his head. "I can't prove it, but I've heard from more than one person that Miguel has helped people to 'disappear' when they got in his way."

"You mean he'd kill me?" Outrage raised her voice several octaves.

"If necessary. He's a Sinaloan Cowboy, Leah."

"I don't understand." If Quin intended to frighten her, he was doing a good job of it. "What's a Sinaloan Cowboy?"

"Sinaloa is one of Mexico's thirty-one states. It's the home base of the Mexican drug cartel. Most of the cocaine and heroin that crosses the U.S. border originates in Sinaloa."

"He's a drug smuggler?"

Quin shrugged. "I'm pretty sure he's a smuggler. I don't know if it's drugs."

"What else would it be?" Fear climbed into the backseat as Leah's journalistic curiosity took over.

"Never mind." He grimaced. "I'm not a source for your damned story. I'm trying to keep you alive." He stood, wrapped a towel around his waist and poured another glass of wine. He downed it in one swallow.

She searched for something to say to defuse his agitation. "That gold belt buckle Lucero wears. It's engraved. Some drug sign?"

His back to her, Quin replied, "Just the letters W-B-P."

"WBP?" She squinted while trying to come up with a suitable combination of letters and words. "The only thing I can think of is the text-messaging acronym for 'write back, please.'" She stood and walked toward him, holding the hem of her robe off the ground to keep from tripping. "What does it mean?"

"Wetback Power, the motto of the Sinaloan Cowboys." He swung around to face her. "Enough kidding around, Leah. This is serious. Tell me what you were doing in that kitchen Wednesday night."

Her chin jutted forward. "Sharing is a two-way street, Quin. I've seen your parents' house, your family told me about your military record, and you told me about your father being in the construction business. All that stuff about you not being able to find another job except as chief of security for a brothel was so much hooey." She took a step toward him and tapped him hard on his bare chest with her index finger. "If you want me to come clean, buster, you go first."

Chapter Twenty-three

Quin met Leah's determined gaze. She should have looked silly: barefoot, dressed in a terry-cloth robe too large for her slender frame and with her wet hair sticking out in all directions. Instead she looked meaner than Papá's dog.

Fearful she would reach under his towel and rip his *huevos* off, he managed to suppress a smile.

The thing is, she has a point. He was demanding that she tell him everything he wanted to know while he withheld information. His sense of fair play warred with his sense of duty.

He suddenly remembered a card Zeke had sent him overseas right after meeting Sandy. He couldn't remember the whole message, but he'd never forgotten one part: "I don't know what it is about this girl, Quin. I've been with better-looking women, but never one who could turn me inside out the way Sandy does. I just look at her, and I'm ready to tell her anything, or do whatever it takes to make her happy. On top of that, she makes me harder than a spike."

Standing there with Leah scowling at him, Quin felt a sense of kinship with his childhood friend. In forty-eight hours, this spitfire had wormed her way into his life and into his thoughts as no woman ever had.

"What's it going to be, Quin? You show me yours, and I show you mine? Or do we just forget about sharing?" Leah demanded.

"You win," he said.

Her evident surprise at his capitulation pleased him. For all her bluster, she hadn't expected him to give in.

He took her hand and led her back into the house. Inside, he pointed to the sofa.

Leah sat without saying a word.

Quin perched on the edge of his favorite recliner across from her.

"Leah, I'm a Dallas undercover cop assigned to keep an eye on Lucero."

He saw the flash of relief in her eyes, but that didn't stop her from pursuing the story. "Keep an eye on him for what?"

Quin drew a deep breath. "We suspect Lucero is bringing Mexican nationals across the border illegally."

She frowned. "That's not a Dallas Police matter."

She's quick. He felt an odd sense of pride. "You're right. It's a joint federal task force being run by the FBI and La Migra."

"La Migra? Immigration?"

"Right. ICE—Immigration and Customs Enforcement. The task force requested local assistance, and I was the perfect choice."

"Why? What made you so perfect?" She tilted her head like a curious sparrow.

"I was an MP in Iraq. I'd just come home. My experience plus Zeke's recommendation got me hired by the DPD. I got tapped for this special assignment before I even set foot in the police station."

"Because you're Mexican-American?"

"Partially. There was also concern Lucero might have an informant in the department. The fact that no one had seen me yet was a huge plus." He hesitated. "My real name is Quin Perez Medina."

A light went off behind Leah's eyes as she processed the information. "That's why your mother looked at me so funny tonight."

He nodded, grinning. "My sister Rita was dying to correct you."

But Leah wasn't about to get sidetracked. "Was that assault charge cooked up as part of your cover?"

"Yeah. They put me in the same cell block as a known associate of Lucero's. I caught a lucky break when four members of the BGF gang cornered Filip in the bathroom."

"BGF?"

"The Black Guerrilla Family, a gang out of California." He leaned forward to rest his elbows on his knees. "I don't have to tell you it's dangerous on the inside. Inmates tend to segregate along racial lines for protection. The BGF caught Filip alone. They had him on the floor, and all four of them were kicking him. I broke the first one's arm and kneed another in the balls. The third lost his taste for the fight and ran. I dunked the fourth one's head in a toilet." He smiled with satisfaction at the memory.

Leah shuddered, catching Quin by surprise. *Careful, Perez. You're scaring her.* He continued, "A month later, when I was released, a Cadillac was waiting outside the county jail to take me to meet Lucero."

"And he gave you a job?"

"Yeah. Things were going great until Wednesday night when you showed up."

Her face clouded. "Quin, that's not fair. I haven't done anything to jeopardize your cover."

He reached out to capture her hands. "Leah, I know you didn't mean to create a problem, but anything that focuses Lucero's attention on me . . . or on you, puts my assignment at risk."

Her chin lifted in a now-familiar gesture. "You're not the only one with a job here, Quin."

"I know that, *cariña*. And I hope you know that I could be fired for what I've just told you."

Her gaze softened, and she squeezed his hand. "I do know that."

"Okay, turnabout is fair play. What were you doing in that kitchen on Wednesday night?"

She bit her lower lip, but then he saw her make a decision. "I was there to meet an informant."

"A member of the club's staff?"

She nodded. "A kitchen worker named Consuelo. She hid when Lucero walked in."

"Have you been in touch with her since?"

She nodded a second time. "Yes, I talked with her last night. She's scared."

"She should be," he said. "If Miguel realizes she's betrayed him, she's dead."

Her face went still, and he could see his words had struck their target. Although he'd only known her for forty-eight hours, Quin was confident that the idea she could be putting Consuelo at risk would cause Leah great distress. He resisted his instinctive urge to offer her comfort. *This isn't a game. She isn't reporting on the latest sex toys. She could get hurt . . . or worse.*

"What has Consuelo told you so far?"

She shook her head. "Nothing. She was going to give me a tour of the club and answer my questions Wednesday."

"When are you supposed to be back in touch with her?"

"I'd decided to give her a chance to settle down before calling her again. I had planned to phone her tomorrow."

He heard the note of doubt in her voice. *You're getting through to her.* Quin drew a calming breath before plunging in. *Careful. She'll eat you alive if she thinks you're being condescending.* "Leah, let's team up on this. Work with me, and I'll make sure you get the exclusive story after it's over."

Her eyes narrowed. "And full access in the meantime?"

The lieutenant will kill me if he finds out. "Yes, on the condition that you promise to sit on your story until the case is closed."

She pulled her hands free while she considered his offer. He crossed his arms and waited. *Please, God, I could use your help here.* He realized his mouth had gone dry.

"All right," she finally said. "I'll work with you."

His shoulders sagged with relief. *Gracias a Dios.*

She stood. "It's late. I should be heading home."

"Don't go." He stood, and the towel began to slip. He tightened it around his waist. "Stay the night." He wrapped his arms around her.

She didn't melt into his embrace, but neither did she stiffen.

"I want you in my bed, next to me tonight." He nuzzled her disheveled hair. "Tomorrow is Saturday. You don't need to be at your desk when the sun comes up. Stay."

Leah rested her hands on his towel-clad hips. "All right." She stood on her tiptoes to kiss his chin.

They walked hand in hand to his bedroom.

He opened the closet and pulled out a long-sleeved dress shirt and a cotton tee. Holding them both out to her, he said, "Your choice of nightgowns, ma'am."

She didn't hesitate; she selected the button-up dress shirt. "This one, thanks."

Pleased he'd guessed right, Quin waved toward his bathroom door. "Ladies first."

She flashed him a quick smile before disappearing.

Quin returned to the back deck to pick up his ankle holster and clothes. He locked the door leading to the pool, but left the deck lights on to provide indirect illumination in his bedroom. Following his usual practice, he placed the holster on his night-stand. The Glock was already in the drawer below.

After pulling down the bedspread, he sat on the edge of the mattress to wait for Leah. *There's nothing in the house to eat. We'll have to go out to breakfast. I'll take her to Café Brazil.*

The bathroom door opened, and Leah appeared. Backlit by the bathroom light, her face without makeup looked young and innocent. His shirt added to the youthful illusion. Its hem fell below her knees, making her look like she was playing dress-up in her papá's clothes.

Quin felt a swell of tenderness. "When's your birthday?" he asked.

"Wha—? April twenty-seventh. When's yours?"

"November eleventh. I'm thirty-four. How old are you?"

"I just turned thirty-two." She approached the bed.

"Have you ever been married before?"

"No. You?"

"No," he said. "Never found a woman I could imagine being married to."

She stopped in front of him, close enough that her thighs lightly pressed against his knees. "Why not?"

He spread his knees so she could move closer. "My parents have been married nearly forty-five years. Forty-two years ago, when Rita was about eighteen months old and Mamá was preg-nant with Rod, they picked up and moved to this country so their children could have a better life." He slid his arms around her waist and tugged her toward him. "My mother didn't want to leave her parents and brothers and sisters to go to a strange new country where she didn't even speak the language, but she trusted Papá." He rested his head against her chest. "I'm looking for a woman with that same courage and strength."

Leah stroked his hair, tunneling her fingers through the strands. "Your mother was willing to sacrifice for your father's vision."

Quin recognized something off in her voice. "What about your parents?"

"Tex had a vision all right, but his dream was all that mattered to him. Mom and I were mostly annoying peripherals." This time, he had no trouble identifying the bitterness in her tone. Warning alarms rang in the back of his brain.

"*Cariña*, how did your mother die?"

She didn't immediately answer, and his stomach clenched. He pulled his head free of her caressing fingers and leaned backward to look up into her face. "Leah?"

She licked her lips and gave a defiant toss of her head. He knew what she was going to say.

"She killed herself. She waited until I left for school and then went upstairs and downed an entire bottle of sleeping pills."

Chapter Twenty-four

Something clicked into place for Quin. Leah's fear of abandonment, her competitive attitude toward her father and her drive to succeed suddenly all made sense.

He reached up to touch her cheek. "Aw, Leah, I'm so sorry."

Her bravado melted away, and tears filled her eyes. "When Mom didn't come downstairs by noon, the maid went into her room and found her."

The tip of his finger halted one tear as it rolled down her cheek. "Baby, don't cry. I'm sorry I brought it up. I wouldn't hurt you for the world."

She brushed at her eyes. "It's not your fault. It's just"—she sniffled—"it's just that I try not to think about it too often . . . 'cause every time I do, this happens." More tears spilled from her brimming eyes.

He pulled her into his lap and cradled her in his arms.

She went willingly, wrapping her left arm around his body and laying her head on his naked chest.

Quin rocked back and forth, his face pressed against her hair.

The room remained quiet—except for an occasional snuffle from Leah. He was struck by how quietly she wept. *Did she cry this silently when she was a child . . . so no one would hear?* Leah coughed, but even that sound was muffled. Once or twice, when she shuddered, he hugged her tighter.

The clock on the nightstand ticked the minutes off, one by

one. Gradually, Leah's body relaxed, and she slumped in his arms. *Good. She's asleep.*

Moving very slowly, Quin laid her on the mattress. She murmured and shifted her limbs restlessly. He froze, waiting for her to settle. When she relaxed back into sleep, he tiptoed to the bathroom and rushed through his nightly routine, not wanting to leave her alone for too long.

He debated whether to leave the bathroom light on or not. *I don't want her to wake in the dark and not know where she is.* He left the light on, but closed the door halfway.

He slid into the bed and across the mattress to press his nude body against Leah's, spooning her back. *"Duerma bien, cariña,"* he whispered. Sleep well, love.

Within minutes, he was fast asleep.

Leah woke with her eyes burning and her head aching. She had a moment of panic. *This isn't my bed. Where am I?*

A man's naked body pressed against her back, a hand rested on her left hip, and a hairy leg lay across her calf. But not just any man. Quin's familiar scent reassured her.

Memories from the previous night flooded her brain. The headache and stinging eyes were souvenirs from her cry fest.

The last thing I remember is him rocking me to sleep. Oh, Lord. Can you be any more lame, Reece? Well, at least he isn't sleeping on the sofa.

Early-morning light filled the room. *It's Saturday morning. I wonder what time it is?* A lawn mower's buzz provided a clue. *Unless Quin has really rude neighbors, it's after eight a.m.*

Since it was the weekend, she was tempted to go back to sleep, but her bladder demanded attention.

Moving carefully so as not to disturb him, she slid sideways, out from under Quin and off the bed. He was sleeping so soundly; beyond one or two snorts, he didn't budge.

Leah winced at her reflection in the bathroom mirror. Tear-salt trails on her face, puffy eyes and disheveled hair did not make an attractive picture. *Would the sound of the shower wake Quin?* The large bathroom held a tub and a shower stall and had an entrance from the hallway and from Quin's bedroom. *Maybe the builder provided extra acoustical protection for a shared bath.*

Quin woke between one breath and the next. He was asleep, then he was awake.

He wondered what had awakened him. Outside, kids shouted to one another in the distance. Inside, there were only the usual noises: the ticking of the clock, the water heater cycling on, and the thrum of the refrigerator.

He glanced to his left. Leah wasn't beside him. *She got up. Maybe that's what woke me. I'm getting soft. A year ago, she wouldn't have been able to leave the bed without waking me.*

The alarm clock said it was almost nine.

Then he heard it: the sound that had disturbed his sleep. An intermittent buzzing. His cell phone.

He sat up and looked around for his slacks. They were in the corner, draped across a stuffed chair.

He crossed the room, retrieved his pants and fumbled to find the phone. The display read "Miguel Lucero."

"*¡Chingado!*" He flipped the cell open. "Medina."

"Quin, I need you in my office by noon."

"I wasn't planning on coming in until tonight, Miguel."

"By noon." The phone went dead.

"Fuck." *So much for spending a leisurely day together.*

The bathroom door was closed. He knocked. "Princess, are you decent?"

No answer. He knocked again, slightly harder. *"Chiquita?"*

When she didn't answer a second time, he walked out of the bedroom to check the hall entrance to the bath. It stood open.

No Leah.

He found traces though. Droplets of water in the sink and tub. A wet towel hanging from the shower curtain rod.

He looked in the kitchen. The smell of freshly made coffee greeted him, but no Leah.

He checked the garage. His car was still there. *She didn't walk home.* He reentered the house and searched for a note. Nothing.

Standing in his den, he tried to decide what to do next. *I could call her cell.*

His gaze swept the room one last time, settling on the glass door. The deck. *Maybe she's out by the pool.*

He went to the door and looked out.

Leah was lying on a chaise lounge, sipping a cup of coffee.

Relief washed over him. The door was unlocked. He stepped outside. "There you are."

"Good morning." Her face was freshly scrubbed and her hair washed and combed back. She looked about eighteen. He suddenly became conscious of the fact that he was completely nude. *Idiot. You should have put something on before walking out here.* "I hope you slept well."

Color flooded her cheeks. "I did." She raised her chin. "Thank you for your kindness last night."

He shrugged. "No need to thank me. I apologize for upsetting you." *We both sound so stiff.*

"It wasn't your fault. You'd think by now I'd be able to discuss an event that happened more than twenty years ago without dissolving into tears." Despite her light tone, Quin could hear the strain in her voice.

"I've known adults driven to their knees by the suicide of a loved one. I can't imagine how an eleven-year-old copes with the suicide of her mother." He rested his right hand on the warm skin left bare by her sundress.

This time it was Leah's turn to shrug. "I coped by keeping busy, by filling the empty spaces with people and noise."

"Maybe that's why it still bothers you. Perhaps you've never let yourself grieve."

"Now you sound like Sandy. I'll tell you what I told her. 'No, thank you.' I have absolutely no interest in wallowing in a pity party over ancient history." She swung her legs off the chaise. "I made coffee. Want a cup?"

The change of subject reminded him of Lucero's call. "Listen, Princess. I planned to spend the day with you, but Miguel just called. He wants me to report in by noon. I'm sorry."

An expression he didn't recognize flashed across her face. Disappointment? Relief?

"That's okay," she said, standing. "I've been neglecting my job. The new issue is near deadline, and I need to look over the layout."

"You don't have to leave right away, do you?" he asked. "At least, let me take you out to breakfast."

While Quin showered, Leah poured him a cup of coffee. She carried the steaming mug into the master bathroom and set it on the counter.

While Quin wielded his washcloth, she caught glimpses of his oh-so-fine body through the glazed glass of the stall. *Mmmmmm.*

Turning to leave the bathroom, she noticed her wet towel was the only one handy. She glanced around for a fresh towel.

The bathroom had a medicine cabinet, but no linen closet. She stepped back into the hallway and found a nearby door that looked like a likely candidate.

Sure enough, the closet contained two shelves with neatly folded bath towels, hand cloths and bedsheets.

She reached in, grabbed a towel and was about to close the door when a box on an upper shelf caught her attention.

Painted a gaudy red, white and blue, the outside of the box included drawings of lightning bolts, stars and improbably colored suns. The big clues were the carefully lettered "Semper Fi" tagline and the eagle, globe and anchor logo.

Leah reached up and took the box down from the shelf.

Chapter Twenty-five

Quin stepped out of the shower and found a fresh towel and a mug of coffee waiting on the counter. *Whoa! Talk about room service.*

He wrapped the towel around his waist before tasting the coffee. *Excellent. The princess knows her way around a grinder and coffee beans. I may just have to marry her. Or at least borrow her once in a while.* He grinned to himself and turned the doorknob to his bedroom.

What the— The door was locked from the bedroom side.

He moved to the hallway door, opened it and stopped dead.

The floor was festooned with red, white and blue confetti. Confetti that looked strangely familiar.

Quin turned toward his bedroom. The door was closed. Hanging over the doorknob was a box. *The box.*

He dropped the empty box on the floor and put his hand—his suddenly sweating hand—on the doorknob. The mental image of Leah's naked rump sent blood rushing to his groin.

He wiped his damp palm on the towel he was wearing, took a deep breath and opened the door.

Dios! She read my mind . . . and my fantasy.

She was on her hands and knees, wearing only a seductive smile. Her back to him, she leaned on her forearms and looked over her right shoulder at him. A pillow under her knees raised her ass high in the air. She wiggled her rump in invitation.

Quin's cock jerked convulsively at the sight of those pale, curvaceous buttocks so blatantly offered to him. He licked dry lips before saying, "Princess, I can't decide whether to praise God or thank Satan for what I see."

Her smile widened. "Instead of giving thanks or praise, why don't you give me some of *that*?" She gestured with her chin toward his bulging towel, where his *verga*, now at full staff, demanded to be set free.

His brain and his balls were at war, pulling him in two directions: his brain wanted him to stay where he was and continue enjoying the sight of her; his balls wanted to fill Leah's body with his flesh.

Quin pulled the edge of his bath towel loose and let the terry cloth fall to the floor. With three quick strides he crossed the room to stand at the foot of the bed.

"Everything you need is right beside you." Leah nodded toward a five-ounce bottle of lubricant, several strands of Thai beads, an anal bead stick, half a dozen condoms and even a jar of antibacterial wipes. He smiled. The butt plug that had also been in the box was noticeably absent. *That's okay. She needs to be comfortable during her first time.*

"*Cariña*, do you know how delicious you look?" he asked, reaching for the bottle of lubricant.

"I want to be sexy for you, Quin."

Another man might not have noticed the tiny quaver in her voice, but Quin had become so attuned to her moods that he had no difficulty hearing it.

"Princess, we are going to take this very slow. If you decide to stop at any point, all you have to do is tell me. All right?"

"Yes."

His buddies hadn't stinted on the gag gift. They'd sprung for the Cadillac of lubricants. In the years since he'd become sexually active, Quin had sampled every kind of lubricant from the petroleum jelly in his parents' medicine cabinet to the well-known blue-and-white tubes found in many nightstands. Although twice as expensive as other lubricants, Astroglide's warming liquid was less sticky and didn't become gummy. *Thanks, guys.*

He opened the bottle. "Leah, we'll start with a massage to help you relax. I'm going to rub some lubricant on your ass cheeks. It will feel warm, so don't be surprised."

No answer. She'd buried her face in a pillow.

Take it slow and easy, Perez. He poured a small amount of the Astroglide on both buttocks.

Despite his warning, she jumped when the liquid touched her skin.

"That's all right, *cariña*. There's nothing to be scared about. I promise to take good care of you." He spread the lubricant, massaging the fluid into her soft skin with a slow, circular motion.

He kept up a gentle patter of nonsense while he worked. "Your muscles are so tight I could bounce a coin off these cheeks. I'm going to massage you until you're putty in my hands."

The warming liquid, his voice and the kneading motion had the intended effect. Leah began to relax.

Quin didn't rush. He started high, just below her waist, and worked his way low, to the backs of her thighs. Not until she started to make small "Mmmmmm" sounds of approval did he move to the next level.

After adding more lubricant, he allowed his hands to drift toward the crack between her buttocks.

She was enjoying the massage so much that she didn't even react when his fingers slid between her buttocks.

"This is special, Princess, knowing that you're sharing yourself in a way you've never shared yourself with another man. I can't believe how much that turns me on."

She made a small sound of encouragement, and he lightly brushed his right index finger across her anal opening.

He felt her buttocks stiffen and immediately moved his left hand south toward her labia. Parting the nether lips, he cruised down her canal until his thumb found her clit.

For the next several minutes, he alternated between stroking her pussy with one hand and moving up and down the valley between her buttocks—from her tailbone to her sphincter—with the other.

He continued his low, sensual patter, telling her how beautiful she was and how badly he wanted to put his cock inside her. "I promise this gorgeous ass is going to enjoy being fucked."

Leah's vagina began to weep, and she started rocking her hips back and forth.

Not yet, Princess. If you want to come, you need to come through the back door first. He grinned at his own pun. He pulled his hands away from her body.

She whimpered at the loss of his touch.

"It's okay, Princess. I have some technical issues to address. I'll be right back."

He examined the sex toys she'd laid out and selected the anal bead stick. Five inches long, it looked like a skewer with six beads arranged in a row along its length. The beads graduated in size from about a half inch in diameter at the tip to a full inch at the other end. The jelly material was flexible, and there were no seams on the beads to tear her tender tissues. The less flexible stick would be easier to insert than the very flexible Thai beads strung on string.

His decision made, he used an antibacterial wipe to thoroughly clean any dust off the bead stick.

After coating his hands with more Astroglide, he was ready. "*Cariña*, I'm going to touch your anus. I have lots of lubricant. But, remember, you have all the control here. If you tell me to stop, I will. Okay?"

"Okay," she said.

Using his right hand, he made small concentric circles around her anal opening. Although he could feel some tension, she was much more relaxed than she had been thirty minutes earlier.

"Okay, Princess, I'm going to slide one finger inside your little rosebud. It may feel strange, but it won't hurt. Ready?"

Ready? What kind of question was that? Who's ready for this? Quin had told her there weren't many sex acts he hadn't done, but Leah was willing to bet he hadn't had a cock stuffed into his rectum. She stifled a nervous giggle by burying her face in a pillow.

His index finger teased her anal opening. Despite her best efforts not to tighten her sphincter muscle, her body tensed.

Without warning, Quin pushed through her back door for the first time.

The lubricant did its job; the invasion didn't hurt.

But the sensation *was* a strange one; an odd sense of fullness even though his finger was barely inside her rectum.

He slid the finger in and out.

"Ohhhh," she squeaked.

"Are you okay?" he asked, immediately pulling his finger out.

"Yes, you just surprised me." She raised her head from the pillow to look over her shoulder at him. "That was the oddest feeling."

"Unpleasant?"

"Noooo." She could hear the uncertainty in her own voice.

Quin pressed his finger against her again and pushed inside. Once more, he slid his finger in and out.

The warm lubricant felt wonderful, and she gradually became accustomed to the full feeling. Her hips even began rocking to and fro in counterpoint to his finger's motion.

"Ready for the next level, Princess?"

"Yes." *I trust him; he's trying so hard.*

"I'm going to insert the anal beads. I promise, once you get used to the sensation, you're going to love these."

I hope you're right.

The first and second beads didn't feel any different than the sensation of his finger pressing past her sphincter. The third beat went deeper into her rectum, increasing that sensation of fullness. She wanted to push back to expel the foreign object from her body. But he continued to nudge the stick into her.

Four beads now. Although she knew it wasn't possible, it felt as though the stick was touching her belly button. She realized she was holding her breath and made an effort to breathe normally. *Don't panic. It's okay.*

She was about to tell Quin he needed to stop when he flicked her clitoris with his index finger. Her gasp of surprise quickly changed to a sigh of delight as he began to massage the tiny organ.

Leah forgot all about the bead stick. The combination of Quin's touch and the warmth of the lubricating liquid was unbelievably erotic. She pressed her pussy into his hand, grinding her clit against his fingers.

Quin continued to manipulate her pleasure button, quickly

bringing her close to coming. She closed her eyes, leaped off the edge into the chasm and soared.

The orgasm broke over her, spreading outward from her core. She lost control of her limbs—almost as though she'd left her body to fly through space.

Colors danced behind her closed eyes, and she joined them, a piece of the whirling rainbow. She was pink and gold, weightless and free.

As the orgasm passed, the rainbow receded and she returned to earth and to her body.

And, at exactly that moment, Quin withdrew the anal beads.

The rippling feeling as each bead popped out was unlike anything she'd ever experienced. By the third bead, the sensation had set off a domino effect, and she tumbled into her second mind-blowing orgasm. She zoned out for several seconds.

When she regained her wits, she collapsed forward on her forearms with her chest flat against the mattress. She could hear Quin behind her, ripping open a condom.

She was panting as though she'd run a foot race. Her womb was contracting, sending wave after wave of pleasure through her body.

"*Cariña*, can you hear me?" Quin asked.

"Yesss," she gasped.

The mattress tilted as he crawled up behind her. "I'm going to rub some more lubricant on you," he told her.

The warm liquid brought her close to another orgasm. Wanting to push herself over the edge for a third time, she slid her right hand under her torso to touch her clitoris.

Quin put his hands between her thighs and spread them so he could kneel between her legs.

She shifted her hand from her clit to the mattress to help prop her body up.

Grabbing her waist, Quin lifted and steadied her. "Princess, I'm going to push my cock into you, but only just inside your rosebud. Ready?"

This time, wanting that third orgasm, she was not only ready but eager. "Do it. Fuck me, Quin. Please."

She felt his hands and thighs trembling with his frantic desire.

He pressed his cock against her anus and pushed forward. With all the lubricant on him and on her, he slid right in.

This time, she felt nothing but pleasure. "Ohhh," she moaned. "Take me, Quin. Take me."

His voice shaking, he ordered, *"Usted. Empuje en mi verga."* You. Push back on my cock. He wanted her to control the rate at which she accepted him into her body.

He was so excited, he'd lost his English. That knowledge thrilled her into action. She rocked back against him, pushing him deeper inside her.

Everything was so tight that Leah felt as though she'd swallowed him. The sense of fullness was the most exquisite pleasure she'd ever known.

Quin pulled back, but not out of her body. *"¿Cariña, está bien usted?"* Sweetheart, are you all right? The words came out in quick pants.

Leah screamed her frustration. "More. Faster, Quin, faster!"

He needed no further encouragement. His thrusts were short and frenzied.

Wanting to seize and hold his cock, Leah tightened her sphincter muscles, making her vagina contract as well as her rectum. Her orgasm was explosive.

When she tightened her muscles around him, Quin came—shouting her name—the rest of his words totally unintelligible. He collapsed against her back, and the two fell forward on the mattress.

Chapter Twenty-six

*L*eah had no idea how long the two of them lay there without moving.

She felt as though every bit of energy had been drained from her body. Although she'd been hungry an hour before, now all she wanted to do was go back to sleep. She drifted off into space on a pleasurable, soft cloud.

She wasn't sure how long she'd been sleeping when Quin moved off her body.

"Jesus, Leah, were you trying to kill me?" he asked.

"You forgot your English," she said with a touch of smugness.

"*Chiquita*, I forgot my own damn name." He got up and moved around the bed to sit beside her on the mattress. "What the hell did you do to me?"

"It wasn't me. You did it to yourself."

"Fuck that. When you squeezed my cock, my heart almost exploded. Thank God I have good genes." He brushed her hair out of her eyes. "If I didn't, you'd be trying to figure out what to do with my dead body."

"Guess I did it okay, then, huh?"

He leaned over to kiss her cheek. "Princess, no one has ever done it so good." He lifted his head to glance at the clock. "Damn. If I'm going to feed you before I drop you off, we need to get going." He licked her bare shoulder. "Want to shower together?"

"Get away from me, you beast. I'm not going anywhere near you. Do you want to cripple me?"

His mood changed instantly. "Did I hurt you? Are you all right?" He started massaging her back with his right hand.

She lifted her head. "I'm better than all right. I just don't want to push my luck. Go shower while I rest here."

Leah waited until he was safely in the shower to slowly and painfully get up. *I don't want him to see me moving around like an old woman.*

She didn't begrudge a single ache or sore spot. She'd earned them honestly, and the fleeting pain would be gone by morning.

After getting off the bed, she found his bathrobe and curled up in a chair in the den to wait for him to finish getting dressed.

Although she would never admit it to him, a part of Leah was relieved that Lucero had called Quin into work. She needed a little "alone" time.

In three days, Quin Perez Medina had turned her world upside down. She'd never encountered a man quite like him. A man capable of being both extremely macho and extraordinarily sensitive.

He might look like just another sexy hunk, but he was way too perceptive. His comments about her mother's death last night had hit their target.

It's all right. He cares about you, a small voice inside her said.

She ignored the voice. Hope was a luxury reserved for her professional life, not her personal one.

She forced her brain into thinking mode, away from her messy feelings.

The news that Quin was a cop had been unsettling. On the one hand, it explained a lot of the things that had seemed so puzzling: why there was no animosity between him and Zeke, why he hadn't told Lucero who she was, and why he kept helping her.

On the other hand, the news that he wore a white hat complicated things. If he expected her not to make a move without his consent, he was in for a surprise. *I'm willing to work with him; I'm not willing to allow him to dictate how I do my job.*

Quin walked into Lucero's office at eleven fifty-seven. Ruben and Domingo sat in chairs along the side wall. *Don't sit down.* He stood behind the chair in front of Lucero's desk and leaned forward, lightly gripping the chair's wooden arms. "You wanted to see me, Miguel?"

Lucero looked up from his desk. "Yeah. I've decided it's time I had a conversation with your little playmate."

Quin had been prepared for this; his face revealed nothing. "Okay, how do you want to handle it?"

Lucero's gaze sharpened. "That's it? I want to bring your girlfriend here, and that's all you have to say about it?"

Quin shrugged. "I told you before, I'm up for whatever you decide. You've treated me right, gave me a good job despite my record. I owe you, and I never welsh on debts."

Lucero nodded. "Okay, good. Were you with her last night?"

Give him a straight answer. "Yeah, I was."

"You supposed to see her tonight?"

"Yeah."

"Okay, plan to bring her back here around two, after the second shift."

"All right." He released his hold on the chair and straightened, ready to get out of that office.

Lucero held up a hand in a "stop" gesture. "Hold on. I need you to do something else for me."

Damn. "Sure, Miguel. What?"

"The receipts coming in from Partido have been light. I want you to take Ruben, go over there and scare the shit out of Isidro." Lucero's face darkened. "Let him know if he tries to fuck with me, I'll cut his *verga* off and feed it to him *poco a poco*."

"Okay, boss. Come on, Ruben." Quin headed toward the door with Lucero's thug lumbering behind him.

Partido de Playa, or Beach Party, was another of Lucero's investments. Located near Bachman Lake in northwest Dallas, Partido was a dance club for Hispanic teenagers. Boys were charged a ten-dollar cover; girls got in free. The venture had been wildly popular since its opening seven months earlier. If the front-door receipts were off, Quin suspected Lucero was right and Isidro Zuazua, the manager, was diddling the books.

Having Ruben with him would complicate making the necessary phone calls to ensure Leah's safety.

Leah had invited him to come to her penthouse for dinner after he'd finished at the club. He'd told her he would phone if there was any change in plans.

There's no way I'm bringing her anywhere near Lucero. I need to talk to Zeke and Hudnell.

Special-Agent-in-Charge Matthew Hudnell was the team leader of the FBI/Immigration task force. To protect his cover, Quin only submitted a written report once a week. The rest of the time, he used a disposable cell phone to update the SAC.

Hudnell isn't going to like this, but we can't risk Leah's safety. Lucero is too unpredictable. We've got to come up with a plan. Maybe I need to call her and tell her to make plans to leave town on unexpected business.

Just before three p.m., Leah walked across Kidd Springs Park toward the gazebo.

She loved the month of May in Dallas. The grass was an impossibly bright shade of green, and the temperatures were still in the mid-seventies.

Somehow, some way, Consuelo had called while she'd been preoccupied with Quin, and Leah had missed the call. Consuelo had left word she wanted to meet with Leah at Kidd Springs Park before her four p.m. shift at the club.

Leah's conversation with Quin had convinced her that she couldn't use Consuelo, thereby putting the woman's life at risk. She had tried to return the call to tell Consuelo of her decision, but the kitchen worker never picked up the phone. Her plan for this afternoon was to pay Consuelo for her time, but to tell her this would be their last meeting.

Leah's conscience was giving her mild fits over not having called Quin to tell him what she was doing. *I'll brief him over dinner tonight.*

As she approached the gazebo, she saw her quarry sitting on the steps at the front of the structure.

"Hello, Consuelo," she greeted the woman.

"Hola, Ms. Reece," Consuelo said in a diffident tone. She wore the white uniform of a kitchen worker and a matching pair of white tennis shoes.

Leah took a seat next to the woman on the gazebo steps. This part of the park was largely unoccupied. A father was taking pictures of his young family in front of the fountain some seventy-five feet away. An elderly couple were walking their standard schnauzer along the sidewalk that bordered the park.

In the distance, a group of high school students played touch football.

"Call me Leah. Thank you for meeting me, Consuelo."

"I cannot meet you again, Ms. . . . Leah. It is too . . ." She hesitated, obviously searching for the English word. *"Peligroso."*

"Dangerous," Leah supplied the missing word. "I agree. I don't think it's a good idea for us to continue meeting."

Consuelo nodded. "It is very dangerous."

Leah's journalistic instincts pushed her to ask one more question. "Why is it so dangerous? What is Miguel Lucero doing that has everyone scared?"

Consuelo shook her head. "I do not know, but there is much secrecy."

"If you had to guess, what would you say is going on?"

Consuelo ducked her head. "I could not say."

"Come on, you must have some idea. Is he selling drugs or smuggling Mexican nationals across the border?"

Consuelo looked down at her hands folded in her lap. "All I know is that the kitchen makes many meals every day, and then Paco and I deliver them to another place each night."

Whoa, what's this? "What other place, Consuelo? Where is it?" She leaned forward.

"I do not know. Paco and I get into the back of a truck that has no windows. Every night, we are taken to a place where boxes are unloaded. . . ."

"Do you mean a loading dock? Like behind a warehouse?" Leah asked.

"Yes, that's it, a loading dock. We carry the boxes of food inside and put them down. We pick up the boxes from the night before, and we leave."

"Have you ever seen what is going on in that warehouse?" Leah pressed.

Consuelo shook her head. "No, ma'am. The guards watch us very carefully to make certain we do not go anywhere we should not."

Damn. "How many meals do you make each night?"

The woman shrugged. "Sometimes it is twenty; sometimes it is twenty-five or thirty."

"And how long does it take you to get to that warehouse each night? Do you know which direction you go?"

Consuelo shook her head for a second time. "No. The truck drives for about fifteen minutes. We stop two or three times on the way."

"When you say you stop, does anyone get out, or is it like stopping for a traffic light?"

"No one gets out. It is like stopping for a red light."

"Good. Okay, you do that two or three times?" Leah reached into her shoulder bag and pulled out a small spiral pad and pen to scribble notes for herself.

Consuelo's only answer was a soft gasp. Leah looked up from her notepad.

Two men in suits stood in front of them, one of them holding a gun pointed at Consuelo.

Leah glanced around. The dog walkers were gone, and the kids playing football were too far away to be of much help. The man with the camera had a wife and three small children. She couldn't put them at risk. Better to just offer them her shoulder bag and hope they would go away.

"Here." She held out her purse. "Take it, and leave us alone."

The man nearest her—middle-aged with dark skin and a

mouth filled with gold teeth—chuckled. "Keep your bag, Miss Reece. Mr. Lucero wants to talk to you." His voice bore the musical lilt of the Caribbean. He smiled at Consuelo. "And I'm betting he'll be really interested in finding out what you're doing here talking to Miss Reece, Consuelo."

The kitchen worker moaned. The despairing sound made the flesh on Leah's arms crawl.

Time seemed to pause, or perhaps she was just hyperaware of her surroundings. Her heart was pounding, and she realized she'd begun to pant. *I'm hyperventilating.* She forced herself to take a surreptitious breath to try and slow her growing panic. *I can't go with them. Quin warned me Lucero could make me disappear. The man in front of me doesn't have a gun. If I jump on him. . . .*

The African-American shook his head. "Don't do it, Leah. If you make a move, my partner here will shoot Consuelo. You'll still end up coming with us, but she'll be dead."

He'd judged her well. While she would risk her own life, she could not gamble on someone else's.

Leah glanced at Consuelo, but the sight was not encouraging. The kitchen worker seemed to be in shock. Her golden skin had turned an ashy beige, and perspiration ran down her face.

Leah looked back at Gold Teeth. "Let her go. Please."

"No can do, *hermana.* Señor Lucero is going to want to talk with her." He did a quick visual check of the park. "Okay, stand up now, real casual like, and we'll walk to our vehicle."

Leah stood, but the guy with the gun had to pull Consuelo to her feet.

"Grab her left arm, Miss Reece. Santiago will take her right arm. We're going to move very slowly and carefully in that direction." He gestured toward the west.

Leah kept looking around, hoping to see someone who had noticed what was going on. No one was paying any attention to them at all.

They were heading toward a panel truck with the logo of a bakery on the side. Gold Teeth moved ahead and opened the rear of the truck. The other man shoved Consuelo inside with a rough arm.

"Hey," Leah protested. Before she could say anything else, the back of her head exploded in pain, and everything went dark.

Chapter Twenty-seven

Just after six, Quin entered the lobby of the *Heat* building.

Felix Warner, the guard he'd met previously, was one of the two men on duty. Something about the way Felix looked at him set off alarms in Quin's brain.

"What's wrong?" he asked.

Felix responded with a question of his own. "Did you talk to Ms. Reece this afternoon?"

Quin's stomach leaped, and bile flooded his mouth. "No, I called her cell about four, but she didn't answer. Where is she?"

"We don't know. She left to keep an appointment around two forty-five, and she hasn't been heard from since."

Jesus, Mary and Joseph. That's why Miguel wanted me over at Partido. He planned to snatch Leah. "Where was she going?"

"We don't know. She'd scribbled something on the notepad she keeps beside her phone." He picked up a piece of paper. "It says, 'three p.m. Consuelo KSP.'"

"What does KSP mean?" Quin had trouble speaking around his fear.

"We don't know." Felix came out from behind the desk to face him. "No one would have thought anything of it except that she had agreed to meet with Kevin and Aggie Curtis about the new issue at four thirty. When she hadn't arrived by five, we started to worry." His eyes narrowed. "What do you know about this?"

"I know she's in trouble. Did she take her car?"

"Yes."

"Does she have a secretary or anyone who might know what KSP stands for?"

"We've already called Celia. She didn't have a clue." Felix took Quin by the arm. "Should we call the police?"

"I am the police," Quin barked. "Think, man! Where would she go to meet a source for a story? She must have favorite restaurants and coffee shops."

Felix's eyes were wide with alarm.

You're just scaring him, Perez. This isn't doing any good. Quin reached for the scrap of paper. "Here's my cell phone number," he said, scribbling. "If you hear anything, call me."

He wheeled around and ran out of the building.

Outside on the sidewalk, he bent over from the waist and breathed deeply, gulping in air. *Panicking isn't going to help.* He pulled his cell out of his pocket and called Zeke's mobile phone.

While he explained to Zeke what had happened, Quin ran to his car and climbed inside. He switched on the ignition and headed toward the 69 Club.

As he drove, the two friends argued. Zeke wanted Quin to call Hudnell and head toward the police department. Quin wanted to go directly to the club to find Leah.

"If you enter that club, you're a dead man walking, and you won't do Leah any good that way. Wait until we have a plan," Zeke insisted.

"What if he kills her while we're diddling around?" Just saying the words made his *huevos* try to creep up inside his body. *If anything happens to her, I don't know what I'll do.*

Leah's return to consciousness was gradual. She first became aware of a nasty headache and then how stiff and uncomfortable she felt. When she tried to straighten her legs, something was in the way.

Opening her eyes, she saw silvery metal girders and a high, white ceiling. *Where am I? What happened?*

She turned her head and saw two young girls staring at her. They appeared to be in their early twenties and were sitting at a cheap kitchen table about six feet from her.

Leah squeezed her eyes shut again. *This doesn't make any sense. Think, Leah, what do you remember?*

She remembered waking in Quin's bed. She remembered him dropping her off at *Heat*. She remembered setting up meetings and . . . oh my God . . . Consuelo.

Leah sat up so suddenly a shooting pain knifed her brain. Her mouth and nose filled with phlegm, and she reached out a hand to grab the sofa arm to balance herself.

She was in a large room in some kind of commercial operation. One door. No windows. The walls had cheesy fiberboard paneling in a wood-grain finish. The paneling stopped about four feet from the ceiling, which as Leah had already noted was criss-crossed with steel ribs. *A warehouse. I'm in Consuelo's warehouse.*

Fear flooded her brain, making it difficult to continue tracking. A roaring sound filled her ears, but she understood the sound did not come from an external source. *I may have a concussion. I need to stay calm. I need to find Consuelo. I need to . . . get the hell out of here.*

She lurched off the uncomfortable sofa she'd been lying on and toward the door. Grabbing the knob, she tried to turn it. *Locked.*

Someone was saying something. It was difficult to understand over the racket in her head. She turned. One of the two girls at the table was talking.

"What. I'm sorry. I can't hear you." She stumbled toward the girl and grabbed the table to keep from falling over. Once she was sure she could stay upright, she tried to steady her trembling arms by placing her hands flat on the table's surface.

"I said the door is locked." The young woman had a Hispanic accent.

"Where are we?" As she spoke, Leah scanned the rest of the room.

Two more girls were huddled in front of a portable TV, watching a Spanish-language telenovela. Consuelo was nowhere in the room.

"We are in Dallas, Texas," the girl responded.

Leah brought her gaze back to the young woman. "Yes, I know that, but where in Dallas?"

"This I cannot say."

"Cannot or won't?" Leah demanded.

"We do not know where we are." For the first time, Leah heard the note of despair in the girl's voice. The sound brought out her protective instincts. *Calm down. This isn't her fault. You're not helping things by snapping at her.*

She took a deep breath, forcing more air into her lungs. Closing her eyes, she focused on breathing evenly and pushing the impending hysteria away.

When she was finally certain she could speak without screaming, Leah opened her eyes again. "My name is Leah Reece. Tell me yours."

"My name is Gloria. This is my friend Dulce." The second girl, who had a very noticeable overbite, nodded and offered a shy smile.

Gloria gestured toward the two girls watching television. "They are Marta and Marisa."

One of the two girls had a fading black eye and a puffy upper lip.

"You're being held prisoner here. Why?"

Gloria's face clouded. "A coyote brought us to this country. He says we must stay here until we pay him back."

Quin was right. Lucero is smuggling illegals across the border. "How can you pay him back if you can't get out of here to get jobs?"

Gloria didn't answer. She lowered her gaze to the Formica tabletop.

For the first time, Leah noticed the way the girls were dressed: in cheap nylon blouses with low-cut tops and in very short skirts. Her mouth went dry. She had to force the words out. "Gloria, is the coyote abusing you?"

The girl raised her gaze to Leah's face, but her expression was confused. *She doesn't recognize the word "abusing."* Leah tried again. "Is the coyote forcing you to do things you don't want to do?"

Gloria nodded once, a quick forceful duck of her head.

Leah's legs threatened to go out from under her again. *Lucero isn't just smuggling immigrants. He's using them as sex slaves.* She dropped her chin to her chest and pressed her hands even harder on the table while she waited for the wave of dizziness to pass. *I have to get help. We need to get out of here.*

My cell phone! It was in my pocket when I met with Consuelo. She slapped at the right-hand pocket of her linen slacks. Nothing. She reversed arms and tried the left-side pocket. Nothing.

"Damn. Damn. Damn!" she snarled.

Hopelessness threatened to swamp her. *What if there isn't a way out of here? Maybe I'll never see Quin again. Or Sandy or Tex.*

The thought of Tex stiffened her spine. *Quin will be looking for me. And Tex will tear up Oak Cliff brick by brick if he has to in order to find me.*

One of the two girls in front of the television—Marta or Marisa—spoke, "Gloria, *ellos vienen.*" They're coming.

All five women listened. Now that the pounding in her ears was receding, Leah could hear the sound of footsteps approaching.

She looked around, frantic to find a weapon, but the room was sparsely furnished: the couch, the table, four chairs, some sleeping bags and the television on its little stand.

Leah heard the sound of a key in the lock, and then the door swung open. Two men she'd not seen before stood in the doorway. "*Es tiempo de ir a trabajar.*" It's time to go to work.

Leah moved toward the men. "I want to see Lucero."

The taller of the two answered. "And he wants to see you, *chica.* Be patient. Your turn will come." He gestured to the four girls. "*Vámonos.*"

One of the two girls—Marta or Marisa—turned off the television set. Then all four walked toward him with obvious reluctance, their heads bowed. Leah tried to follow, but when she got to the doorway, the second man held his hand up to block her. "No."

"I want to see Lucero."

The first man laughed. "What you want doesn't matter here, Princess."

Hearing Quin's affectionate term for her on this thug's lips filled her with anger. "This is kidnapping. I'll prosecute and see you put in jail," she threatened.

"Ah, but first I'll see you." The words sounded like a promise. "Maybe I'll even bid on you. What do you think, Juan? Should I bid on the *puta flaca?*" Skinny whore.

The two men laughed as they slammed the door shut in her face.

If his words were meant to intimidate her, he'd failed. The sight of the four girls meekly obeying orders and the contempt in the man's voice gave birth to a rage the like of which Leah had never experienced before.

She picked up one of the kitchen chairs and flung it at the door. The chair bounced off the wood and fell to the floor, bending one of its aluminum legs.

She heard the snicker of a key in the lock. "We'll be back for you later, little wildcat. Perhaps Juan and I will put our money together to bid on you. Then, maybe you will show us some of that passion up close and personal, yes?"

The sound of their laughter echoed down the hall.

Leah looked around at the four walls of her prison. *There has to be a way out of this place.*

Although the walls didn't go all the way to the ceiling, there was no possibility that she could climb up and over them.

She walked to the nearest wall and examined the wood-grain paneling by pressing her fingers along the edges. It felt like they had been glued onto steel frames with nails about every two feet. *Maybe I can find a place where one isn't stuck on tightly enough.*

Quin slammed his fist down on the conference table. "We're fucking around here, and Lucero has Leah. We need to go to the club and get her back."

Lieutenant Pete Olson turned to FBI Special-Agent-in-Charge Matthew Hudnell, who had just snapped his cell phone shut. "Did you get the warrant?"

Hudnell shook his head. "The DA won't even take our application to a judge."

The lieutenant, nominally the host of the meeting taking

place at the Dallas Police Department headquarters, wasn't satisfied with the answer. "Why won't he seek the warrant?"

"The DA doesn't think we have enough evidence tying Ms. Reece's disappearance to Miguel Lucero."

"What are you talking about?" Quin could hear the volume of his voice rising, but he couldn't seem to help it. "Lucero told me to bring her to him."

"I misspoke. What I should have said"—Hudnell's voice was heavy with sarcasm—"was that the DA doesn't believe we have enough 'disinterested' evidence to go to a judge."

"Special Agent Hudnell, I've already apologized for not telling you about Leah sooner, but the truth is she only showed up at the club seventy-two hours ago." Quin leaned across the large table toward Hudnell. "I know. I should have called you, and I didn't. Discipline me if you must, but don't punish Leah for my failure to act." His voice cracked. "Please."

Hudnell's frosty gaze melted a fraction, and he sighed. "Perez, I want to take action, but you haven't given me anything that would justify a search of the 69 Club."

"Lucero runs an illegal sex club."

"Yes, an illegal sex club that has been under surveillance for more than three months. You heard the report from the guys on the scene this afternoon. They didn't see anyone resembling Ms. Reece enter the premises." He shrugged. "That makes it hard to argue the case that we need to search the place."

"They reported on several cars and vans that pulled in and out of that three-car garage."

"Yes, but Lucero asked *you* to bring Ms. Reece to him. If anything, your deposition supports his being innocent of her kidnapping—if she was even kidnapped to begin with."

"What about an ICE raid?" Zeke interrupted before Quin could rip Hudnell a new one.

"Yeah, La Migra is happy to break down doors for its own purposes," Quin snarled. "Why not ask them to break down one or two for us?"

"What about it, Hudnell?" Olson asked.

"We could probably justify a raid, but my counterpart at ICE, Eduardo Trevino, is in Washington this weekend for a fund-raising event."

"When I'm out of touch, I have a second in command qualified to take over," the lieutenant said in a mild voice.

Without warning, the door to the conference room slammed open and an elderly man in a plaid chambray shirt, jeans and worn boots marched in, followed by an agitated administrative assistant.

"I'm Benjamin Franklin Reece," the cowboy announced. "And I'm here to find out where the hell my daughter is."

Chapter Twenty-eight

While the group of law enforcement professionals gaped at him, the white-haired cowboy raked the room with his penetrating gaze. His focus settled on one man.

"Zeke Prada, where's my girl? What have you gotten her into?"

Zeke opened his mouth to speak, but before he could say anything, Quin jumped in. Waving the administrative assistant away, he said, "Mr. Reece, my name is Quin Perez. Leah has been working on a story about a man suspected of smuggling Mexican nationals into this country. We think he may have her."

Tex Reece's eyes narrowed. "Then what are you all doing sitting here?" He turned to Hudnell. "You, in the suit, FBI, right? I know your boss."

"Stephen Claussen?" Hudnell asked.

"No," Reece snorted. "I'm talking about Warren Revel, Director of the FBI. We had dinner last month in Washington. Warren's known my daughter since she was twelve." The old man rested his fisted hands on the conference table. "You've got about two minutes to tell me why I shouldn't pull out my cell and call my friend Warren to tell him his man in Dallas is sitting around jawing while my little girl is in trouble."

Special-Agent-in-Charge Matthew Hudnell's mouth opened and closed a couple of times, making him look like a fish gasping for air.

Pete Olson came to the agent's rescue. "We were just getting ready to arrange an Immigration raid on the 69 Club, where we believe your daughter is being held, weren't we, Hudnell?"

"Uh, yes," SAC Hudnell said. "Yes, yes, we were." He reached into his pocket, pulled out a cell phone and flipped it open.

Tex Reece turned to Quin. "My daughter's people tell me that your name is Medina. You say it's Perez. Which is it, son?"

"My name is Quin Perez Medina, sir." Quin studied Tex's face for signs of Leah. Father and daughter had the same lean frame and startling blue eyes. "I'm curious," he said. "How did you find us?"

"Felix Warner is a retired cop. He figured you must be undercover, and I knew Zeke is undercover with Vice. I made a few calls, tracked down Olson there"—Tex nodded toward the lieutenant—"and here I am." He pulled out a chair. "While we're waiting on the Fibbie there, tell me the whole story."

Leah lay on her side on the floor of the room in which she'd awakened. She'd found a spot on the wall behind the sofa where the paneling was loose. For the past thirty minutes she'd been trying to work it free from its steel frame anchor. She'd managed to pop out a couple of nails and create a small opening.

By bending the cheap piece of paneling back, she could peek through the gap in the wall to the other side—the back of another paneled wall. *If I could make a big enough opening here and then get the paneling on that wall free, I might be able to crawl through to the next room.*

Encouraged by the possibility of creating an escape route, Leah redoubled her efforts to open an exit out of her present circumstances.

As she worked, her mind wandered from the task at hand.

This is all my fault. Quin warned me about Lucero. He took a big risk by sharing his cover with me—a freaking journalist—and he even offered to work with me.

And what did I do? Go off and meet with the informant on my own.

What's that about? Why does it always have to be my way? What am I trying to prove?

"That's the third time you've checked your watch in the last fifteen minutes, son. Didn't your mama ever tell you about watched pots?"

Quin glanced at Tex, seated across from him in the large panel van parked outside the 69 Club.

"They just seem to be taking an awfully long time to clear the house out," he complained.

Immigration and Customs Enforcement—with the support of the Dallas Police Department and the local FBI field office—was conducting a sweep of the premises.

Quin and Tex had been allowed to go along as long as they agreed to stay out of sight. The van they were in was outfitted with cameras and directional mikes so they could watch and hear the activity around them.

Federal agents had escorted everyone outside the mansion, where they were relieved of cell phones and segregated into groups to be interviewed.

Neither Lucero nor Leah had been brought out yet.

"You sleeping with my daughter?" Tex asked.

Taken aback by the question, Quin stared at the old man. "Yeah," he answered, not bothering to hide the edge in his voice.

"But Thursday night was the first time, right?"

"Leah didn't tell you that." Quin was very certain of this.

"In a way, she did," Tex said. "Leah never lies to me. We had lunch together yesterday, and she told me there was no one she'd been out with more than once lately. Ergo, you and she could only have been together one time." He offered Quin a small smile of satisfaction. "My guessing Thursday night was a gamble, but as worried as you are, I figured it had to have been pretty recent."

"Are these the kinds of mind games you played with Leah while she was growing up?" Quin knew he sounded unfriendly, but he didn't care.

Tex appeared surprised by Quin's tone. "I encouraged my daughter to stay on her toes. That's the way one succeeds in this life."

Quin's first impulse was to tell the old man off. Instead, he took a deep breath and remained quiet. *Leah wouldn't want me getting into a fight with her father. Besides, he's not the one I want to tear to pieces.*

Both men were silent for several long minutes.

"It probably would have been better if Leah had been a boy," Tex said suddenly. "I would've known how to raise a boy on my own. But a girl . . . well, I don't mind confessing she nearly defeated me. I didn't have a clue what to do with her after her mother died." He hesitated. "I know I made mistakes, but it wasn't for want of trying."

Quin didn't speak. He wasn't sure what to say.

"Are you in love with Leah?" Tex asked.

Quin temporized. "I care for her a great deal."

"Don't give me that crap. You either love her or you don't."

Quin nodded. "I love her."

"Good," Tex said. "Then you'll find her and keep her safe."

Quin stared at the white-haired man. *God, I hope he's right.*

The door to the rear of the van opened. Pete Olson looked in on the two men. "ICE tells me neither Lucero nor Leah are anywhere on the premises."

Quin's heart sank. "What about Consuelo?"

The lieutenant shook his head.

"Lieu, let me talk to the kitchen staff. Maybe I can find out something."

Olson shook his head a second time. "Nope. You stay in this van. I'll get Prada to talk to them."

Quin didn't waste time arguing. "Are you sure you got everyone's cell phone? We can't afford to have anyone calling and warning Lucero. He might panic and hurt Leah."

Olson rolled his eyes. "This isn't our first rodeo, Perez. You and Mr. Reece just stay put. We'll let you know as soon as we have something." He slammed the van door shut on them.

Following Olson's directions, Zeke leaned against a Mercedes coupe, eyeing the group of five kitchen workers huddled together nearby.

Two of the men interested him.

The first, a teenage male, was obviously an undocumented Mexican national. He alternated between watching the ICE agents and peering around as though seeking an escape route.

The second man was more interesting. He was middle-aged, clean and well groomed. Unlike his fellow workers, he did not chatter excitedly with the others. Instead, he stood a little apart from the group, smoking a cigarette and looking anxious. More than anxious; he looked heartsick.

Zeke drifted closer to him. "Hey, do you have a cigarette I could borrow?"

The man studied him for a second and then reached into his pocket, removed a pack and held it out.

Zeke tapped a cigarette loose and put it between his lips. His new friend offered him a light.

"Thanks. I gave it up more than ten years ago, but whenever I'm nervous or scared, I crave a smoke."

The kitchen worker tilted his head to one side. "You work for La Migra, and you're scared? Something is not right."

"I'm not an immigration agent. I'm a Dallas cop. I'm looking for two women: a writer named Leah Reece and a kitchen worker named Consuelo. I'm afraid they're in trouble."

The man's eyes widened in alarm. "Consuelo? Something has happened to Consuelo?"

Bingo! "You know her?"

"We work together. She is my good friend." The man threw his cigarette away and grabbed Zeke's forearms. "Tell me. What has happened?"

"First, tell me your name."

"I am Paco Martinez. Please tell me where Consuelo is."

"Paco, I'm Zeke Prada. We don't know where she is. She and Leah Reece disappeared around three this afternoon."

"I spoke to Consuelo just after noon. She said she had a meeting at Kidd Springs Park."

KSP! Of course. "Did she say anything else, Paco?"

"Just that she would be at work at the regular time." He released Zeke's arms. "When she didn't show up, I knew something was wrong."

"This raid has only one purpose: to find Consuelo and Leah. They are not here. Do you know where they might have been taken?"

Paco worried his lower lip with his teeth. "The only place I can think of is the warehouse."

"What warehouse? Where is it?" Zeke gripped Paco's shoulders. "This is important, man. Where is the warehouse?"

"Yo no sé." I don't know. "We are taken there in the back of a truck. I have never seen how we get there."

"Come with me, Paco." With his hands still on the worker's shoulders, Zeke turned him toward the van where Quin was waiting. "I have someone you need to talk with."

Chapter Twenty-nine

The police van was crowded. Quin and Tex had been joined by Pete Olson, SAC Hudnell, Zeke, an agent from ICE whose name Quin hadn't caught and a kitchen worker named Paco.

Paco had answered questions for twenty minutes about the warehouse where he and Consuelo had been taken on multiple occasions. Since Quin's Spanish was better than any of the others', in the interest of time, he had handled the questioning.

Although he had never been able to watch how the truck got to and from the warehouse, Paco was certain the driver went west from the club and across the Trinity River into West Dallas.

Olson's people had accessed the computer database for the City of Dallas's property appraisals. They'd searched for any properties held by the 69 Real Estate Trust, the legal owner of the club. They'd found four warehouses in West Dallas that might fit the bill. Quin had been with Lucero to one of them. Since it didn't have a loading dock behind the building, it was crossed off the list. That left three.

Olson dispatched undercover officers to check out the remaining locations, hoping to discover some signs of activity at one of them. The surveillance teams were instructed to remain at a distance and not to approach the buildings.

Quin sent Paco back out to join the kitchen workers, who were still being interrogated by ICE. The six men remaining in the van continued to argue over possible strategies.

In less than thirty minutes, the three scout teams reported

back. None of them had found any suspicious activity at the three warehouses. "There has to be another location we don't know about," Olson told the crew in the van.

A cell phone buzzed, and all the men jumped. Quin fished his cell out of his pocket and checked the display. "It's Lucero," he told the others.

"Don't let him know you realize he has Leah," Zeke cautioned.

Quin cleared his throat before he flipped the phone open. "Hey, Miguel," he said.

"Where are you?" Lucero asked.

"At my place. I've just climbed out of the shower. In a couple of minutes I'll head out to pick the girl up."

"Change of plans. I need for you to go back to Partido. Isidro is . . . indisposed. I want someone I trust to close out the till."

"Sure thing, Miguel. As soon as I get dressed, I'll head over there." He paused. "What about Leah Reece?"

"She's not going anywhere. She'll keep for another night. As soon as you finish the first tally, bring the receipts to me at the club. We'll talk more then." Lucero disconnected without giving Quin a chance to say anything.

Quin brought the others up to speed.

"I don't like it," Olson said. "Something's wrong."

"Yeah," Hudnell jumped in. "It's just too much of a coincidence that he's calling right now."

"Shit!" Zeke leaped up and opened the van door. "I'll bet he's got a GPS on your car."

"I scanned my car with a bug detector this morning, the way I do every morning," Quin said.

"Yeah, but you spent part of the day at that teen club. What do you want to bet they tagged you then?" Olson nodded toward Zeke. "Go check his car."

Zeke jumped down from the van, leaving the door open behind him.

Hudnell looked at Olson. "So what do we do?"

"What do you mean, what do we do?" Quin asked. "We still have no idea where he's holding Leah." He glanced at his watch. "It's after ten now. We've got no choice. I have to go along with Lucero until we find her."

Olson frowned. "I don't like it." He sighed. "But I agree, we don't have many options. Let's get a wire on you."

Quin shook his head. "No way. Miguel will be looking for that."

"Then you're not going in." Olson stabbed a finger in the air at Quin. "I am not sending one of my men into what is probably a trap—"

"Definitely a trap," Zeke interrupted, climbing back into the van. "There's a GPS under the body of your Jeep, Quin. Lucero knows you were at DPD headquarters earlier tonight and outside his club while you talked to him a minute ago." He turned to Olson. "I didn't disturb it."

"So that means he won't be coming back here later. And that's why he wants you to come to him," Olson said to Quin.

"I don't understand." Tex spoke for the first time since the group had assembled in the van. "Why is this Lucero still hanging around? He's gotta know you're onto him. Why not just hightail it back across the border into Mexico? He can always return later when the heat dies down."

The unidentified ICE agent shook his head. "Lucero is a member of the Sinaloa Cartel, the largest of the Mexican traffickers and the most vicious. They kill with impunity in their own country." He looked across to Quin. "Lucero has at least three reasons to kill you." He ticked them off on his fingers. "First, to eliminate someone who could possibly testify against him. Second, to provide a warning to other cops who might be thinking about trying to infiltrate the cartel." He tapped his ring finger. "And finally, because you betrayed him, and the Sinaloan Cowboys kill traitors. They live for revenge."

Hudnell nodded. "Infighting with rival cartels and with the federal government in Mexico has killed more than seven thousand people over the last three years in their own country."

"So you're telling me Quin here is signing his death warrant by walking into that Partido tonight." Tex's voice was flat, without any inflection.

"Probably," Hudnell agreed.

"Hey, I'm not dead yet." Quin allowed his annoyance to show. "Don't be in such a rush to write my obituary."

Olson rubbed his forehead, a habit his men joked about, claiming he did it to massage his brain cells when he was thinking. "We can put our own GPS on your Jeep, but that's not likely to do us any good once you arrive at Partido." He looked at Zeke. "We can put surveillance teams outside the place, but do we have anyone we can send inside to keep an eye on things?"

"A club for Hispanic teens?" Zeke shrugged. "We don't have anyone who looks young enough unless you want to send one of our informants in."

"No." Quin shook his head. "We'd be signing the kid's death warrant." He stood. "I'd better get moving."

"Listen." Hudnell held a hand out to stop him. "The bureau has bugs that can pass for quarters. Let me give you one of them.

You can stick it in your pocket just like any coin, and we'd still be able to pick up your conversations."

"Will it get past a bug detector scan?" Quin asked.

"What do you care?" Hudnell snorted. "You're dead already. You think Lucero is going to give extra points because you didn't try to fool him?"

Tex spoke up. "What if you put two bugs on him? Plant a more obvious bug that's physically close to the coin. Maybe Quin will get lucky. If the guy checking him is sloppy, he might grab only the first bug and miss the second."

Hudnell nodded. "It's worth a try. We could stick an old-fashioned bug in your wallet and leave the coin loose in the same pocket."

"Let's go for it," Olson said.

Hudnell nodded and climbed out of the van. "It will take me five minutes," he said over his shoulder.

Olson ran his hands through his thinning hair. "Who knows? Maybe it will work. What do we have to lose?" He reached for his cell phone. "I'm going to put a surveillance team out front in the parking lot and another behind the club, in case they try to sneak you out the back door."

"Thanks, Lieu. I appreciate it," Quin said. "I'm going to take a piss while we're waiting." He edged his way across the van's interior and jumped down to the pavement.

Zeke followed on his heels. They crossed the parking lot side by side, and headed toward the mansion.

"Anything you need me to take care of?" Zeke asked.

"If something happens to me, I'm counting on you to find Leah and get her out safely for me."

Zeke threw his arm around Quin's shoulders. "You got it.

Just make sure that nothing does happen to you." He released the other man. "I'm going to get myself assigned to one of those surveillance teams. See you later."

"Take care of yourself." Quin slapped his friend on the back.

Quin entered the mansion and walked into the men's room.

As he washed his hands, he stared at his reflection in the mirror. The eyes of the man looking back were haunted.

When he'd been overseas, he'd experienced a constant low level of anxiety about the safety of the men who fought beside him. But that apprehension was nothing next to the fear he now felt for Leah. Terror permeated his entire being and interfered with his thinking, his decision making and even his ability to breathe. Despite the years he'd spent fighting in the Mideast, he'd never before had fear hunker like a lump of coal in his gullet.

We're going to get her out. There's no other option. Lord, I'll pay any price you ask. Just let her be safe.

When he stepped outside into the night, Tex Reece was waiting for him.

"If I could go in your stead tonight, I would." Quin heard the sincerity in his voice. "But since I can't, I wanted to say thank you." Leah's father thrust his hand out.

"I'll bring her back if I can," Quin replied, shaking hands.

Leah had broken or chipped every one of her fingernails. She had long angry scratches on her wrists and forearms and on both legs where the wall had fought back, tearing holes in her pants and her skin. *If I'd known I was going to be doing construction work, I'd have worn jeans instead of linen slacks. Now I'm going to need a tetanus shot.*

The good news was that she'd opened up a space in the wall on her side large enough to scrunch through. Over the past couple of hours, she'd been pushing and shoving on the paneling in the next room, trying to separate it from its steel frame.

The temptation to kick at the paneling was enormous, but she didn't know who might be able to hear if she started kicking. *Keep quiet* had become her mantra. That and *I'm getting out; I'm getting out.* The thought that she was doing something positive to help herself kept the god-awful fear at bay.

She also managed—thanks to a couple of broken fingernails and the heel of her shoe—to work two nails out of the paneling. She'd tucked them away in her pants pocket. *They may not be much of a weapon, but they're all I've got.*

Suddenly, without warning, the frame released its hold on one edge of the paneling.

Leah ignored the new scratch on her right ankle. She pulled her legs out of the hole and swiveled her hips so she could sit up and examine the paneling.

She'd pushed the lower-right corner free. Now all she needed to do was enlarge the hole enough so that she could crawl through to the other side. *The room's empty. Why lock an empty room? If there's a phone in there, I can call for help. If there's no phone, I'll just let myself out of the room and look for an exit.*

Reenergized, she went back to pushing on the paneling. This time, she concentrated her efforts right above the place where it had come loose.

A noise distracted her. Footsteps coming down the hall. More than one person.

She leaped up, pushed the sofa back against the wall and lay down on the cushions. *Maybe they're just checking on me. I'll pretend to be sleeping.*

A key snickered in the lock.

She offered a quick prayer and closed her eyes.

Chapter Thirty

Quin pulled into one of the reserved spaces outside of Partido de Playa and parked his Jeep. "Okay, I'm here," he announced to the listening cops. "Heading inside. Wish me luck."

The parking lot was jammed with teens, noise and activity. Boys cruised up and down the lot and the street in their cars, fronting for the girls. The girls, who mostly traveled in packs, did some posturing of their own. Along the dark fringes of the lot, couples sat together in cars, mackin' it.

Usually the kids amused him. Tonight he barely noticed them. He bypassed the long line waiting to gain entrance to Partido and went straight to the front door.

Tomas, acting as doorman, stepped out of his way, clearing the path.

Inside, a sea of flashing lights, moving bodies, blaring instruments and laughing voices greeted him. This world belonged to its teen patrons; adults were neither needed nor wanted.

Quin waved to one of the bartenders and skirted the edge of the perimeter created by the bar that ran across the room. Fifteen-year-old girls flirted with him, striking poses and batting their eyes. It was a familiar routine, and—conscious of their fragile egos—he always shook his head regretfully as he walked on by them.

One part of his brain concentrated on functioning as though nothing were wrong. The rest of his consciousness focused on finding Leah and getting the hell out.

At the end of the bar, an unobtrusive door marked STAFF ONLY opened onto the hallway that led to Isidro's office. "Time to party," Quin murmured for the benefit of the team on the other end of the bug. He pushed the door open and entered.

The hall had been built in a T shape, dead-ending after fifteen feet, but offering two side passages. Isidro's office was to the left. The hall to the right led to the kitchen. *If they're waiting for me, it's at the end of the hall.*

He covered the space in a few strides and turned left, as though he expected nothing to be wrong.

In front of him, Santiago stood, pointing a .44 at him.

The unmistakable sound a gun makes when the hammer is pulled back came from behind Quin.

"That's right. I have my weapon pointed at your head. Put your hands up where I can see them and turn around very slowly." The voice seemed better suited to sultry Jamaican nights than guns and bullets.

Quin obeyed and turned to face Tyree, another of Lucero's men.

"What's up, Tyree? Miguel asked me to come over here and collect the receipts from tonight's take."

"Yeah, well, he told me to come over here and collect a no-good informer." Tyree's bright smile didn't quite reach his eyes. "Pat him down, Santiago."

Expecting this, Quin had left his Glock and his throwaway piece with Zeke. "I'd rather you have them than Lucero's button men," he'd told his friend.

When he came up clean, Tyree raised his eyebrows. "You usually carry," he said.

"Yeah, well, I wasn't expecting any trouble tonight."

"Let's go to Isidro's office. I am suspicious of your sudden pacifism."

The three men walked the rest of the way to the tiny office at the end of the hall. The room was only large enough for a desk, chair, file cabinet and one visitor's seat.

"Check him for bugs," Tyree directed his number two.

Santiago retrieved a scanner from the top drawer of the file cabinet. When he passed the bug detector over Quin's torso, the device began chirping.

"I'll get it," Quin said, reaching into his pocket for his wallet. He removed the small silver bug that resembled a lithium battery and handed it over.

Santiago dropped the little device into a glass on the desk half filled with what looked like rum. *"Vámonos,"* he said. Let's go.

Hallelujah! But Quin's elation was short-lived.

"Scan him again," Tyree ordered.

The door opened and Leah heard a rush of movement and the clatter of furniture.

"Better luck next time. Maybe then someone will want a bitch with beaver teeth." It was the same guy who'd called Leah a skinny whore earlier.

The door slammed.

Leah opened her eyes to see Gloria's friend Dulce standing in the center of the room, crying.

She jumped up from the sofa and ran to comfort the girl. "Are you okay?" she asked.

Dulce turned her head away and continued to sob quietly.

Leah touched the girl's shoulder and repeated the question in Spanish, but Dulce pulled away and refused to answer.

Leah told her in Spanish, "I'm here if you want to talk, but I'm going to leave you alone until you're ready."

She returned to the sofa, pulled it out from the wall and got down on her back to continue trying to push through to the other side.

Although she didn't watch Dulce, the girl soon stopped crying and came over to kneel beside her.

"What are you doing?" she asked in Spanish.

What does it look like? "I'm trying to escape," she answered in the same language.

"If they find you doing this, they will hurt you badly."

Leah lifted an eyebrow. "From the way you were crying, they're going to hurt me either way. I'd rather get hurt trying to help myself."

Dulce chewed her lower lip in obvious indecision. She looked over her shoulder at the door and then said, "Move over. I'll help."

Leah scooted over. For several minutes, she worked to peel more of the paneling up on their side to make room for the two of them to work. In the meantime, Dulce continued pushing on the paneling on the other side of the hole.

With the pressure being applied by both of them, the wall soon gave way, opening a hole big enough for them to squeeze through one by one.

Leah was elated. "Come on," she said. "Let's hurry."

Dulce stood and backed up. "No," she said. "I'm not going."

"What are you talking about?" Leah asked. "Of course you're coming."

Dulce shook her head. "No. If they find you, they will kill you." She walked across the room and turned on the television. "I'll stay here."

"Dulce, they're still going to hurt you. What are you going to tell them when they ask why you didn't call them?"

"I will say I was asleep." The girl's jaw was set. "You had better hurry. They will be coming for you soon."

Leah stood there in an agony of indecision. Dulce's back was toward her, rigid and uncompromising.

"All right. I'll go for help. Can you at least tell me which way the door to the outside is?"

Dulce's shoulders raised a fraction, but she did not turn around to face Leah. "I am not certain. There are many hallways. I think it is that way." She pointed toward the left.

"Okay, thanks. Don't worry. Someone will be coming to rescue you soon."

She knelt down and started wiggling her way through the opening. She thought she heard a soft voice say, *"Buena suerte"*— Good luck—behind her, but she wasn't sure.

The room next door was dark. She scrambled to her feet and waited a few moments for her eyes to grow accustomed to the dim light.

Moving slowly, she started across the room toward where she guessed the door would be. She maneuvered her way around a desk, but bumped into a small table on the way. Fortunately, nothing crashed to the floor.

When she reached the wall, she felt her way cautiously along it and nearly screamed with frustration when she came to the interior wall that ran perpendicular to her wall. Taking a deep breath, she edged back in the direction from which she'd come and soon came to the doorjamb.

This is it. Please, dear God, let the door be unlocked.

Almost afraid to hope, she grabbed hold of the doorknob.

And it turned in her hand.

Her relief was so great, she almost sank to her knees in thanks.

Cautiously, she opened the door, but she waited a few seconds before sticking her head out into the hall.

About eight feet away, a bare 60-watt bulb dangling from a wire overhead provided enough illumination for her to see in both directions.

She was looking at a very long corridor that stretched more than a hundred feet in each direction from where she stood. *This place must be enormous.*

The walls out here were ordinary white plasterboard. *As opposed to the "elegant" faux paneling inside the rooms,* a sarcastic voice inside her sniped. But like the rooms, the walls out here didn't go all the way to the ceiling.

There were no handy red EXIT signs to point her way, but Dulce had said to go left. *So, left it is.*

Despite her anxiety to get away, she couldn't bring herself to step out into the hallway. Her legs seemed frozen in place. The idea of being out in the open in that long corridor was terrifying. She stalled by bending over to remove her flat shoes.

Okay, I admit it's scary, but not as scary as it's going to be when you have to face Lucero. Get moving, Reece.

With great reluctance, she stepped outside the room. *Should I lock the door behind me? No, I may have to run back here to hide.*

I need to try every door along the hall as I come to each in case I need to duck inside a room.

Her heart was beating so loudly, she was afraid Lucero's men would hear it even behind a closed door.

With her shoes in one hand and one of her two stolen nails in the other, she started down the long corridor.

Chapter Thirty-one

"Thought you were going to put one over on us, didn't you?" Tyree asked, examining the FBI "coin" bug in his hand.

Quin didn't bother answering. *What's the point?*

"This is such a fine piece of work that I hate to fry its little circuits. But"—Tyree dropped the bug into the glass of rum— "we can't be transmitting our conversations, now can we?"

Quin had negotiated a deal with the lieutenant. If Lucero's people found the second bug, the clock would start running. He had sixty minutes before the wrath of the Dallas Police Department came down on Partido de Playa. He stole a glance at his wristwatch.

"What! You got someplace better to be?" Tyree asked. "Santiago, we are boring our man Quin here. He is looking at his watch."

"Maybe he needs some more excitement in his life." Santiago grinned.

"Perhaps you are right, in which case we can help him. Let's go visit Miguel and the beauteous Ms. Reece."

Quin's head snapped around, and he stared at Tyree with narrowed eyes. "What do you know about Leah?"

"Ahhh, Santiago and I met your lovely lady in the park this afternoon. We took a ride together. Now it's your turn." Tyree gestured with his .44 toward the hallway.

Santiago led the way toward the kitchen with Quin behind him and Tyree bringing up the rear. Halfway down the hall, Santiago opened a closet. He pressed up on two of the shelves simultaneously and the back of the closet swung open. After producing a small flashlight from his pocket, he stepped through the open space.

Quin hesitated, but Tyree's weapon at his back was a powerful incentive. He followed the first man into a storage room. "Where are we?" he asked, wrinkling his nose at the exotic and pungent odors that filled the small space.

"In the back of the Thai restaurant next door," Tyree told him. "They closed for the night about an hour ago." He laughed. "Didn't you know Miguel owns this entire strip center?"

"No. No, I didn't." Although he maintained a neutral façade, Quin's optimism took a nosedive. He had a good idea what was coming, and the next few minutes proved him right.

Moving from business to business via a series of hidden doors, the three men took a tour through the back offices of a dry cleaner's and a photo shop before ending up in the rear of the used-book store on the opposite end of the shopping center from the teen club where they'd started.

The surveillance teams are sitting outside the front and back doors of Partido. They'll never see us leaving from this end of the strip.

Leah reached the end of the corridor without incident. There was only one direction to go—to the right—down yet another long hallway with no red EXIT signs in sight.

I wish I had some sense of the geography of this place. As big as it feels, I could be lost here for hours. And the longer I wander around, the greater the chances that someone will spot me.

She was about midway down the new hallway when she heard footsteps approaching from a perpendicular corridor. The nearest door had a plaque reading PRIVATE—MAINTENANCE. She pushed the door open and slipped inside, surprised to find herself at the bottom of a dimly lit stairwell.

Great. I had no idea this place had more than one floor. She looked up the staircase, trying to decide whether to wait a couple of minutes before returning to the corridor, or to climb. *I haven't seen a window yet. Maybe if I go upstairs, I can get a look outside the building. It's probably safer, too, than the first floor. I doubt I'm going to run into a maintenance man this late at night.*

Decision made, she started climbing. The stairwell was narrow and clearly intended for use by maintenance staff only. It dead-ended one flight up with another door. *End of the line. Decision time. I can go through here or back down the way I came.*

After listening outside the door for a moment, she pushed it open.

She faced a narrow wooden catwalk. The space was enclosed and tight—a tall man would have to stoop—and full of odd noises.

One of Leah's former boyfriends had been the manager of a local theater. During the time they'd dated, she'd spent hours with him backstage, and this catwalk reminded her of the one above the theater.

Pipes and electrical conduit ran along both sides of the three-foot-wide wooden floor. A maze of silver air-conditioning duct-work added to the claustrophobic feel of the space. The sounds she was hearing were the electrical systems switching on and off throughout the building and water flow in the pipes. Somewhere ahead of her, voices floated into the crawl space from below.

The temptation to stay right there on the catwalk was enormous. For the first time in hours, she felt relatively safe. *I could hide here until everyone goes home or until Quin finds me. By now, he knows I'm missing.*

A small voice in the back of her head reminded her that Consuelo and the other women weren't as safe as she was.

While she debated whether to return to the first floor and continue searching for a way out of the building, a high-pitched scream echoed through her hideaway.

Leah dropped her shoes. One hit the wooden floor hard; the other bounced off the catwalk into the cluster of pipes beneath.

Sweet Lord, what was that?

She could hear the shouts of men along with outraged feminine shrieks. The men sounded as though they were cheering. *Cheering what?*

It took a minute before she calmed down enough to retrieve her shoes. By then, the women had gone quiet, but the men's cheering laughter had grown in volume.

The women's silence decided her. *I need to find out what's happening down there.*

She crept toward the source of the noise. Her breathing sounded unnaturally loud to her ears, and fear nearly clogged her throat.

Ahead of her, the catwalk appeared to be illuminated from below. As she drew closer, the mystery of the light source resolved itself.

The maintenance crew had obviously been working to get the air-conditioning system operational before summer. Their tools lay discarded along the wooden floor. A line of aluminum-colored ductwork ended six feet from where she stood.

Immediately to her left was a ventilation grate. The workmen had not yet secured the ductwork to the grille. All the light and noise radiated upward from the room below.

Her desire to get out of the place warred with her anxiety over Consuelo and the four other girls she'd met. *If I'm careful, no one should see me. I'm above them, so unless I make a noise, they probably won't look up. And they sound totally preoccupied.*

Aware that she was just playing mind games with herself, Leah yielded to her need to know. She dropped to her knees, crawled to the edge of the grate and peered through.

From her angle, she could see a large, well-lit room below, but she couldn't see any people. She set her shoes down on the cat-walk, put the nail back into her pocket and prepared to inch her way toward the opposite end of the grille. Once there, she leaned forward to peek through the grate.

And froze in horror.

While the sale Wednesday night at the 69 Club had been bi-zarre, it had been obvious that both the bidders and the "mer-chandise" were willing participants in the event.

The scene below had none of the lighthearted flavor of that earlier auction.

A dozen women stood in a row, secured to a long wall. Chains around their wrists held their arms high above their heads.

The females were in various states of undress. Some were completely naked, while others still wore remnants of the clothes that had been ripped from their bodies.

Three dozen men wandered up and down in front of the pris-oners, "sampling" the wares. Some contented themselves with lifting a chin in order to examine a face and with squeezing a bare breast here or a nipple there. Others probed the genitals of their helpless victims with greedy fingers.

Most of the women seemed resigned to their fate. They bowed their heads so their long hair hung forward to hide their faces.

Leah searched the row of victims for anyone she knew. She whimpered when she found Gloria. A large red-haired man in a custom-made suit was pumping his hand in and out of her pussy, heedless of the distress on her face.

But it wasn't until she located Consuelo that Leah needed to shove a fist into her mouth to keep from screaming out loud.

The shrieks she'd heard earlier had been Consuelo's. The kitchen worker still sobbed with fear and outrage, but her mouth worked soundlessly. *She has no voice left.*

Two men held Consuelo's body out from the wall so that she was almost horizontal. One supported her torso in the air while the other plucked her pubic hairs out one by one.

Leah had never known anger as intense as what she experienced in that moment watching Consuelo being tortured by a pair of sexual sadists. If she'd had access to a weapon, she would have killed them both without hesitation.

She was still struggling to get her rage under control when Lucero's voice cut through the noise and laughter below.

"Gentlemen. Gentlemen. It's nearly time for our auction to begin." He moved into Leah's line of sight. "I'm very happy to see the level of enthusiasm that this week's offerings are inspiring. I'm just hopeful that your bids are as lively as your inspection of the merchandise."

Male laughter greeted his announcement.

"I'm also pleased to be able to report that we have a very special surprise for the discriminating among you tonight."

Leah's hand was still in her mouth. She bit her right knuckle. *No. No. He can't mean* me!

Lucero strutted around the room, moving in and out of her sight line. "Occasionally, the 69 Club attracts unwanted attention from the media." He paused dramatically. "Can you imagine how much their interest would be heightened if they knew about our little get-togethers here on Saturday night?"

This time, the group of men did not laugh. An uneasy murmur went through the crowd.

"Relax, my friends. There's nothing to be concerned about. I have the journalist involved safely tucked away in another room right now."

Leah couldn't see him, but she could hear the smug satisfaction in his voice.

"She's quite the beauty. Unlike this group, she's blond and blue-eyed. And she's accustomed to getting her own way. I anticipate she will give her new owner quite a spirited ride." He chuckled. "The sale price includes free disposal when the purchaser grows weary of his new toy."

Leah's stomach roiled, and her mouth filled with the taste of copper. She looked down and realized she'd bitten her knuckle. The coppery taste was blood.

Lucero's clients were once more laughing, confident that their private activities would remain secret.

Is Lucero insane? He can't really believe he can just dispose of me like yesterday's garbage.

How can anyone be so arrogant, so callous, so evil?

She was shivering. Trying to warm herself, she rubbed her bare arms. Her skin felt cold and clammy. *I'm shocky. I need to get out of here. When he realizes I'm missing, he'll tear the place down by the rafters.*

In her agitation, Leah had missed several beats. She suddenly realized something had happened downstairs that she'd missed. Leaning forward, she listened.

"Excuse me, gentlemen. I need your attention. There's a matter that requires all our cooperation." The anger in his voice leaked out. "It seems our prize lot managed to escape her holding pen. The master alarm panel has not signaled an alert so I'm confident she is still on the premises. Let's split up and locate her as quickly as possible, please."

No! Oh, God. What do I do?

In her agitation, Leah began crawling backward on the cat-walk. Her foot hit something that clattered down onto the pipes. Her shoe.

A moment of silence.

Then she heard Lucero's drawl. "Gentlemen, I think we've found our pretty little bird. Now would someone please climb up the tree and bring her down for me?"

Chapter Thirty-two

As Quin anticipated, the parking lot outside the used-book store was deserted. No one noticed the black coupe pulling out into the traffic on Northwest Highway.

His only comfort was that they were taking him to Leah. *She's got to be terrified. At least we'll be together.*

During the drive to West Dallas, Tyree and Santiago joked with each other and made cracks at his expense. He ignored them. Instead he focused on thoughts of Leah. The prospect of dying had never terrified him the way it had some of the men he'd served with. It was ironic that now that he'd met Leah, life was more precious to him. *But there's no way I'm going to make it out of this alive. If I can just find some way to get her out, I'll be satisfied.*

The warehouse they brought him to was not one of those they'd been looking at. *Even if Olson raids all of the warehouses on his list, it won't do any good.*

The front of the property looked deserted, but when Santiago drove around to the rear, there were dozens of parked cars. *A special group of bidders for even more exclusive merchandise?*

He stole a glance at his watch. *Olson hasn't even raided Partido yet.*

Santiago parked, and the three men got out. They entered the warehouse through a side door, using keypad access.

The building was enormous, but his two guides knew the layout well. As they directed him through the dimly lit corridors, Quin could hear shouting voices coming from somewhere deeper in the warehouse.

"Excellent," Tyree murmured. "I was afraid we'd miss all the action."

"Something is going on," Santiago said. "And it's not just an auction."

They finally came to a large open space deep in the bowels of the building. There was so much activity and excitement in the room that it took Quin a few seconds to assimilate it all.

His inspection of the scene was interrupted by a familiar voice.

"Tyree! You've brought my traitorous employee back to me." Lucero came striding toward the three men.

"Hello, Miguel." Quin kept his tone mild.

"Quin! I'm so glad you could make it. We've been waiting for you to arrive." Quin was familiar with all of Miguel Lucero's mercurial moods. Although the club owner's attitude seemed welcoming, even jubilant, Quin recognized the underlying rage.

"Come, come. Let me show you around." Lucero grabbed his arm and led him to a bar. "Jose, my friend here drinks single-malt scotch. In a little while he is going to die a long, very painful death. The least we can do is give him a drink before dying. Pour one for him, please."

Quin accepted the glass with real gratitude. He took one deep swallow and nodded at the bartender, a man he'd never see before. "Thanks, *amigo*."

"*De nada*," the fellow answered. His brown eyes looked troubled. *Maybe not everyone here is happy with the place.*

Lucero still had a grip on his left arm. The club owner now pulled Quin through the crowd of men. "Here's this night's merchandise."

Quin's eyes widened with surprise. While he'd expected another, perhaps more exclusive, auction, he hadn't expected to see these listless, abused Mexican girls chained up like dogs. And they were just girls; most were scarcely out of their teens. A killing rage filled his chest. Rage and something else.

Fear. *Leah! Where the fuck is Leah?*

Despite the emotions churning inside him, Quin kept his voice light while his anxious gaze continued to scan the room. "Miguel, what are you running here? A private club for perverts? I have to say I'm a little surprised. I was expecting more from you."

For a second or two, Lucero's own anger blazed in the depths of his eyes, but was quickly extinguished. "Come, now, my friend. You know I have always catered to the 'special' tastes of men who can afford to pay for their pleasures." He waved a hand toward his crowd of customers. "And this clientele pays very well."

Quin gestured toward the row of imprisoned women. "So this is your new wetback power? A bunch of terrorized teenagers?" He allowed his scorn to show.

Lucero's jaw tightened, and Quin watched his fight to retain control. *If I can get him to blow up, maybe he'll forget about Leah and take his anger out on me. I can't let him see that she matters to me.*

Quin knew the exact moment when Lucero regained his composure. It was as if a switch had been thrown somewhere deep inside the man. One minute the club owner was nearly bubbling over with fury, the next he was smiling as though nothing had happened.

"Of course, I do have better merchandise than what you see on display here. In fact, we've been waiting for you to arrive so we could put my 'special stock' up for auction."

An icy knife lanced through Quin's gut. *Careful, Perez. If you let him see how you feel about her, he will tear her to pieces in front of you.*

"Glad to hear it. It isn't going to have to be much to improve upon this lot." He waved toward the row of chained women.

"This way, my friend. I'm sure you'll agree my 'special label' is something very special indeed."

The crowd of men parted as Lucero, Quin, Tyree and Santiago moved past them.

"Out of the way. Out of the way," Lucero ordered as the foursome approached a small knot of his clients. The men stood with their backs to the newcomers in a rough semicircle.

Quin drew a surreptitious breath, instinctively girding himself against what he knew was coming.

The onlookers parted, and he saw what they'd been ogling.

Leah stood, chained to the wall with her wrists above her head. Her clothes had been ripped off her. The shreds of her blouse still hung from her body.

She wasn't completely nude; she wore a lacy black bra and a matching V-cut thong.

But the thing that differentiated her from the other women wasn't just the sexy lingerie. It was the attitude.

Although she stood there a prisoner, she had the posture of a warrior queen. She held her head high and dared any man to touch her. She wore her anger and disdain like a shield, holding the perverts at a distance.

Quin had to struggle to keep his face expressionless while his emotions careened all over the place. Relief, concern, pride, and male outrage all took a turn, only to be shoved back down again. With one glance, he recorded her every scratch, bruise, bit of dried blood and broken fingernail.

"*Hola, chiquita.* Looks like you're having a bad night."

She whipped her head around to meet his gaze. He held his breath, hoping she'd understand.

"What are you doing here?" she drawled.

Despite the danger and the god-awful odds, Quin felt a surge of pure joy. She trusted him and was willing to go along with whatever game he played. *The thing is, cariña, I'm clean out of aces. I've got no cards left to play.*

"Me and Miguel have some unfinished business to take care of." He jerked his head toward Lucero.

"Are you going to bid on me, too?" Her voice was scornful.

"Nah. Why buy the cow when you've already drank all the milk." He turned back to Lucero, dismissing her.

When he met Lucero's gaze, he was rewarded by the confusion in the club owner's eyes.

"I thought you cared about her."

Quin grinned. "Yeah, Miguel, I care about her the same way I care about my next meal. I told you all I wanted to do was fuck her."

Lucero narrowed his eyes. "I don't believe you."

Quin shrugged. "Believe what you want. In the meantime, you and I have business to discuss."

Lucero shook his head, unwilling to give up an opportunity to torture an enemy. Anger and doubt battled for control of his face.

Quin's attention was diverted by the sight of the men closing their circle around Leah like a pack of jackals surrounding a wounded lioness. He wanted to leap on them and tear them to shreds.

One of the perverts had his hand on Leah's belly. *I'll kill the fucking bastard.* Only the knowledge that Leah would suffer much worse if Lucero realized he loved her kept Quin from leaping on the man.

"Let's test your indifference, shall we?" Lucero suggested. His eyes now gleamed with calculation, and Quin's heart tripped.

Lucero motioned to Tyree to watch Quin. When Tyree nodded, the club owner strode to stand beside Leah.

"Gentlemen, it's time for you to bid. I'd like to suggest that
we begin our auction with this lovely bit of fluff." He reached out
and dragged his hand down Leah's naked shoulder to her breast.
He fondled the black lace bra, watching Quin all the while.

Quin forced himself to remain still. *Think, Perez! What can you do?*

Leah stood there, looking off into the distance, seemingly in-
different to Lucero, the perverts and the entire auction.

Quin stole a glance at Tyree. The man smiled back, too much the
professional to allow himself to be distracted by a slave auction.

What the hell am I going to do?

Although Leah acted as if she wasn't aware of her surroundings,
she knew everything that was going on. Most of all, she watched
Quin from a corner of her eye.

She'd expected him to come, but she hadn't anticipated that
he would simply throw his lot in with hers. She'd been hoping for
cops, lots of firepower and paddy wagons to round up all these
sexual sadists.

Instead it looked like he'd allowed himself to be captured.
*Maybe he's wearing a wire, or a GPS device. Any minute now, the cops are going
to break in and save us.*

The truth was, she didn't care what the plan was, or even if
there was a plan. She was just happy he was there with her.

She had been on the thin edge teetering on hysteria when he
arrived. *If he hadn't walked in when he did, I would have been sobbing and
begging just like Consuelo.*

Lucero's hand stroked her right breast. *He's trying to provoke Quin
into a response.*

She let her gaze rake across the audience, but paused. *Something's wrong. Some of these creeps aren't paying attention. What's going on?*

At the back of the room, a few of the bidders had dropped their paddles and were running for the doors.

She tilted her head to listen. *Oh. My. God. It's the police. We're being raided.*

Lucero was still so caught up in his auctioneering patter that he hadn't caught on yet. Excited members of the audience were still bidding. Because she was facing the audience, she could see what was going on at the back of the room.

She looked for Quin and gave him a brilliant smile. He frowned, and she flicked his eyes toward the rear of the room.

He swung around and said something to the Jamaican man who had kidnapped her. The guy looked over his shoulder. In that second, Quin brought his arm up to deflect the gun trained on him and slammed his head into the other guy's face.

The gun went off in the air, and the room went nuts. Men started running for the doors, and the stampede created a logjam at the exits. Leah watched with glee as the perverts shoved and punched each other in their desperation to get away. "You're all going to jail," she screamed.

Lucero ran past her toward a door in the corner of the room. Quin scooped up the gun the Jamaican had dropped and followed. "Hey, what about me?" she shouted.

He didn't answer.

"Well, this is just great," she said. *I'm practically naked, chained to a wall, and my guy just ran off and left me.*

She could hear shots all over the building, but fortunately none seemed to be in her vicinity.

Her fellow prisoners had roused from their stupors and were staring around in amazement. She knew exactly how they felt.

A familiar voice popped up nearby. "Well, girlfriend, it looks like you've had a busy night."

"Zeke!" she shrieked. "Come get me free."

"Actually, I was just enjoying the view."

"I mean it. Get me out of here."

"Sweetheart, do you happen to know where the keys are?"

"Lucero's got them, and Quin's chasing him."

"Then it's a safe bet he'll be bringing the keys back shortly."

"Well, don't just stand there. Take the coats off those guys and cover the girls."

He obeyed instantly, walking up to the now corralled perverts to demand their jackets. A few of the men complained, but the look Zeke gave them quickly ended any debates.

By the time Quin returned, half dragging and half carrying Lucero, Zeke had draped a navy blue suit jacket over her, tying the sleeves around her neck.

Lucero looked like he'd been through a meat grinder. His face was covered in blood, one arm hung at an odd angle and it looked like his other shoulder had a gunshot wound. He seemed barely conscious.

Zeke greeted his friend. "How many times did he fall down while you were chasing him?"

"I lost count," Quin responded, dropping the beaten Cowboy on the floor in front of Zeke. "He tripped over Tyree's gun once, too."

"Clumsy bastard," Zeke commented. He pulled his right leg back and delivered a vicious kick to Lucero's side.

Quin turned his attention to Leah. "Are you okay, baby?"

"Never better." She managed a watery smile. When he got the chains unlocked, she collapsed into his arms.

Quin handed the key chain off to another cop. He untied the jacket sleeves and helped her slip inside the garment.

"How'd you find us?" he asked Zeke.

"Well, you know, I'm a suspicious kind of guy. I was just cruising around the strip center, waiting for you to come out, when I saw a big black sedan parked in front of a used-book store. I decided to hang around and see who belonged to the vehicle." He grinned. "Imagine my surprise when you came out with two button men, climbed into it and drove away."

"You always were a nosy bastard," Quin said. "Thanks."

"No problem." Zeke looked around the room. "Damn, the paperwork on this mess is going to last for weeks. You'd better take your woman out of here before Olson notices you and starts asking questions. I'd go that way." He pointed to the door Lucero had tried to escape through. "I'll just tell the lieu I found this pile of garbage myself."

Quin nodded. "I'd appreciate it." He reached into his pocket and pulled a gun out. "This belongs to Tyree. Lucero must have picked it up in the excitement."

"Right before he fell and it discharged. I know." Zeke glanced around. "Now get out of here, both of you, before I change my mind."

Quin scooped Leah up in his arms and asked, "Ready to go home, Princess?"

"I was ready hours ago," she answered.

The two of them walked through the chaos and out of the warehouse.

Chapter Thirty-three

The evening after the police raid on the warehouse, Leah and Quin relaxed in the hot tub on the third floor of the *Heat* building.

The warm water felt good on her body. Her arms still ached from being chained above her head for so long.

She sat in Quin's lap, feeding him grapes and strawberries from a bowl alongside the hot tub.

"I had a job offer today," he said.

"Oh, from whom?"

"Your father."

She shook her head. *I should have known.* "What did he offer you?"

He leaned forward to kiss her right ear. "Well, it seems he's been looking for a man of my talents to help manage security for the Reece Media Group. Do you think he's trying to buy me off?"

She turned her head so her mouth could touch his. He tasted of strawberries. "Mmmmm. You taste good. No, I think you saved his daughter's life so he did a quick background check on you. Your military record impressed him, and he wants to get to know you better."

Quin pulled his head back so he could look her in the eyes. "And you know all this because . . ."

"Because I talked to my father today, too. He came by to check on me." She ran her tongue across his lips one last time before reaching into the bowl again. "What did you tell him?"

"That I was happy being a cop. He seemed disappointed."

"Don't worry. I guarantee that won't be the last offer he makes you." She held a new strawberry up to his lips.

"What makes you say that?"

"As long as we're dating, you're an element he can't control. Offering you a job is a way to correct that situation." She popped the strawberry into his mouth.

While he chewed, she continued. "Last night was hard on Tex. All his money and power couldn't save me and that realization must have shaken him to his core."

Quin made a "keep talking" gesture with his hand.

"He actually told me he hadn't been a very good father, and he wants to make it up to me." She shook her head. *If only things were that easy.*

Quin swallowed. "So is he going to start taking you camping and fishing and stuff to make up for lost time?"

"God forbid!" She laughed. "No, but I did decide to take advantage of his moment of weakness. I asked him to do something for me."

"You want him to buy Mexico for us?"

She slapped his bicep. "No, but you're close. I asked him to make sure that all those girls Lucero victimized get to stay in this country."

He stared at her. "Princess, they crossed into the U.S. illegally."

"And they paid for it. The least we can do is help them to start a new life here."

"Well, if anyone can pull that trick off, your father can." He stroked her shoulder. "I've been thinking."

"Hmmmm?"

"Why don't we go upstairs to your bedroom and play hide the *chorizo*?"

"Hide the *chorizo*? I'm not familiar with that game," she teased.

"It's the Mexican version of that all-American pastime, hide the sausage. My people have added some spicy variations."

"I don't know. I'm awfully comfortable here." She snuggled against his chest. Although it had been less than an hour since they'd fucked, his cock was already semihard beneath her thighs.

Without warning, he stood, lifting her at the same time, and walked to the steps. She didn't bother to make even a token protest. *I love it when he carries me.*

He shifted her in his arms so she was lying across his shoulder and headed toward the door. She shrieked, "Wait, Quin, we're dripping water everywhere."

"I told you once before, Princess, water dries." He put his hand on the doorknob.

"But we can't run around the building naked. Someone will see us."

"I hate to break it to you, but a whole lot of people saw you almost naked last night." He grabbed a towel off a nearby rack and draped it across her bare buttocks. "There. You're decent. Let's go upstairs."

"You're a maniac, you know it, don't you?" she complained while he crossed the hall and pushed the elevator button for the fourth floor.

They didn't encounter any *Heat* staffers on the way upstairs. Leah's great view of Quin's buns from her position over his shoulder helped to distract her.

When they reached her apartment, he headed straight for her

room. They'd left the lights on and the sheets rumpled from their last romp.

He dropped her on the bed and crawled up beside her. "Now where were we?"

She sat up. "Actually, I wanted to talk about your views on equality between the sexes." *It's really hard to concentrate when he's naked and kneeling in front of me like this.*

"I'm all for equality. What are we talking about?"

"Well, you know how on Saturday morning we played with your box of sex toys?"

"*Chiquita*, I'll never forget it." He grabbed her ankles in his hands and spread her legs.

She shoved him backward with one hand.

"I need for you to listen to me," she complained.

"I'm sorry." He sat back on his haunches and assumed an attentive expression. "Equality between the sexes."

"That's right." Leah slid off the bed and went to her closet, where she removed a large square box with a huge purple bow on top. She returned and put it in front of him.

"What's this?" he asked.

"You remember that Aggie has been working on a spread on sex toys?"

He nodded and that grin she loved so much spread across his face. "More sex toys?"

"Yes, except this time they're for me."

"Equality between the sexes. I get it." He flopped onto his back on the mattress. "Bring them on, *hermana*. I can take it."

She removed the lid from the box. "There are all kinds of goodies in here, but there were a couple of things that I really, really wanted to try."

"Anything you want, Princess. I'm at your service."

She reached into the box and pulled out two pairs of handcuffs. "How about these?"

"Who's doing the cuffing and who's doing the wearing?" he asked.

"Since I spent half of last night chained to a wall, I'd think you'd be willing to take one for the team."

He sat up. "*Chiquita*, I'm a cop. Handcuffs are not something to be taken lightly." He tapped her on the nose. "For a cop to allow a civilian to cuff him requires an enormous amount of trust."

She nodded. "I can understand that. Along the same lines as trusting one's partner to stick his cock up your ass?"

He grinned and shook his head. "Admit it. You enjoyed the experience."

"I did," she agreed. "And you're gonna love this." She pulled on his shoulders. "Move a little bit this way. No, more to your left. That's good. Okay, raise your arm here. Yes, just like that."

Within minutes, she'd handcuffed both his wrists to her headboard. She sat back to admire her handiwork.

The contrast of his dusky skin and the dark-inked tattoos against her white sheets was wonderful. "You are a beautiful specimen," she said.

"Why, thank you, ma'am. I appreciate that."

She straddled his body with her torso over his chest. "But now that you're my prisoner, you need to obey my every wish."

"Yes, ma'am," he responded.

"First, I want you to eat my pussy," she ordered.

"Yes, ma'am," he repeated.

She edged closer to the headboard, grabbing it for balance and lowering her body so he could easily reach her.

He swiped her labia with his tongue. "*Chiquita*, I may need some help here. This is hard to do without my hands."

"Improvise," she ordered.

And improvise he did. He buried his face in her pussy, using his nose and his tongue and, even once, his chin.

She gave herself up to the experience, shifting her hips and moving around to give him easier access.

He concentrated on her clit with his tongue and teeth, alternately nibbling and licking the pleasure button.

She encouraged him with sighs and moans. As her pussy began to produce the lubricating moisture that signaled her excitement, Quin eagerly lapped it up.

The heat spread from her core to her belly. "Quin, wait. I'm getting close."

Instead of listening to her, he redoubled his efforts, lightly gnawing on her labial lips.

But her desire to share this orgasm with him was enormous. She lifted her hips, taking away his access.

"Princess, what are you doing?" he complained. "You were about to come. I could feel it."

"Yes, but I have other plans for us tonight."

She scrambled off his body and crawled back to the box of sex toys. Reaching inside, she pulled out the peach-colored cock ring Abby had brought with her from Los Angeles. She held it up so he could see it. "Know what this is?" she asked.

He squinted and a smile spread across his face. "I've seen cock rings before, but that looks like one souped-up baby."

"Yeah, Aggie promised something for everyone with this model."

His cock was pointed toward the ceiling—almost like a living Tower of Pisa. She reached into the box and pulled out a familiar bottle.

He strained his neck, trying to see what she was doing.

"What's going on down there?" he asked.

"This time it's your turn to test-drive the Astroglide." She poured a generous amount onto one palm and then rubbed her hands together. Reaching for his cock, she started massaging the warming liquid into his skin.

"Ahhhh," he moaned. "That feels so good."

"Not as good as it's going to feel." She picked the bottle up and poured a bit more directly on his penis.

He began to pant. "Slow down, *chiquita*. I don't want to come too soon. Damn, that feels good."

When his hips began to rock, she stopped and reached for a condom and the cock ring.

After she had sheathed his cock, she said, "Okay, let's see how this slipper fits, Cinderella." Following the directions she'd read, she worked the ring over the head of his penis and slid it one-third of the way down the shaft. Once it was in place, she turned the vibrator on.

"Oh, babe, do that some more," he moaned.

"Okay, cowboy, ready for action?" she asked.

"Hi Yo, Silver."

Climbing across his body, she straddled him again, this time balancing above his hips. She stifled a grin. Looking down at his cock from above, it appeared to be wearing an oddly shaped Easter bonnet.

She lowered herself onto him. The cock ring was made from

a silicone gel, making it easier than she expected. However, the vibrator complicated matters. Quin's hips were moving all over the place, and it was a few minutes before she was firmly seated.

"Leah," he gasped. "I hope you're ready because I'm gonna come any second."

She didn't even bother to answer. Leaning a bit forward, she slammed down on his torso. The movement elicited a scream from her and a groan from him.

Neither one wanted to wait. She rode him hard and fast like a cowboy breaking a wild mustang. The vibrating ring enhanced and emphasized the effect of the smallest movement either one made.

For his part, Quin raised his hips on the upstroke and fell back toward the mattress on the downstroke.

The bed rocked and groaned from their wild exertions.

"Leah?" he wheezed.

"Now!" she screamed.

They came together, in a mingling of breath, sweat and soul. She froze for a second above him, but then collapsed onto his chest.

The two lay there, panting. While they'd been dripping from the hot tub when they'd arrived, they were drenched from forehead to thigh now.

"Are you okay, *cariña*?" he asked.

"Mmmm," she responded.

A few minutes later, he said, "If the stud service was okay, how about removing the cuffs now?"

She lifted her head. "Or I could keep you here overnight to do whatever I demanded."

"But what I really want to do is hug you," he said, a wheedling note in his voice.

Leah sat up. "I just thought of something." She rolled off his body and jumped down from the bed.

"Where are you going?" he asked.

She didn't answer, just ran out of the room.

"Leah," he yelled. "Get back here right now. Don't leave me like this."

She returned, carrying her cell phone.

"What are you doing with that?" he asked.

"Just taking a photo of you like this."

"The hell you are."

She raised her head from the phone's menu. "Afraid?"

"Leah, don't." He meant it.

"Okay, but you owe me." She put the phone down on the nightstand. "How are you going to repay me?"

"I have a gift right here for you," he said.

She looked pointedly at his now shrunken cock. "I don't think so," she drawled.

"No, not there. Let me loose, and I'll show you."

She retrieved the handcuff keys and unlocked him.

He sat up, rubbing his wrists. Then he removed the cock ring and discarded the condom.

"Okay, don't welsh on me," she said. "Let's see you deliver."

He turned sideways so she could see the back of his left shoulder.

There, among the stylized tattoos of his heritage, was an un-finished heart with her name in it.

Leah was struck dumb. "I thought you didn't get tattoos with names or other stuff."

"I never have before. Only for you would I wear a brand."

Her heart leaped into her throat, and tears began to pool in the corners of her eyes. "But it isn't finished."

"Look carefully, *cariña*."

She leaned forward. The tattoo was three-quarters finished. It read "Leah" with the first initial of her last name, but the leg of the "R" was missing.

"You need to tell me how to finish it," he said.

She looked first at him with a quizzical expression, then back at the tattoo. Her heart began to swell. "It's a *P* right now."

He nodded. "For Perez."

She didn't say anything.

He cleared his throat. "Or I can finish the *R* for Reece. Either way, you still own my heart, and I'll wear your brand."

She heard the hesitation in his voice and turned back to him. "Are you asking me to marry you, Quin?"

He nodded. "Last night when I thought I was going to lose you, I realized that I didn't want to stay in a world where you weren't."

"Quin—"

"No, let me finish. I want to do this properly. I love you, and I want to spend the rest of my days with you. Leah Reece, do you suppose you could bring yourself to marry me?"

"Yes!" She threw herself on him.

He wrapped his arms around her and buried his face in her hair. "Even though we've only known each other four days?"

"Yes!"

"Even though I'm a Mexican peon and you're Anglo royalty?"

"Stop talking nonsense and kiss me." She pressed her mouth to his.

The kiss was unbelievably sweet, holding the promise of bright days and warm nights.

"I didn't tell you everything about my conversation with your father earlier," he said a few minutes later.

"Oh?"

"He didn't call me. I called him."

She pushed back to look into his eyes. "Why?"

He grimaced. "I wanted to do this right. I called him to ask for his permission to propose to you."

Her stomach turned over. "Is that when he offered you the job. To go away?"

He shook his head. "No. He'd asked me last night if I was in love with you."

"What did you say to him?"

"I told him yes." He smiled ruefully. "He said that was good because it meant I'd find you."

She stroked his cheek. "He was right. Tex is always right."

"When I called him this morning, I reminded him of the conversation and said that—even if you turned me down—I'd earned the right to ask you to marry me."

She drew a deep breath. "And what did he say?"

Quin shook his head, his expression filled with wonder. "He agreed with me." His gaze met hers. "Your father wished me luck and said he'd be proud to have me as his son-in-law."

She couldn't hold the tears back any longer. "He really said that?"

Quin nodded. "Yeah, and then he said, 'No matter what Leah says, I'd like for you to come work for me.'"

"I can't believe my ears." She shook her head. "If you only

knew how many times he's mocked my boyfriends and shoved lawyers or surgeons at me."

"I don't think you've given him enough credit, *cariña*. He wants you to be happy and safe. He knows I'll die before I let anything hurt you ever again."

"Oh, Quin." She leaned forward, letting her forehead rest against his.

"You still haven't told me that you love me yet," he reminded her.

"No, I haven't. Let me correct that oversight." She sat up straight and looked into his eyes. "Quin Perez Medina, I love you with all my heart. I want to marry you and make little Perez Reece babies."

"Good, because my mother wants lots of grandchildren."

"My father will want us to pop out a baseball team," she countered.

"Well, then, we'll have to get started fast." He grabbed her hand. "Come on, *cariña*, let's get dressed and go get my tattoo finished before you change your mind. Afterward, we can start working on Quin, Jr."

Sweet Cheeks rode his stationary bicycle, his back to Sandy. His tight ass moved rhythmically up and down and side to side as his muscular legs pedaled furiously. The bike's whirling noise and his heavy breathing muffled the sound of her footsteps behind him.

He wasn't wearing anything except bike shorts. Sandy admired his broad shoulders, now shiny with perspiration. Although he was only two minutes into his routine, his hair was already plastered to his head, the long, dark curls clinging to his face and neck.

She slid one hand across his damp back to squeeze his left shoulder. His deltoid muscle was as hard and firm as the rest of his body. She leaned forward and kissed his right shoulder.

He tasted hot and salty. Sandy clenched her thighs together as she felt the rush of moisture between her legs that always accompanied the sight of his nearly naked body.

Sweet Cheeks stopped pedaling and turned, pivoting to pull her toward him while remaining perched on the bike.

When she moved into the vee between his thighs, his bulging cock pressed against her naked belly. She arched, stretching and rubbing against his erection, eliciting a moan from him. His hands shifted to her ample hips, where his fingers kneaded her fleshy ass, encouraging her to continue what she'd started.

His gaze was fixed on her bare chest, and she took a deep breath. The movement raised her nipples, displaying her full breasts to advantage. Her lungs filled with his musky man-scent.

Beads of perspiration clung to his chest, and she leaned forward to capture a single droplet with her tongue. When she licked him, his muscles convulsed. Sliding her hands to his rear, she cupped those sweet ass cheeks, trying to insert her fingers between his body and the bike seat.

He nudged her backward so he could step off the bike. His large hands encircled her waist and he lifted her—as easily as if she were a size six, not a sixteen.

She wrapped her legs around his hips, bringing her aching cunt in line with his cock and making it nearly impossible for him to free himself from his bike shorts on his own. Still clinging to his body, she tried to help him remove the pants. They were both frantic, their movements jerky and awkward.

When the garment fell to the floor, he stepped out of it and shifted her weight in order to get his hand between their bodies. He fumbled for a minute, trying to maneuver himself into the creamy channel that already dripped with readiness for him.

She squirmed eagerly, licking and nibbling at his ear. The tip of his thick cock pressed against her, promising fulfillment.

When he entered her, she let out a little gasp of pleasure and bowed her back, raising her breasts so he could reach them with his mouth.

He filled her completely . . . they were two bodies with one mind and one purpose. She undulated against him, increasing the friction. His groan brought an answering sigh from her.

He staggered, struggling to retain his hold on her. Stumbling forward, he anchored her body on the wall.

The unforgiving plaster pressed against her bare shoulders and buttocks as he pounded into her. She clutched at him, not caring if she scratched him with her nails, knowing it would only excite him more. She needed to reach her peak. . . .

A horn sounded abruptly from the street below, shattering her vision and denying her climax. He stopped pedaling.

Sandy blinked into the eyepiece of the telescope as the familiar fantasy slipped away.

Across the street, the object of her lust reached for the sports drink sitting on the table next to his bicycle and tilted his head back to swallow.

"Damn." Sandy shook her head to clear the fantasy's lingering image, smiling ruefully. "You need to work on your staying power, Sweet Cheeks. You let me down."

Unknowing, her gorgeous neighbor resumed his exercise routine.

Sandy swiveled her telescope to scan the front of his building again.

Beyond her balcony, Uptown was coming alive for the night. If she leaned over, she could look down and see people drifting in and out of boutiques, eating at outdoor cafes or standing in line for tickets at the art house movie down the block.

Her sixth-floor condo was just north of downtown Dallas, in the shadow of the skyscrapers that dominated the north Texas sky.

Sandy focused on the apartments directly across from hers, checking to see if any of her regulars were home yet.

Her spying on the neighbors had begun accidentally a few months earlier, but during that time she'd become attached to many of the people who lived across the street. In a curious sort of way, she felt like their guardian, keeping an eye on them to make certain everything was all right.

Yes, there were Mr. and Mrs. Kinky, the young couple on the fifth floor. They were in their kitchen preparing dinner. Knowing them, dinner would be part of the evening's foreplay.

Mr. Dominant, the penthouse tenant, wasn't home yet. She frowned and wondered if he was traveling again. He'd been gone a great deal recently, and she half hoped he was moving out. His sexual escapades made her queasy, but she couldn't stop herself from watching.

Unlike the apartments across the street with their open latticework balconies, Sandy's balcony was solid brick. She hadn't furnished it with hanging plants or wind chimes or anything that might draw attention. The only item on hers was a tall ficus tree. The hundreds of dark green leaves quivered in the pleasant September air and, more important, helped to conceal her telescope.

Her hands trembled, and she felt the fluttering of excitement in her belly from her fantasy workout. It was the same each weekend. No matter how often she spied on her neighbors, the thrill never waned.

More tenants returned home and switched on their lamps. The flat face of the building across the street resembled a checkerboard with alternating squares of light and dark. She slowly rotated the body of the telescope, trying to find activity. Mrs. Blue Hair, the elderly woman on the fourth floor, had been sick lately. Sandy was glad to see she was feeling well enough to host her Friday night bridge group. Three other women sat at a table in the living room, playing cards and chatting.

She checked Mr. and Mrs. Kinky's apartment again.

"Oh, wow! Hey, guys, that's some gourmet meal you're whipping up there."

The good-looking young couple was stark naked, lying on their sides in the sixty-nine position on a Chinese black lacquered dining table. The wife was busy sucking her husband's penis while the husband masturbated his wife.

Sandy shook her head. "You two are unbelievable. Every time I think I've seen it all, you raise the bar another notch." She tightened the knob to focus on the action and smiled as the wife reached orgasm with a mouth-open scream. "You go, girl."

Mr. K's hips moved more rapidly now and, using one hand, he tried to press his wife's head closer toward his erection.

Mrs. K was in no condition to meet his needs. Sandy saw the young blonde's face go slack. For the moment, the wife was in her own world. Her husband's dick slipped out of her mouth.

"Oh, oh. He's about to explode," Sandy whispered.

Sure enough, his cock began spewing ropes of cum.

Mrs. K resurfaced, came alert and made a grab for her husband's wildly pumping penis, but it was too late. He bathed her with his cream.

"That's one virile man," Sandy said to herself. The young couple began to laugh. As they scrambled to sit up on the table, they held on to each other for support. The blonde wiped the cum off her face and neck and smeared it on her husband's chest. He leaned forward and licked her lips.

"That's it, guys," Sandy encouraged. "Celebrate each other."

The sight of the happily married couple made her feel wistful and even more alone than usual. It had been so long since she'd been part of a couple. Her sense of isolation brought her back to this balcony again and again. Sometimes she felt more connected to these anonymous neighbors than to anyone else in her life.

Sandy shifted the body of the telescope again. The tenant she called Mr. Dominant was just returning home. A beautiful brunette woman Sandy had never seen before accompanied him. They sat on leather chairs in his living room, sipping wine and talking.

Sandy tightened her focus on the girl, who looked about twenty and had the porcelain skin and perfect features of an expensive doll. "Dolly, that's what I'll call you," she muttered. The woman's polite, attentive, yet somewhat blank expression suggested she was no stranger to the D/s world of Mr. Dominant.

He leaned back against the leather cushions and studied his guest before barking a short command. Sandy saw his lips move and watched the girl stand and begin to unbutton her blouse.

Dolly never took her eyes off Mr. Dominant, who remained seated, watching as she slid the shirt off her shoulders. The black lacy bra she wore drew attention to her smooth white skin and made her look more vulnerable.

Sandy saw Mr. Dominant's lips move again. In response, Dolly unbuttoned her skirt. She pushed the material down over her hips until the garment puddled at her feet. Her sexy thong matched the bra.

Sandy wondered what it would be like to stand almost naked before a man sitting in cold judgment of her. A tremor rippled through her body at the thought. Did Dolly know what came next?

Dolly stood passively and waited. From past spying on Mr. Dom, Sandy knew his partner would take no action without being told to do so. Her heart began to beat faster, and she wondered if the girl felt half the tension she did.

He spoke again. Dolly leaned forward and reached behind her back to unhook her bra. As she freed the last hook, the lacy scrap fell off, and her breasts tumbled forward.

Dom stood and snapped out a command. The woman removed her panties, then stepped forward and knelt before him.

Sandy shivered. The sight of a naked Dolly at Dom's feet, staring worshipfully up into his eyes, disturbed her. At the same time, it was unquestionably erotic. Sandy opened and closed her fist, resisting the temptation to touch her tightening nipples.

Dom reached out his right hand to cup his companion's cheek. Dolly pressed her face into his hand and kissed it.

Dom shifted and slid his hand into Dolly's thick brown hair. *If she's a true submissive, she likes to subjugate herself to a master,* Sandy reminded herself, but when she saw him tighten his grip, she couldn't help whispering, "No, don't."

He seized Dolly by the hair and dragged the girl off her knees. She hung there, suspended in air between his fist and the floor, her face twisted in pain.

Still fully dressed, Dom pulled his nude captive across the room by her hair toward an ottoman in front of the fireplace. He shoved her in the direction of the oversized piece of furniture, and Dolly obediently crawled onto it. She knelt on top of the ottoman on her hands and knees with Dom towering over her.

Sandy knew what was coming. She had seen Dom place a submissive on the ottoman before. She squeezed her thighs together, savoring the feeling of warmth uncoiling between her legs.

He walked to an umbrella stand near the front door. After removing what appeared to be a rattan walking cane, he returned to stand behind Dolly. Sandy could not see his face and did not know if he said anything before he raised the cane and brought it down on Dolly's bare buttocks.

The girl arched her back as the rattan connected with her skin. Dom immediately raised his arm and brought the cane down in another wide arc, slapping it hard against Dolly's ass.

The ringing of her telephone distracted Sandy from the scene across the street. For the space of another ring, she debated whether to answer it. If it was her mother, a nonresponse would start a cycle of calls every twenty minutes until Sandy picked up—even if it took until two in the morning. *Better get it over with now.*

She rushed toward the living room, brushing past the closed drapes, and picked up the phone on the fourth ring—right before the answering machine kicked in.

"Hello," she said breathlessly.

"You've been a bad girl, Alexandra Davis," a male voice greeted her.

"Who's this?" she demanded.

"You've been spying on your neighbors. How do you think they'd feel if they knew?"

Sandy's heart stuttered. *No! This couldn't be happening.* No one could have seen her. She'd been too careful.

"I don't know what you're talking about," she replied in her coldest voice. "I'm going to hang up. If you call me again, I'll report you to the police." She slammed the receiver down.

OhgodOhgodOhgod! She bit her lip and stared at the phone. What if someone *had* seen her? Maybe someone knew. Reality came crashing down. If this came out, she could be arrested. She'd lose her job. And her mother! Oh, dear heaven, what would her mother say?

Sandy forced her mind to function through the mounting panic. First, she needed to get the telescope off the balcony. She needed to sit down and think this through. . . .

The phone started to ring again. Sandy stared at it like a field mouse cowering before a snake. She made no move to pick it up. It rang a second . . . a third . . . and, finally . . . a fourth time.

The answering machine kicked in, and Sandy heard the male voice from before. "It's no good, Alexandra. You can't hide from

Justice. If you don't believe me, go check outside your door. I'll wait."

Sandy's stomach muscles clenched. She looked toward the door and took an involuntary step backward. Was this a trick? Maybe he was waiting out there to grab her.

Almost as if he'd heard her thoughts, he said, "I'm not out there. Leave the chain on and look. I've left something for you."

She gnawed on her lower lip as she walked toward the door and looked through the peephole. No one outside. Didn't mean anything. He could be standing beyond the peephole's range of vision.

"Go ahead, Alexandra. Look," the voice from the machine encouraged.

Sandy unlocked the dead bolt but left the safety chain in place. She eased the door open.

A large brown envelope sat on her welcome mat.

Making a sudden decision, Sandy unlatched the chain, opened the door, grabbed the envelope, pulled back inside and slammed the door shut. It rattled in the door frame.

"Good girl. Now look in the envelope. I'll call you back in a few minutes." The dial tone replaced his voice.

She stared in horror at the telephone. How had he known she'd opened the door? Was he standing at the end of the hall, watching? *Sweet Lord, maybe I'd better call the police.*

Sandy staggered across the room toward a chair and dropped into it. If she called the police, what would she say to them? She stared at the envelope.

It was a plain brown nine-by-twelve envelope with a single clasp. There were no markings on it, not even her name. Sandy opened it and a group of photos fell out. She flipped through the pictures, and bile rushed into her mouth.

All of the photos were shots of her balcony. They had been taken with a telephoto lens from somewhere across the street.

In every picture, the telescope was obvious. So was Sandy. There were photos of her looking out from behind her draperies, carrying the telescope out to the balcony, adjusting the settings. It was clear that her telescope was not directed toward the night sky; it was almost level.

She stared in horror at images of herself looking into the telescope while rubbing her breasts and—sweet mercy!—with her hand inside her slacks, touching herself.

The phone rang again. This time, she didn't hesitate. She walked straight to the telephone and picked it up. "What do you want?" she snarled.

"Alexandra, Alexandra," the voice said in an admonishing tone. "You sound so angry. Now you know how your victims will feel once they realize what you've been doing. How you've invaded their privacy—"

"I asked, what do you want?" Sandy interrupted.

"Justice. Like I said before." The voice became businesslike. "There's something waiting for you downstairs at the desk. Go get it. I'll call you back."

"I'm not going any—" Before she could finish the sentence, he hung up again.

Downstairs, Russell the security guard greeted her with a smile. There were two boxes sitting on his desk. Both were wrapped in plain brown paper. One was large and square; the other was longer and shallower.

Sandy tried to sound casual when she said, "Hi, Russell. Is one of these mine?"

He laughed. "You must be celebrating Christmas early. Both of these are for you."

"Both?" she squeaked, looking at the tops of the boxes. Sure enough, "Alexandra Davis" was printed in block capitals on each wrapper. "Did you see who dropped them off?"

"Nope. I was helping Mr. Caruthers from the third floor carry his groceries in. When I got back, they were waiting here. One of them is pretty heavy."

"Thanks, Russell. I think I can manage."

When the elevator reached six, she carried the boxes to her condo. Once safely inside, she put them down and glared at them. No matter what they contained, it wasn't good news.

She decided to start with the larger one first. After finding a steak knife in the kitchen, she cut the strapping tape that secured the package. With trembling fingers, she slit the tape across the top and opened the flaps.

Inside were several items, each carefully packed in Bubble Wrap. Sandy lifted the first one out and began to unwind the protective layers.

"Oh, God. No."

It was a video camera.

She was *not* going to perform for this sick bastard. The photos were bad enough. If she gave him videos, she'd never be free.

The phone rang again, interrupting her thoughts. She snatched up the receiver. "Who are you?" she demanded.

"Call me Justice," he replied. "Because that's what I'm going to get. Justice for all those people you exploited. Now, have you opened both boxes?"

"Just the camera. I am not going to—"

"You're going to do exactly what I say," he snapped. "If you don't, the police will be on your doorstep in fifteen minutes. Open the other box."

Sandy closed her mouth so hard her teeth clicked audibly. She shifted the receiver to her shoulder and grabbed the second, smaller box.

When she'd opened the flaps, white paper peeked out. She reached in, removed the top item and tore off its tissue wrapping.

Inside was a red satin, flowered jacquard bustier with black lace accents. It had a lace-up front and garters.

"No, no way," she whispered into the receiver.

"You'll look beautiful in it. I can't wait to see those big gorgeous breasts filling that up." Justice's voice had gone low and gravelly. "I'm getting hard just thinking about it."

Sandy was so shocked, she forgot to be scared for a moment. She licked her lips nervously. No man had ever said anything like that to her before. And she'd never owned anything so . . . sexy.

Appalled to realize she was even thinking about it, she cried, "I won't do this."

"Yes, yes, you will, Alexandra. I'll—"

"It's Sandy," she butted in. "I hate 'Alexandra.' "

"Okay. *Sandy.* I can't stand it any longer. I need for you to put it on."

Sandy's breath caught in her throat. If she refused outright, he'd already made it clear that he'd report her. Besides, even if she did film herself, it didn't mean she had to hand the video over to him.

"Put it on, baby."

The sound of the endearment hung in the room, making Sandy's heart beat faster. Only a short while ago, she had felt chilled with fear; now she felt flushed, hot. He really expected her to do this. She should be disgusted. But, at some point, her body had started to respond to the low, intimate sound of his voice. That voice was the stuff of her fantasies. Warm, sexy, even tender.

What was wrong with her? What was he doing to her?

Sandy fingered the satin and lace material of the bustier. She could pretend to be doing it. He wouldn't know. He couldn't see her, after all.

"My cock is hard just thinking about you."

Sandy's sex clenched at his words; her panties were soaked. Was he big? The question popped into her mind unbidden and, with it, an image. A man seated, his face in shadow, his thick shaft jutting proudly from between splayed legs. Waiting for her.

"All right," she said. "I'll put it on."

"Tell me what you're doing, everything you're doing." His voice was lower now, little more than a rough growl. Sandy felt her own excitement growing in response.

"I'm . . . removing my pullover," she mumbled, grabbing the hem of her shirt and yanking it up over her head.

"You're wearing black. You always wear black. It makes your skin seem even more pale and perfect."

His words calmed and emboldened her. Sandy unbuttoned her slacks and removed them. "I'm taking off my pants."

"That's the girl. Now your bra. What color is it?"

"Flesh-toned." She grimaced. For once, she wished she were wearing a hot, lacy bra like the ones in the lingerie catalogs.

"Oh, baby, you need to wear black to contrast with all that luscious skin." His breathing sounded harsh. "I want to suck your breasts until you come. Have you ever come just from having your nipples sucked?"

"No," she whispered.

"Too bad. Sounds like you've been running around with the wrong guys. Now your panties. Are they flesh-colored, too?"

"Yes," she lied, unwilling to describe the plain white cotton underwear she was actually wearing.

"Okay, Sandy. Slide them down. Now I want you to touch your pussy for me."

Sandy stifled a gasp. No man had ever used that word with her before. It was the word reserved for her fantasies—forbidden, sensual fantasies. Despite her fevered body, she shivered. Her imaginary world was merging with her real world. Where would it take her?

"Pretend that it's me fingering you, making you wet."

Mesmerized by Justice's voice, Sandy lay down on the couch and spread her legs. She slipped two fingers into her cleft and wasn't surprised to find herself dripping. It was that voice. He had the sexiest, most erotic voice she'd ever heard.

"I . . . I'm touching myself," she said out loud.

"Good, sweetheart. So am I. I had to open my pants and let my dick out because it was getting too tight in there."

"What does it look like?"

Her question met with silence, and Sandy felt herself blush. What was the matter with her? She didn't even know this man, and she was asking him to describe his cock. *He's blackmailing me, for Pete's sake.*

"What does *what* look like?" She heard the smile in his voice.

Whether it was the wickedness of what they were doing or the sound of his voice, Justice's teasing emboldened her. "Your dick," she said boldly. "Describe it to me."

He inhaled sharply. Sandy smiled to herself, pleased to have surprised him.

"It's about eight inches long. I'm not circumcised so it's thicker than most guys'. It's hard as a pike, and the tip is all purple with wanting you."

Sandy's breath caught at the image. "I wish I could see it," she breathed.

"I wish you could, too, baby. But, for now, reach into that box the bustier came in, and you'll find another gift from me. . . ."